Make time for friends. Make time for **Debbie Macomber**.

Debbie Macomber is a number one *New York Times* bestselling author. Her recent books include *Hannah's List, 1022 Evergreen Place* and *1105 Yakima Street*. She has become a leading voice in women's fiction worldwide and her work has appeared on every major bestseller list. There are more than a hundred million copies of her books in print. For more information on Debbie and her books, visit www.DebbieMacomber.com.

A Merry Little Christmas

Debbie Macomber

featuring *1225 Christmas Tree Lane* and *5-B Poppy Lane*

MIRA

Published in Great Britain 2012
MIRA Books, an imprint of Harlequin (UK) Limited,
Eton House, 18-24 Paradise Road,
Richmond, Surrey, TW9 1SR

A MERRY LITTLE CHRISTMAS © Harlequin Books S.A. 2012

The publisher acknowledges the copyright holder of the individual works as follows:

1225 Christmas Tree Lane © Debbie Macomber 2011
5-B Poppy Lane © Debbie Macomber 2006

ISBN 978 1 848 45144 5

58-1012

MIRA's policy is to use papers that are natural, renewable and recyclable products and made from wood grown in sustainable forests. The logging and manufacturing processes conform to the legal environmental regulations of the country of origin.

Printed and bound by
CPI Group (UK) Ltd, Croydon, CR0 4YY

CONTENTS

1225 Christmas Tree Lane

Paula Eykelhof
my wonderful editor
for more than twenty-five years

One

"Mom!"

The front door slammed and Beth Morehouse hurried out of the kitchen. Three days before Christmas, and her daughters were home from college—at last! Her foreman, Jeff, had been kind enough to pick them up at the airport while Beth dealt with last-minute chores. She'd been looking forward to seeing them for weeks. Throwing her arms wide, she ran toward Bailey and Sophie. "Merry Christmas, girls."

Squealing with delight, they dropped their bags and rushed into her embrace.

"I can't believe it's snowing. It's so beautiful," Bailey said, holding Beth in a tight hug. At twenty-one, she was the oldest by fourteen months. She resembled her father in so many ways. She was tall like Kent and had his dark brown hair, which she'd tucked under a knitted cap. Her eyes shone with a quiet joy. She was the thoughtful one and that, too, reminded Beth of her ex-husband. Three years after the divorce, she still missed him, although pride would never allow her to admit that. Even her budding relationship with Ted Reynolds, the local veterinarian, paled when she thought about her life with Kent and their history together.

"My turn." Displacing Bailey, Sophie snuggled into Beth's embrace. "The house looks fabulous, Mom. Really Christmassy." This child was more like Beth. A few inches shorter than her sister, Sophie had curly auburn hair and eyes so blue they seemed to reflect a summer sky. Releasing Beth, Sophie added, "And it smells wonderful."

Beth had done her best to make the house as festive and bright as possible for her daughters. She'd spent long hours draping fresh evergreen boughs on the staircase leading to the second-floor bedrooms. Two of the three Christmas trees were loaded with ornaments. The main tree in the family room was still bare, awaiting their arrival so they could decorate it together, which was a family tradition.

A trio of four-foot-tall snowmen stood guard in the hallway near the family room where the Nativity scene was displayed on the fireplace mantel. Decorating had helped take Beth's mind off the fact that her ex-husband would be joining them for Christmas. This would be the first time she'd seen him in three years. Oh, they'd spoken often enough, but every conversation had revolved around their daughters. Nothing else. No questions asked. No comments of a personal nature. Just the girls and only the girls. It'd been strictly business. Until now.

Until Christmas.

They both loved the holidays. It was Kent who'd first suggested they have several Christmas trees. Always fresh ones, which was one reason Beth had been attracted to the Christmas tree farm when she started her new life.

"I've got lunch ready," Beth said, trying to turn her attention away from her ex-husband. He still lived in California, as did the girls. He'd stayed in their hometown of Sacramento, while Bailey and Sophie both attended university in San Diego. According to their daughters, Kent had asked to come for Christmas. She'd known for almost two weeks that he'd made reservations at the Thyme and Tide B and B in Cedar Cove. The news that he'd be in town had initially come as a shock to Beth. He hadn't discussed it with her at all. Instead, he'd had their daughters do his talking for him. That made everything more awkward, because it wasn't as if she could refuse, not with Bailey and Sophie so excited about spending Christmas together as a family. But Kent's plans had left her with a host of unanswered questions. Was this his way of telling Beth he missed her? Was he looking for a reconciliation? Was she? The questions swarmed in her head, but the answers wouldn't be clear until he arrived. At least she'd be better able to judge his reasons. His intentions. And her own...

"Just like it used to be," Bailey finished. Beth had missed whatever she'd said before that, although it wasn't hard to guess.

Just like it used to be. These were magic words, but Beth had recognized long ago that the clock only moved forward. Yet the girls' eagerness, Kent's apparent insistence and her nostalgia for what they'd once shared swept aside her customary reserve.

"Mom?" Bailey said when she didn't respond. "We're talking.... Where are you?"

Beth gave a quick shake of her head. "Woolgathering. Sorry. I haven't had much sleep lately." Exhausted as she was, managing the tree farm and getting ready for Christmas with her daughters—and Kent—she'd hardly slept. She couldn't. Every time she closed her eyes, Kent was there. Kent with his boyish smile and his eyes twinkling with mischief and fun. They'd been happy once and somehow they'd lost that and so much more. Beth had never been able to put her finger on what exactly had gone wrong; she only knew that it had. In the end they'd lived separate lives, going their own ways. Their daughters had kept them together—and then they were off at college, and suddenly it was just Kent and Beth. That was when they discovered they no longer had anything in common.

"You're not sleeping?" Bailey's eyes widened with concern.

Sophie elbowed her sister. "Bailey, think about it. This is the busiest time of year for a Christmas tree farm. Then there's all this decorating. And, if we're really lucky—"

"Mom made date candy?" Bailey cut in.

"And caramel corn?" Sophie asked hopefully, hands folded in prayer.

"Yes to you both. It wouldn't be Christmas without our special treats."

"You're the best mom in the world."

Beth smiled. She'd had less than three hours' sleep, thanks to all the Christmas preparations, her dogs and... her incessant memories of Kent. Traffic at the tree farm had thinned out now that Christmas was only three days away. But families were still stopping by and there was quite a bit to do, including cleanup. Her ten-man crew was down to four and they'd coped just fine without either her or Jeff this morning. While he drove out to the airport, she'd been getting ready for her daughters' arrival. However, as soon as lunch was over, she needed to head back outside.

Beth and the girls had booked a skiing trip between Christmas and New Year's, and after the hectic schedule of the past two months, she was counting on a few relaxing days with her daughters. Their reservations were made and she was eager to go. Ted Reynolds, good friend that he was, had offered to take care of her animals, which reminded her of the one hitch in her perfectly planned holiday escape.

"Before we sit down to eat, I need to tell you we have special guests this Christmas."

"You mean Dad, right?" Bailey led the way into the other room, where there was more greenery and a beautifully arranged table with three place settings.

"Well, yes, your father. But he's not the only one...."

"Mom." Bailey tensed as she spoke. "Don't tell me you have a boyfriend. It's that vet, isn't it?"

"Ten guests, actually," she said, ignoring the comment about Ted, "and they aren't all boys."

"Puppies?" Sophie guessed.

"Puppies," Beth confirmed, not surprised that her daughter had figured it out. "Ten of them."

"Ten?" Sophie cried, aghast.

Without asking, Bailey went straight to the laundry room off the kitchen. "Where did you get ten puppies?" The instant she opened the door, all ten black puppies scampered into the kitchen, scrambling about, skidding across the polished hardwood floor.

"They're adorable." Sharing Beth's love for animals, both girls were immediately down on the floor, scooping the puppies into their arms. Before long, each held at least two of the Lab-mix puppies, the little creatures intent on licking their faces.

Unable to resist, Beth joined her daughters and gathered the remaining puppies onto her lap. One curled into a tight ball. Another climbed onto her shoulder and began licking her ear. The others squirmed until one wriggled free and chased his tail with determined vigor, completely preoccupied. They really were adorable, which was good because in every other way they were a nuisance.

Sophie held a puppy to her cheek. "Where'd you get them, Mom?"

"They were…a gift," she explained, turning her face away to avoid more wet, slurpy kisses.

"A gift?"

"But why'd you take all ten?" Bailey asked, astonished.

"I didn't have any choice. They showed up on my porch in a basket a week ago." Beth didn't say that discovering these puppies had been the proverbial last straw. They'd literally appeared on her doorstep the same day she'd learned Kent was coming here for Christmas. For an insane moment she'd considered running away, grabbing a plane to Fiji or Bora-Bora. Instead, she'd run over to the Hardings' and ended up spilling her heart out to Grace. Under normal conditions, Beth wasn't one to share her burdens with others. However, this was simply too much—an ex-husband's unexpected visit and the arrival of ten abandoned puppies, all during the busiest season of the year. The Hardings had given her tea and sympathy; Ted had been wonderful, too. Beth was grateful for his willingness to watch her animals but she refused to leave him with these ten additional dogs. So she'd made it her goal to find homes for all of them before Christmas. Which didn't give her a lot of time…

"How could someone just drop off ten puppies?" Bailey asked as she lifted one intrepid little guy off her shoulder and settled him in her lap.

"Who could do that and not be seen?" Sophie added. "I mean, you have people working all over this place."

Beth had certainly asked around. "Jeff saw a woman with a huge basket at my door. He thought he recognized her from his church, but when he asked her, she denied it. Then later, Pete, one of the drivers, claimed he saw a man on my porch with a basket. I talked to five different people and got five different stories. All I know is that I've got to find homes for these puppies before we leave for Whistler." And preferably before Kent arrived, although that was highly unlikely.

"Have you found any yet?" Bailey asked.

"No…but I've put out the word."

"You'll do it, Mom," Sophie said confidently. "I know you will."

"How old are they?" Bailey stroked a soft, floppy ear.

"Ted thinks about two months. Between six and eight weeks, anyway."

"They're irresistible. You won't have trouble finding homes," Sophie said.

Beth wished she had even a fraction of her daughter's

faith. In October, she'd found homes for four part-golden-retriever puppies. Coming up with those homes had been hard enough—and now ten more. She hoped the season would help.

She'd offer assistance with training if the new owners wanted it—and she'd push the all-important spay-and-neuter message. Ted had promised to give the owners a break on the price, too.

Working together, Beth and the girls corralled the puppies and got them back inside the laundry room. Then they washed up for lunch. Thankfully the girls' favorites didn't require much effort; the tomato basil soup and toasted cheese sandwiches were on the table within minutes.

"Now I truly feel like we're home," Bailey said, spooning up the thick soup.

Sophie sighed contentedly. "This place is starting to feel more like home all the time."

Beth had moved to Washington State following her divorce. For fifteen years she'd taught business and management classes at an agricultural college outside Sacramento. After she and Kent had split up, Beth felt she needed a change. A big one. An escape. She'd read about this Christmas tree farm for sale while browsing on the internet and had become intrigued. As soon as she'd visited the property and toured the house, she was sold.

Her general knowledge of farm life and crop cultivation had come in handy. She knew just enough about trees not to be intimidated. Besides, Wes Klein, the previous owners' son, had helped the first couple of years. She'd soon picked up everything else she needed to know. She hired the same crew each season and was pleasantly surprised by how smoothly things had gone this year, the first year she was on her own.

In addition to Christmas trees, she sold wreaths and garlands, which were created by three members of her staff who devoted all their time to this endeavor. The Kleins used to have only a handful of orders for holiday wreaths. Beth had turned that into a thriving aspect of the business. Plus, overseas sales of Christmas trees had doubled in the past three years. Beth had always enjoyed the season, but never more than now. She felt she was actively contributing to a lot of families' happiness this Christmas.

The girls cleared the table and put their plates and bowls in the dishwasher.

"I've got to get back outside, but before I go, I need you to tell me what's going on with your father." From the girls' startled expressions Beth realized she should have led into the conversation with a bit more finesse. But subtlety wasn't exactly her strong suit and she was short on time.

"Dad wanted to come for Christmas," Bailey answered, as if that was all the explanation required.

"Did he give you any particular reason?" she asked suspiciously.

Sophie shook her head. "None that he mentioned."

That wasn't too helpful; still, Beth persisted. "But why this year?"

Bailey shrugged. "Don't know. All I can tell you is that he said he missed us and asked if he could join us for Christmas. We couldn't say no. You wouldn't want us to, would you, Mom?"

"Of course not." Beth looked from one daughter to the other. "He didn't say anything more than that? You're sure?"

"Positive." Both girls widened their eyes, expressions innocent as could be.

Convinced there was more to this sudden desire to be with them—and remembering Grace's suggestion that the girls might be more involved than they were letting on—Beth hesitated. She wanted to probe deeper but really needed to get to work. As it was, she'd lingered with her daughters well into Jeff's lunch hour.

"You'll be okay without me?" Beth asked, abandoning all inquiries for the moment.

"Mom, it isn't like we're six years old!"

"I know, I know, it's just that I hate leaving you so soon after you got here."

"Go," Bailey said, ushering her toward the door. "We'll be fine. We'll unpack our suitcases and put *It's a Wonderful Life* in the DVD player."

"I want to watch it, too," Beth protested. It was their favorite Christmas movie.

"Okay, we'll hold off until tonight. Now go."

Walking out the door, Beth blew them a kiss, the same way she had every time she left for work when they were youngsters.

The second the door closed, Bailey turned to her sister. "Do you think Mom suspects anything?"

"I'm not sure...."

"I told you we needed to get our story straight before we saw her!"

"I didn't think she'd drill us with questions the instant we walked in the door. Just remember, this whole idea was yours," Sophie reminded her.

"But you agreed! Dad's miserable without Mom, and Mom needs Dad whether she's willing to admit it or not."

"Well, she's *not* willing to admit it, not yet," Sophie said. She rinsed out the soup pan and placed it in the dishwasher. "I never really understood why they got divorced," she mused.

"Yeah." Bailey was wiping off the kitchen counter. "It didn't make any sense."

"When they told us I thought they were joking. Some joke, huh?"

"Could there be anyone else involved?" Bailey asked, growing introspective. "Mom mentioned that vet again. Ted something."

"Ted Reynolds. She hasn't dated in ages, but she seems to like him. He could be trouble."

Bailey frowned. "The problem with Mom is that she's living inside an…an emotional cocoon." She nodded, pleased with that description. "She's consumed by this tree farm so she doesn't have to think about Dad or the divorce or anything else."

"Who made you the expert?" Sophie muttered.

Bailey ignored the sarcasm. "I took this really great psychology class, and I recognized what Mom's been doing for the past few years. We've got to shake her up, make her realize the divorce was a terrible mistake."

"It's not just the tree farm, it's those darn puppies," Sophie lamented. "With puppies constantly showing up on Mom's porch, she can focus all her attention on them. She spends a lot of time training her dogs for those canine therapy programs—"

"And being the unofficial rescue facility," Bailey threw in.

Sophie nodded. "And now there's this Ted guy. Getting Mom and Dad together isn't going to be as easy as you think."

"What did you tell Dad?" Bailey asked.

Sophie slouched into a chair and stared at her sister. "Just that it's important to Mom that we all spend Christmas together."

"Did he ask why?"

"Not really. He said he didn't have any fixed plans for Christmas, and if Mom wanted him to come he would."

"What are we going to tell them when they discover we arranged this?"

"What we should've said when they told us they were getting divorced. This is stupid. They should've tried harder."

"They just grew apart, that's all, but if they'd made an effort they could've gotten close again, right?"

"Right."

"Marriage takes work," Bailey said, feeling wise. The research for her recent psych essay on "Family in the New Millennium" had made that very clear to her.

"I just don't want them to be upset with us," Sophie said, worried.

"They can't. It's Christmas. We brought them together… okay, under false pretenses, but they can't be mad because we're only doing what's best for them."

"Amen. Sing it, sister."

"We'll sing it in two-part harmony."

"Dad gets here when?"

"Tomorrow afternoon."

"Perfect." Sophie held up two crossed fingers. "I believe. I believe."

"So do I," Bailey echoed. This was going to be the most wonderful Christmas of their lives and it didn't have a sin-

gle thing to do with the wrapped packages under the tree. It
was because of the gift they intended to give their parents.

And each other.

The snow had stopped falling, and the grounds were so
pristine and lovely, they could've been on a book cover. Or
a Christmas card. The evergreens were daubed with snow,
giving them a flocked look that was more beautiful than
anything Beth could reproduce with the sticky artificial
stuff her crew applied to the more elaborately decorated
trees in the shop.

"We're back," Bruce Peyton said as he approached Beth.
"And this time, we're definitely going home with a tree."

His pregnant wife, Rachel, looked so much better than
she had two weeks ago. Beth had learned later that Rachel
was hospitalized with food poisoning that same evening.
Bruce's teenage daughter, Jolene, was with them today, as
she'd been before.

"Are all the best trees taken?" the girl asked, her eyes
wide with concern.

She had a point. The trees closer to the house had been
thinned out, but there were still a number of excellent
spruces and firs in the far lot. "Not to worry," she assured
Jolene. "I always save the best for last." She handed the
girl a cup of warm cocoa. "If you'd like, I'll have my foreman take you to the back twenty in the ATV and you can
see for yourself."

"Really?"

"Really," Beth confirmed. She led them over to Jeff, made introductions and gave him Jolene's request.

The ATVs were built for two, so Jeff took one and Jolene climbed on behind him. Bruce took the second vehicle. Rachel looked at the hard seat, then eyed the dirt road speculatively.

"I think I'll stay here and visit with Beth while you two choose the tree."

"You can't," Jolene said loudly. "You *have* to help pick out the tree. That's the most fun part."

"I'm just not sure I'm up to this."

"Let me take you for a test run," Bruce suggested.

Rachel remained hesitant, then nodded. "Okay, but don't be upset if I decide to stay back."

"I won't," Bruce said.

"I really want you to come with us," Jolene insisted.

"I know, honey. I will next year. I'll come with you and your little sister. Don't forget, it'll be her very first Christmas."

Jolene hugged her quickly. "Okay."

Ten minutes later, Rachel was sitting in the office, drinking a bottle of apple juice as Beth finished her paperwork.

"I doubt they'll be long," Beth told her. "The trees there are gorgeous, especially with this afternoon's snow."

"I hope Bruce and Jolene don't go overboard and choose the biggest tree on the farm."

Beth chuckled. "Jeff knows that people look at a tree and have no idea how large it is until they try to get it in the house. He'll keep them realistic."

"Oh, good. Jolene loves Christmas." Rachel leaned back in her chair. "I consider this our first real Christmas as a family. We were married last year but I was so busy cleaning and moving that it didn't feel very Christmassy."

"There seem to be a lot of firsts for your family," Beth said gently.

"I agree. It hasn't been a smooth transition for us, but everything's come together in the past couple of weeks."

"I'm glad," Beth said. She wasn't entirely sure what Rachel meant. Busy though she'd been, when the Peytons originally came for their tree, Beth couldn't help noticing the tension between Rachel and Jolene. The change in attitude, particularly on Jolene's part, was encouraging.

Twenty minutes later, the two ATVs roared into the yard. As soon as the engine was shut off, Jolene leaped off the back of her father's vehicle and raced toward Rachel.

"We found the most beautiful tree," she said excitedly. "It's just *perfect*."

"Where is it?" Rachel asked, laughing at Jolene's unabashed enthusiasm.

"You should've seen her," Bruce said, joining them. "Jolene was like a rabbit, hopping from one tree to the next."

"Dad, you're embarrassing me," the girl protested, but

not too vigorously. In fact, it looked as if a smile was permanently affixed to her face.

"Exactly where is this wonderful, perfect Christmas tree?" Rachel asked again.

"Jeff's going back in the pickup for it now," Bruce explained. He reached into his pocket for his wallet. "While he's doing that, I'll pay for the tree and get out the rope so we can tie it to the top of the car."

"When we take it home, we're all going to decorate it together," Jolene said happily.

"My girls and I do that," Beth told her. "I always decorate several trees, but I leave one undecorated so the four… three of us can do it together once they're home from college."

Jolene looked at her father and Rachel. "Will you wait for me when I'm in college, too?"

"You bet," Rachel said, raising one thumb.

That seemed to satisfy the teenager. "It won't be that long, you know."

"No need to rush it," Bruce commented.

The phone rang, and since Jeff was busy, Beth grabbed it. "Cedar Cove Tree Farm," she said. "Beth speaking."

"Oh, Beth, I'm so glad I caught you."

It was her friend, Grace Harding, the head librarian who'd adopted a golden-retriever mix from the previous batch of puppies. She sounded harried.

"What can I do for you, Grace?" Beth asked.

"We need a small tree."

"How small?"

"One that'll fit in a hotel room. It's for a family who just arrived in town. Friends of ours."

"Sure. I can have Jeff cut one for you and deliver it myself."

"Oh, would you? I know this is last-minute, but these are two special friends who once rented our house on Rosewood Lane. That was years ago—but Ian's in the navy and it looks like they're moving back. They have two children. They're only here for a few days, but I can't bear the thought of them spending Christmas in Cedar Cove without a tree."

"I'm on it," Beth said. "Don't worry, I'll see to everything, including lights and decorations. Shall I bring it to your place?"

"Yes, please. I don't know how to thank you."

"You already have," Beth said. Replacing the phone she looked at Bruce. "Now, I don't suppose I could interest you in adopting a puppy?"

"A puppy?" Jolene perked right up. "Could we, Dad? Rachel? *Could* we?"

Bruce shrugged uncomfortably. "I don't think so, sweetheart. With the baby coming and everything..."

"What kind of puppy?" Rachel asked, reaching for Bruce's hand.

"They're a Labrador mix. They're all black and extremely cute. You could have the pick of the litter."

Jolene clasped her hands and turned pleading eyes to her father.

Bruce held Rachel's gaze and after a moment nodded. "But remember, Jolene, you're responsible for training and taking care of the puppy."

"I will, Dad, I promise. I've always wanted a dog! I want a girl and I'm going to name her Poppy."

"Poppy's a good name," Rachel said.

"I can help with the training," Beth offered, leading all three of them to the laundry room. It didn't take Jolene long to choose the puppy she wanted.

One down, nine to go.

Two

Earlier in the month, Grace had been pleasantly surprised to get a phone call from Cecilia and Ian Randall, who were stationed in San Diego. They phoned again once they got into town.

"Would it be possible for Ian and me to stop by and visit?" Cecilia asked.

"Cecilia, of course! How are you? I hoped I'd get a chance to see you and Ian and the kids." Grace had a hundred questions. The young couple had always been close to her heart, and she was thrilled at the prospect of having them back in the area.

"Remember I told you the navy transferred Ian back to Bremerton?" Cecilia said. "He's going to be working in the shipyard instead of on the aircraft carrier. Cedar Cove feels like home to us, so we're really happy about coming back."

"That's wonderful!" The Randalls reminded Grace of when she and her first husband, Dan, had purchased their house almost forty years ago. They'd been young, too, with a child and another on the way. Maryellen was a toddler and Grace had been pregnant with Kelly, and 204 Rosewood Lane had been their first real home. In fact, Grace had lived in that house most of her adult life. She'd raised her children there, buried her husband and learned to deal with life as a widow all on Rosewood Lane. The place held a great deal of sentimental value for her and she hadn't been able to let it go, even after marrying Cliff Harding. So she'd decided to rent it out.

The Randalls had been ideal tenants, but the navy had transferred them all too soon. Over the years, Grace had seen a number of renters come and go. Faith Beckwith had resided there for a while; she'd had a difficult time with break-ins perpetrated by the tenants preceding her. That was long past now and the culprits were behind bars, thanks to Sheriff Davis. The most recent renters had left, and the house was sitting empty.

"I think I mentioned that Ian has leave over Christmas. We flew out here yesterday. We came to see my dad and look for housing." She paused. "Dad lives in a small apartment, so we're staying at the Comfort Inn."

Grace had assumed as much, based on their previous conversation. And other than the Beldons' B and B, the Comfort Inn was the only hotel in downtown Cedar Cove.

"Do you have a car?" she asked.

"A rental."

"Come over today if you can and we'll chat."

"What time?"

"Two," she suggested. "Olivia is planning to stop by around then, and I know she'd love to see you."

"Judge Lockhart...I mean, Judge Griffin?"

"Yes."

"I'd love to see her, too. Ian and I owe her so much."

Indeed they did owe a debt of gratitude to Olivia, as did many others in the community. Despite her decades as an attorney and then a family court judge, Olivia had never become jaded or cynical. She looked at each case individually. Over the years she'd made some controversial judgments. In Ian and Cecilia's case, she'd denied their divorce. That decision had caused quite a stir in the courtroom and around town. She'd used a technicality, urging the couple to try harder and not to give up on each other so soon.

As it happened, Jack Griffin, the new *Chronicle* editor, had been visiting the court that day and had written an article about her decision, which had greatly embarrassed poor Olivia. Nevertheless, his inflammatory piece had been the start of their relationship. And look where that had led! Grace couldn't hold back a smile.

"We'll be there at two," Cecilia said.

"Be sure to bring the kids," Grace told her. "Cliff is

boarding a pony over the holidays. She's very gentle, and the owner said we can give rides to anyone we want."

"Oh! Aaron and Mia will love it. See you at two."

Grace finished addressing the last of her Christmas cards and walked down to the mailbox to send them off, knowing they'd be late this year. She wondered how she'd gotten so far behind.

Cliff helped her prepare by setting out a plate of cookies, although Grace suspected he ate as many as he put on the plate. The cocoa was warming on the stove when a car rolled into the driveway.

Beau, her puppy and guard dog, barked, warning them of impending visitors. "Is it the Randalls or Olivia?" Grace asked.

Cliff peered out the kitchen window. "Looks like Olivia." He reached for his coat. "I'll be outside with Pixie, saddling her up for the Randall kids."

"Thanks." Grace dried her hands and hurried to the door. Olivia immediately handed her a fruitcake wrapped in aluminum foil.

"From Mom," she announced, stooping to pet Beau. "She baked them while she was living with Jack and me, and wanted to be sure you got one."

Grace wasn't a fruitcake fan—except for Charlotte's, which included green tomato mincemeat and pecans. She put it on the counter next to an evergreen spray in a narrow vase.

"That's so thoughtful. How's Charlotte doing?" Grace was well aware that Charlotte and Ben's recent move into the assisted-living complex hadn't been easy.

"She has good days and bad days." Olivia removed her gloves, stuffing them in her pocket, then slipped off her coat and draped it across the back of a kitchen chair. "On Tuesday, Mom phoned and told me she'd made a big mistake and wanted to return to the house."

"But Will's living there now."

"I didn't remind Mom of that. I figured out what was wrong. It's Christmas and she misses all the things that represent the holidays to her. She associates them with the house."

"Poor Charlotte."

"It *is* hard to make such a huge move at this point in her life."

As Beau settled on the rug by the kitchen door, Grace poured them each a cup of coffee. She carried the mugs to the table, then pulled out a chair. "So what did you do?"

"I found the crèche she'd tucked away in the basement and brought it over to their apartment, along with a small Christmas tree and a few other decorations. Then we sat and chatted over tea for a while. After about an hour, Mom said she'd had a change of heart and the assisted-living complex would suit her just fine."

"That's a relief." Grace knew this had been as difficult for Will and Olivia as it was for their mother and Ben.

On the whole, though, the new arrangement seemed to be working out.

"I had a call earlier today," Grace said.

"Oh?" Olivia sipped her coffee.

"Remember I mentioned that Ian and Cecilia Randall were coming to town? In fact, Beth was by just a short while ago to drop off a tree for them."

"So they're here?"

"Yes. Since Ian's been transferred to the Bremerton shipyard, they came to spend Christmas with Cecilia's father, and look for a place to live. They're staying at the Comfort Inn."

"When did they get in?"

"Yesterday. Cecilia phoned and they'll be stopping by—" She paused to glance at the kitchen clock. "Anytime now," she finished.

"Why the Christmas tree?" Olivia asked.

"You know as well as I do that Bobby Merrick isn't going to have a Christmas tree for those kids. I explained the situation to Beth and she brought over the cutest tree you can imagine. It's in a pot and won't take up much space. They should be able to set it in a corner of the hotel room without a problem. She even threw in lights and a few ornaments." Grace appreciated all the effort Beth had put into this spur-of-the-moment idea.

"She owes you big-time after you decided to keep Beau," Olivia said.

On hearing his name, Beau scampered from his place by the door to Grace's feet. When she picked him up and held him in her lap, Beau licked her hand, then settled down to snooze, content to be close to his mistress.

"I'm the one who owes Beth," Grace said, brushing her hand along Beau's soft fur. She'd resisted her affection for Beau as long as she could, but his sweet temperament had eventually won her over.

"I heard Beth has ten more puppies to find homes for now."

"Nine," Grace was pleased to tell her. "Beth is elated. Bruce and Rachel Peyton let Jolene have a puppy for Christmas. She's named her Poppy."

"I hope everything's okay," Olivia said, frowning slightly. "I don't want to see them in my courtroom."

"The situation seems to have resolved itself. When I spoke to Rachel, she said all three of them were in counseling and making great strides." Then Grace added, "I'll be grateful when Rachel returns to the salon. My nails are a mess without her."

"Grace!"

"Well, it's true."

They heard a car door slam in the distance. Beau's head came up and he leaped down from his resting place on Grace's lap. Barking, he ran to the front door, tail wagging furiously.

She followed him and opened the door to Cecilia Randall.

"Merry Christmas," Cecilia said, giving her a bright red poinsettia.

Cecilia didn't seem to have changed since the last time Grace had seen her. True, her dark hair was shorter now, stylishly cut, but she was as slim and elegant as ever.

Cecilia broke into a big grin. "You look exactly the same as I remember."

"I was just thinking the same thing about you." Grace set the plant on a small table near the entry. As she closed the door she glanced over at the barn. Ian and the two children were already talking to Cliff, who'd led the pony into the yard. Cliff had Pixie saddled and was introducing her to the children. Grace would serve them cookies and hot chocolate later when they came in. "Olivia's here."

"Oh, good! I was hoping for a chance to see her." As Cecilia moved into the kitchen, Grace hung up her scarf and wool coat.

"Hello, hello," Olivia said. Standing, the two women exchanged hugs.

"Sit, please," Grace said. She took out another mug and filled it with coffee.

There was a lot of laughter and smiling as they caught up with one another, but then Cecilia grew serious. She turned toward Olivia. "I was out to see Allison this morning." She bowed her head slightly. "Do...do you ever visit your son's grave?" she asked in a small voice.

"Yes," Olivia admitted softly. "On Jordan's birthday, Justine and I put flowers by his headstone."

"Ian and I went this morning and cleaned off her grave. The kids brought her a poinsettia."

"It's still difficult, isn't it?" Olivia said, reaching across the table to squeeze Cecilia's hand.

Grace leaned over to grab a tissue and passed it to the young woman.

"Do you still cry?" Cecilia asked, unmistakable pain in her voice. The loss of her infant daughter was an anguish that might fade but would never disappear. Grace knew that from her own experience, losing Dan.

"Yes," Olivia said. "We don't forget our children. Ever. We can't. There's been a gaping hole in my heart—in my life—ever since we lost Jordan. He was only thirteen...." She cleared her throat. "I've chosen to fill that hole with love."

"I have, too," Cecilia whispered. "Love for Ian and our other children. Both Aaron and Mia know they had an older sister. On Allison's birthday last year, Aaron wanted to bake her a cake."

"Did you?"

Cecilia nodded. "It never felt right to leave Allison when Ian was transferred. I'm so glad we're moving back."

"We're glad, too," Grace told her. Then because she was

afraid they'd all end up weeping, she changed the subject. "So, you're looking for a house...."

"Oh, yes." Cecilia wiped the tears from her eyes and straightened. "Ian and I want to talk to you about the house on Rosewood Lane."

Grace smiled happily. "Well, as I said, my last renters left when their lease expired, and the house is empty. Cliff and I would be delighted to rent it to you."

Olivia checked her watch. "Sorry to rush off, but Justine needs me to baby-sit this afternoon."

"Of course." Grace stood, too, and hugged her friend. "If I don't see Charlotte, make sure you thank her for the fruitcake."

"Will do."

"See you Christmas Eve at Noelle's birthday party, right after church." She briefly explained, for Cecilia's benefit, who Noelle was and that she'd been born here at the ranch a year earlier.

"Yes, see you then," Olivia confirmed. She put on her coat and gloves and wished Cecilia a merry Christmas. Grace walked her out, returning to find Cecilia by the back door, looking at her children, who were taking turns on the pony. "About the house," Cecilia began, moving back to the kitchen table. "Ian and I—"

A polite knock sounded at the door, but before Grace could reach it, Ian Randall came inside. "Hello, Grace," he said warmly. "Cliff said I should go on in. He's taking the kids into the barn to feed the horses." Giving an obligatory bark, Beau trotted over to him and Ian crouched down to stroke the sleek, soft head.

"They're going to love that," Cecilia said. "Aaron is such an animal person." She might as well have said, *And so is Ian.*

"Would he like a puppy for Christmas?" Grace rushed to ask, knowing how desperate Beth was to find good homes.

"He'd love one," Cecilia replied, "but with the move, a puppy—"

"He can pick one out. They're at a tree farm owned by Beth Morehouse, a friend of ours. If you get a puppy, Cliff and I can keep him here with Beau until you're back in Cedar Cove."

Cecilia and Ian exchanged a glance. "That's too much to ask."

"Not at all. And it would be a huge help to Beth. Someone abandoned ten puppies on her porch and she needs good homes for them before Christmas."

"Aaron's responsible, and he'd love it," Cecilia prompted. "Besides, we'd be rescuing a puppy. What do you think?" She looked at her husband, obviously attracted to the idea.

Ian shrugged. "A puppy for Aaron would be a great gift…if you're positive you don't mind keeping him for a few weeks."

"We wouldn't mind in the least," Grace assured him.

"Okay, that's settled. We'll go and see your friend, pick

out a puppy." Ian pulled out a chair and sat down next to his wife. "Did Cecilia mention the house on Rosewood Lane?"

"We'd just started to talk about it," Grace said. "I told her it's available and we'd love to rent it to you again."

Ian shook his head.

"You don't want it?" This surprised Grace because she remembered how fond Cecilia had been of the place and all the small homey changes she'd made. "My mistake. I'm sorry," she said with some embarrassment.

"Actually, Cecilia and I were wondering," Ian said, clasping his wife's hand, "if you and Cliff would consider selling us the house."

"Selling," Grace repeated. "Oh…I hadn't thought of that."

"I brought it up to Cliff," Ian continued, "and he said the decision was yours."

"Well…yes, I suppose it is," Grace murmured. Her immediate reaction was not to sell. Her emotional attachment to the house on Rosewood Lane remained strong. "Can I think about it and get back to you sometime in the next couple of days?"

"Of course," Ian said.

The back door opened again and Cliff came in with the two children. Aaron was instantly on the floor, playing with Beau, and Mia ran to tell her mother all about riding Pixie.

The rest of the visit passed in a blur for Grace, preoccupied as she was with Ian's request. She served cocoa and cookies and presented the Randalls with the small Christmas tree, which thrilled the kids, but she was hardly aware of anything that was said. The young family left soon afterward.

Grace and Cliff waved them off and returned to the house.

"From the look on your face, Ian must have said something about wanting to buy the house." Cliff walked over to the coffeepot and refilled his mug. He leaned against the counter as he waited for her reply.

"He did."

"And?"

"I…don't know if I can give it up."

"Then tell them it's only available to rent," he said matter-of-factly.

"But…this is exactly the type of family I'd want to sell the house to." Grace found she couldn't keep still. She walked over to the refrigerator and opened it for no reason. Closing it, she circled the kitchen table.

"I understand." Cliff came up behind her, placing his hands on her shoulders. "It's a big decision."

Grace exhaled slowly. "It is…but I think it's time," she said with sudden resolve. "My old life was on Rosewood Lane. My new life is here with you—and Beau."

Lying on the braided carpet beneath the kitchen table, Beau raised his head and barked once. Apparently, he was in full agreement.

Three

Two down and eight puppies to go.

Saturday morning, the day before Christmas Eve, Aaron Randall—as well as his parents and little sister—had stopped by and picked out a puppy. Grace, bless her, had agreed to keep tiny Poko until the Randalls returned to Cedar Cove in the second week of January. He was with her now, as it would've been too difficult to look after the puppy in the hotel room.

The Randalls' rental car pulled out of the driveway just as another vehicle turned in.

Kent. Obviously driving a rental, too. It was a bright blue sedan, not his usual style at all.

It couldn't be anyone else. He'd phoned shortly after he'd arrived at Thyme and Tide, and said he was on his way over.

Despite herself, Beth felt another wave of excitement. She hadn't slept all night, trying to make sense of his unexpected need to connect as a family again. Granted, he saw their daughters more often than she did, since both attended college in California. But all four of them together at Christmas… It had been a long time. Even if, as she suspected, Bailey and Sophie were involved in this, Kent didn't have to go along with it. But he had.…

Still, she wondered if she was reading more into the situation than it warranted; all the same, she considered scenarios of what this Christmas would be like. Then there was Ted. He was a close friend, and while they'd shared little more than a few chaste kisses, the relationship looked promising. She felt it and thought he did, too.

Beth remembered Christmases when the girls were young. She remembered laughing with Kent, the two of them shushing each other as they stayed up half the night assembling tricycles and later bicycles and then fell into bed exhausted. In an hour or two, Bailey and Sophie would be jumping up and down on the mattress, shrieking that Santa had come.

One Christmas Eve they'd gone for a sleigh ride in freshly fallen snow, snuggling under a blanket, keeping one another warm. Kent had stolen a few hot kisses while the girls giggled and hid their eyes, complaining that it was "yucky" to see their parents kiss.

Beth smiled. They'd had some really good years together. Somewhere along the way, though, their lives had changed. No, their marriage had. They'd grown apart. It wasn't any big disagreement, no betrayal or unforeseen revelation. Instead, an accumulation of small slights and annoyances had eventually grown from a small distance into a huge crevasse. One that had deepened and widened over the years until they'd been unable to reach across it....

Was it possible? Did Kent regret the divorce? Beth had more than a few regrets herself. They'd both been so stubborn, so unreasonable, so eager to prove they didn't need each other anymore.

Perhaps if they'd been the kind of people who yelled and stomped around the house, everything might have gone differently. Instead, once the subject of divorce had been broached, they'd been so darned polite. Attorneys said there was no such thing as a "friendly" divorce, but that hadn't been Beth's experience. Theirs had been not only friendly but accommodating and fair. But maybe that was just on the surface. Maybe going ahead with the divorce was *unfair*—to both of them.

She'd gotten busy at the college and Kent had his engineering company. They'd been like those ships in the old cliché, passing in the night, each drifting in a different direction. She had her life and he had his.

Kent claimed he found her friends stuffy and boring, and stopped attending social functions with her. Beth decided *his* friends were snobs. He didn't seem to mind that she stayed home when he had an event, and after a while she wondered if he'd met someone else. It wouldn't have surprised her. Although he'd never admitted it… They were so remote at that point, spending almost no time together. Oh, they slept in the same bed but rarely touched, rarely communicated about anything other than routine or functional things. Like who was picking up milk or paying the electricity bill.

She was the one who'd suggested divorce. At first Kent had seemed shocked. But he'd recovered quickly enough. He'd simply said that if she wanted a divorce, he wouldn't stop her…and he hadn't.

They'd divided everything as equitably as possible, sold the house and parted ways. It'd all been so civilized, so straightforward, as if twenty-three years as husband and wife meant nothing.

When the final decree came through, Beth decided to leave the academic world. She'd been seeking a geographical cure, she supposed, considering it now. The Christmas tree farm had been the solution she'd been looking for. She had her dogs and a menagerie of other pets, including two canaries, a guinea pig and now the puppies. Eight puppies. She also fed a number of feral cats. And she'd made new friends and found new purpose….

Kent—and, yes, it was Kent, as she'd expected—parked the car and turned off the engine. Beth pretended she was busy. Too busy to even glance in his direction. But despite herself, she was excited. Happy.

All she'd ever wanted from him was some indication that he still loved her, that he still cared. His insistence on spending Christmas with her and the girls, no matter how it had come about, was the first time either of them had made a move toward the other. Could this be the start of a reconciliation?

Her heart rate accelerated and she brushed her hair behind both ears. She wished now that she'd worn something other than her ever-present jeans. Dressing up a bit would've been a subtle way of letting Kent know how pleased she was that he'd extended an olive branch. She had on a long-sleeved shirt beneath her red V-neck sweater, which would have gone nicely with her black wool pants. Oh, how she wished she'd put on her black wool pants.

The car door closed, and Kent stood there, looking at her.

"Hello," she said, surprised by how shaky her voice sounded. "Welcome to Christmas Tree Lane—and Cedar Cove Tree Farm."

He zipped up his jacket and grinned. "The house is fabulous. The girls were right."

"Thank you." The porch railing was covered with swags of evergreen and twinkling white lights. More lights hung from the roofline, glittering brightly in the dull gray winter morning.

The passenger car door opened and Beth saw that Kent hadn't come alone. A lovely, young—much younger than Beth—woman climbed out. She was tall, lithe and stylishly dressed in a full-length black coat and long, high-heeled black boots. She towered an inch or two above Kent, who stood at nearly six feet. Her blond, shoulder-length hair was perfect.... Actually, everything about her seemed perfect in an urban, sophisticated way that contrasted painfully with Beth's farm clothes, disheveled hair and work-roughened hands.

Beth blinked and her heart almost stopped as reality hit her. *Kent had brought another woman.* They were together. A couple. He was seeing someone else now. This little fantasy she'd built around a reconciliation was only that—wishful thinking.

It took her a moment to recover and realize that every assumption she'd made was completely and totally off-base. Kent hadn't come to spend Christmas with her and the girls. His sole purpose was to show off this...this model.

Nothing had changed. Nothing ever would.

"Hello." Beth greeted the other woman with a forced smile and an extended hand. "I'm Beth Morehouse. The ex-wife."

"I know," the woman said in a sultry voice that was sweet enough to caramelize sugar. "I'm Danielle."

Just Danielle? No last name? Like Cher or Madonna or Beyoncé?

"Welcome to *my* Christmas tree farm," she said, placing emphasis on her ownership.

The screen door flew open and Bailey raced onto the porch. "Dad!"

Sophie was directly behind her sister. They darted down the stairs like young fawns in their rush to hug Kent.

Her ex-husband opened his arms, and his daughters launched themselves into his wide embrace.

"How are my girls?" he asked, his voice warm with affection.

"Missing you, Daddy," Sophie murmured.

"Who's that?" Bailey asked starkly, frowning at Danielle. Apparently, she was as shocked as Beth.

"This is Danielle Martin," he said, sliding his arms around each of their waists.

Oh, so there was a last name.

"What's *she* doing here?" Sophie demanded.

"Sophie," Beth snapped, appalled at her daughter's lack of manners.

"Danielle's a friend from work who traveled with me," he said by way of introduction.

"Why don't we all step inside, out of the cold," Beth suggested, and marched into the house, assuming everyone else would follow.

The girls had obviously been playing with the puppies when Kent arrived because the second the door opened they swarmed onto the porch, eager as jailbirds to make an escape. Four were already out the door and racing down the porch steps.

"Don't just stand there," Beth cried to her daughters. "Help me."

Laughing, Sophie and Bailey hurried in one direction while Beth went in the other. Even Kent got involved in the chase. The only one who didn't move was Danielle. With her arms crossed, she remained immobile, as if moving a single inch would have dire consequences.

Once the puppies were all inside the house, Beth brought Kent and Danielle in. Danielle perched on the arm of a recliner with her feet off the carpet. She seemed to fear that all the puppies would rush toward her at one time.

Beth called out instructions. "Get the puppies into the laundry room," she told the girls. "I'll give them some treats." This was not the way she'd planned to greet Kent, with puppies creating havoc.

In the momentary quiet of the laundry room, Beth pressed one hand to her chest, which felt as though it was knotted with pain. She would not, *could* not, yield to the icy tide of disappointment or to the surprising burst of white-hot anger. Not now. Not here. She'd rather be dipped in Christmas-tree sap and rolled in holly leaves before she made a fool of herself in front of the girls.

With a deep breath, Beth squared her shoulders and opened a bag of canine treats just as the girls herded in the last three pups. Whether it was the rustle of the bag or the distinctive aroma, Beth didn't care, only that they all came on the run. On another calming breath, she promised to deal with her emotions later as she distributed the miniature bone-shaped biscuits.

She slowly and deliberately wiped her hands on her jeans while arranging her features in her best hostess smile. Returning to the living room, she motioned Sophie and Bailey to the couch and nodded at her guests. "Now, where were we?"

The girls exchanged a puzzled look and obeyed. At Beth's question, they fixed their gazes on their father.

"Are all those dogs...yours?" Danielle asked incredulously.

"No, no. I'm finding homes for them."

"Where are *your* dogs?" Kent asked. "Do you still have Lucy and Bixby?"

"Of course. They're in the heated kennel in the back."

"It's huge. You should see it, Dad," Sophie said, growing more animated as she spoke. "Mom's got six dogs of her own, and she helps with the Reading with Rover program at the library and...and she trains dogs and she just got a puppy herself." She was out of breath by the time she completed her list.

"He's been sickly so she keeps him upstairs," Bailey added.

"In your *bedroom?*" Danielle's eyes widened with what appeared to be horror.

"You started to tell us about Danielle," Bailey reminded her father, turning away from the other woman.

"Well, yes." Kent looked at Danielle. "She's a…friend."

"A good friend," Danielle murmured. "A *very* good friend."

"I can't believe this." Bailey paced their bedroom with her hands locked behind her back. "This is all wrong! Nothing is working out like we planned."

"When did Dad meet Danielle?" Sophie, the practical one, asked. "And where?"

"Why are you asking me? I don't know any more than you do."

Sitting on the edge of the bed with her hands in her hair—as if trying to pull out an answer—Sophie said, "Well, she wasn't there when we visited him at Thanksgiving. And he didn't say a word about her to me, but I thought he might've mentioned it to you."

"I wish." Bailey threw a scowl at her sister. "If he had, we never would've invited him for Christmas. That's for sure. Besides, I'd have told you. What's Dad thinking? Or *is* he thinking? Anyone with half a brain can see she's all wrong for him."

"She can't be much older than we are."

"Did you see how she reacted to the puppies?" Bailey cried. "Like they were diseased or something. Sitting with her feet in the air, as if they'd mistake her leg for a tree trunk. Too bad they didn't."

Sophie groaned. "And did you hear how she talked to me? Like I'm ten years old. For a minute I thought she was going to pinch my cheek and tell me how cute I was."

"Dad and Danielle? It's a joke," Bailey muttered. "A terrible joke."

"That's what you said about the divorce—until it happened."

"I know. I just don't want to believe this…whatever it is." But she'd seen the way Danielle had looked at their father. Clearly, he didn't have a clue. This woman was set on getting a big diamond ring from him. Bailey was bound and determined that wasn't going to happen. Not on her watch. If ever their father had needed help, it was now. They had to do something before he made the second-biggest mistake of his life. The first had been going through with the divorce.

"Well, you'd better come up with an idea fast, or you'll be spending next Thanksgiving with Dad and your new stepmother. Just you and Danielle and Dad. 'Cause I'm not going. I'll be here with Mom."

"Don't say that," Bailey moaned. "Besides, you'll *have* to come."

"Nope. I don't like Danielle."

"Me, neither."

"There's got to be something we can do," Sophie said.

"What?" Bailey asked in frustration, which was immediately followed by discouragement. "We can't let this happen. We just can't."

"I agree. Think, Bailey. You always come up with good plans."

"I'm trying, I'm trying."

Sophie kicked off her shoes and sat cross-legged on the bed. "First, we have to figure out what Danielle wants. No woman that young and perfect-looking would ever date our dad."

Bailey nodded. As harsh as it sounded, Sophie wasn't saying anything she hadn't already considered.

"We could introduce her to a younger man."

"Who?" Bailey asked.

"Jeff is cute."

"Mom's foreman? He's married. I don't want to be responsible for breaking up a marriage in order to get our parents back together."

"Yeah, that's bad," Sophie agreed. "Okay, who else is there? It's got to be somebody young. I mean, Dad's way over forty."

"So is Mom."

"Oh, Mom," Sophie said miserably, flopping back onto the bed. "She knew. She was so stoic when she introduced herself to Danielle, I wanted to scream."

Bailey had been too shocked to tear her eyes from her father. When she did look at her mother, she couldn't bear the return of the polite frozen smile. From the moment she and Sophie had mentioned that their father would be coming for Christmas, they'd both noticed a change in her.

In the beginning, when she'd heard the news, Beth had seemed confused and a bit panicky. Over dinner the night before, she'd peppered them with questions about their father. She was interested, all right. Interested and intrigued and, after a while, Bailey had sensed a definite excitement. She'd seemed happy, and for the first time since the divorce, they'd seen a brightness in her eyes.

It was exactly the reaction Bailey and Sophie had been looking for. Over the past three years, Mom had put on a great act. To all outward appearances, she was content; she certainly claimed to be. Her new life suited her just fine, she said. What had frightened the girls into taking action was the fact that their mother had started to casually drop Ted Reynolds's name into their conversations.

Beth's eagerness about seeing their dad convinced both Bailey and Sophie that all this talk about contentment was false. They'd been up half the night whispering in the dark, so sure they were right—and now this.

"Have you got any ideas yet?" Sophie sounded worried.

"Where's Mom?"

"Where she always goes when she's upset. She's with her dogs."

"With her dogs," Bailey echoed. The kennel was a place of comfort for Beth, a place of solace. The thought of her mom sitting on the ground with her precious animals gathered around her made Bailey want to weep.

"Where did Dad and Danielle go for lunch?"

"I don't know…."

He'd invited Bailey and Sophie to join them, but of course they'd declined.

"We should've gone with him," Bailey said.

"No way." Sophie shook her head. "I am not socializing with *her*."

Bailey reviewed various options that began occurring to her. Yes, it would work. She hopped onto the bed and tucked her legs underneath her.

Sophie stared at her. "What are you thinking?"

"We need to show Dad that Danielle's completely wrong for him."

"Well, duh. Just how are we going to do that?"

"There *are* ways." Bailey gave a conspiratorial smile.

Immediately, Sophie straightened. "You think we can do it?"

"I don't just think, I know. Watch out, Danielle. You're in for it now."

Four

Judge Olivia Griffin pulled into the parking lot at the Pancake Palace. She'd ordered two coconut cream pies for their Christmas Eve dinner at Justine's. After the meal, they'd attend church services, then head over to Noelle's birthday party. Picking up the pies was on the list of errands she needed to run before collecting Mom and Ben that evening.

The restaurant was packed, which surprised her. She hadn't expected it to be this busy on Christmas Eve Day. But she should have, she mused, as she hunted for a parking space at the back of the lot. Based on last year's experience, her daughter had warned her. With a firm conviction that family came first, Justine had decided to close the Tea Room for Christmas Eve as well as Christmas Day. Her staff was thrilled with the unexpected gift of this extra time off.

Inside the restaurant, Olivia stood in line at the counter waiting her turn. Wave upon wave of happy voices washed through the room. Looking around, she noticed the painted windows, decorated with a variety of holiday scenes. Holly on one window, a snowman on another. She gazed across the room and saw the Randall family in a booth with Cecilia's father, Bobby Merrick. Holding fistfuls of crayons, the two Randall children were bent over their place mats, solving puzzles, connecting the dots or just coloring.

Remembering her conversation with Cecilia the day before, Olivia couldn't help releasing a sigh. The young mother had asked about Jordan, Olivia's son and Justine's twin brother.

It seemed to Olivia that her entire life was divided by that summer. Life before Jordan died and life afterward. Her world had imploded that summer afternoon. No sooner had they buried their son than Stan, her husband, announced that he wanted a divorce. Within a matter of months, she'd lost her son *and* her marriage.

Watching Cecilia and Ian Randall now, sitting close together, so attuned to each other, so much in love, she didn't regret denying their divorce. How could she? She would've given anything if someone had done the same for her and Stan. The pain of losing their son had been so horrific that, instead of bringing them together, it had driven a wedge between them.

When Stan remarried only months after their divorce, Olivia's friends had speculated that he'd been involved with Marge long before Jordan's death. It'd been easy to believe, especially then. Her mother, who was reluctant to say anything bad about anyone, felt Stan had acted irrationally in leaving his family.

Irrationally? Their son was dead. How could either of them remain rational? The grief had killed them, too.

It was all a moot point. Stan had married Marge, and some years later they'd divorced, as well. For a time it seemed that he wanted to get back together with Olivia and had done his best to thwart her budding romance with Jack Griffin. By then, however, Olivia had fallen for Jack, and her sights were set on the future instead of resurrecting the past. It was far too late for her and Stan. When it became apparent that she wasn't interested, he'd found someone else. Justine had told her that Susan, the new woman in his life, was living with him now. Olivia assumed he wasn't willing to try marriage a third time.

Yesterday, Cecilia had asked if she still cried over Jordan. Did a mother ever stop weeping over a lost child? Olivia doubted it. While going through cancer treatments a couple of years ago, Olivia had become desperately ill with an infection. From what others told her later, she knew she'd been close to death. It was while her fever raged that

Jordan had come to her. For the briefest of moments she'd seen him as he was that summer, a skinny thirteen-year-old, full of life, eager to prove himself. He'd been a happy boy, smart and witty. Even now when she heard his favorite song by the group Air Supply, tears would prick her eyes. When she thought of her son, she remembered his ready smile, his ease with people, a natural charm that never failed to endear him to others.

Once again, Olivia wondered what would have become of her son had he lived. He had a variety of interests. He'd been good at math and loved to take things apart, then put them back together. He might have been an engineer. Then, too, he was often the go-between when Justine and James argued, helping his siblings settle their differences. Perhaps he would've followed in her footsteps and become an attorney.

Olivia felt a thickening in her throat and blinked back tears. This was silly. Christmas was supposed to be joyous, festive. Now wasn't the time to reminisce about Jordan.

Cecilia glanced up and, seeing Olivia, she smiled. Their eyes connected—mother to mother. Heart to heart. Cecilia knew Olivia was remembering Jordan. And Olivia knew Cecilia was remembering the infant daughter she'd held so briefly in her arms.

Cecilia nodded and rested her head against Ian's shoulder. For an instant Ian looked surprised, and then Olivia saw him reach for his wife's hand and give it a gentle squeeze.

Tammy, the hostess, touched Olivia's arm. "I have your pies, Judge Griffin."

"Oh...oh, sorry, I got distracted." Olivia pulled out her wallet, paid for the pies and carried them out to the car without looking back.

Olivia had just opened the driver's-side door when her cell phone chirped. She dug it out of her purse, saw it was her husband and pushed the talk button.

"Hello, sweetheart," she said.

"Where are you?" he asked, sounding rushed.

"The Pancake Palace, why?"

"Eric and Shelly arrived with the boys."

"I didn't think they were due until five." Her stepson and his family were hours early. They'd driven from Reno to spend Christmas Eve with Jack and Olivia at Justine's, and Christmas Day with Shelly's family. "Can you feed them lunch or do you want me to come home?" she asked.

"Lunch isn't a problem. I'm calling because I need to know if Beth Morehouse has any of those puppies left."

"I'm sure she does."

"Great. Eric was saying he wanted to get Tedd and Todd each a dog after the first of the year, and he was hoping to find a couple of Labs. I told him about Beth's situation and he's interested."

"Oh, Jack, Beth would be so grateful!"

"That's what I thought. I'll give her a call and take Eric and the boys out to her place later this afternoon. Do you want to meet us there?"

"If I have time…"

"Okay. Love you."

"Love you, too." She ended the call and dropped her cell back in her purse. Beth would be thrilled to find homes for two more puppies.

Olivia's next stop was the Sanford assisted-living complex, where her mother and stepfather had recently moved. The snow had been cleared from the parking lot and the sidewalk swept and salted. Hugging her coat around her, she hunched her shoulders against the wind and hurried inside.

A large, beautifully decorated Christmas tree sparkling with lights and classic ornaments graced the entry. Red bows were attached to a set of twin chandeliers. Six fresh wreaths festooned the second-floor railing and left a lingering scent of pine. The complex had a homey, welcoming appeal.

Olivia saw Ben first. He was in the card room set off to the side of the main room. He was apparently playing either pinochle or bridge, his two favorite games. Olivia knew Charlotte was waiting for her upstairs. Her mother insisted on reviewing their Christmas-dinner menu, although Olivia had already prepared most of the dishes in advance. Tonight and tomorrow were for family. She had no intention of spending Christmas Day in the kitchen, although she planned to put the turkey in the oven sometime Christmas morning.

The menu was the same one they had almost every year, many of the recipes directly from the cookbook Charlotte had compiled for Justine. Last Christmas, Justine had made copies of her grandmother Charlotte's favorites for the extended family and it was a much-loved treasure.

Olivia headed for the elevator without interrupting Ben's game and went up to the third floor. Charlotte and Ben's small apartment was at the end of the hall. The door was propped open, a sign to all who came that they were welcome.

"Come in, come in," Charlotte said, putting aside her knitting and getting up. She was definitely moving more slowly, struggling a bit. Harry had arranged himself on the back of the recliner, his tail hanging straight down.

Olivia kissed her mother's cheek and urged her to sit again. She herself sat down in Ben's recliner. An end table served as a catchall between the two chairs, and Olivia saw not only Charlotte's knitting but Ben's current crossword. Dutifully, she took out a pad and pen. "You wanted to talk about Christmas dinner."

"Oh, yes. I do hope you intend to serve that wonderful artichoke appetizer."

"Got it," Olivia assured her. It was done and ready to go in the oven. The artichoke and caramelized onion filling was baked in a flaky dough. Everyone loved it. In fact, Olivia had made two because they were sure to disappear quickly.

"The potato casserole?"

"Wouldn't be Christmas without it," Olivia told her.

"Ben likes it with bacon crumbled on top."

"I can do that." Olivia made a notation on her pad to add bacon to please Ben.

"Did Jack make his special cookies?"

Generally speaking, Jack in the kitchen was a laughing matter but he had managed to prepare his favorite cookies—chocolate-dipped crackers sandwiched with peanut butter. They were a hit every Christmas. The cookie had been his own invention, and considering Jack's pride in the recipe, anyone would think it had won him a Cooking Channel top-chef award.

"The cookies are ready, as well."

"And what did the kitchen look like afterward?" Charlotte asked with a knowing gleam in her eye.

"A disaster. I helped with the cleanup."

"You're a good wife."

Her mother had set a good example.

"Justine wanted to serve beef Wellington, so I thought we'd do a turkey tomorrow."

"You can't go wrong with that," Charlotte said.

"No, you can't," Olivia agreed. There'd be stuffing and plenty of gravy, too. Her mother would work with her and add her personal assortment of herbs and spices to create the distinct taste everyone loved. Although Olivia had watched carefully and taken notes, hers never turned out quite the same.

"Anything else?"

Olivia hesitated. With her mother, everything was homemade, from the dinner rolls to the desserts, of which there was always a wide variety. Pecan pie, fruitcake, rum cake, apple strudel and more.

"I bought a couple of coconut cream pies from the Pancake Palace." Half expecting her mother to berate her for taking the easy road, Olivia held her breath.

"Oh, that's wonderful."

Wonderful? Olivia could hardly believe it. Her tensed shoulders sagged with relief.

"Everyone knows the Pancake Palace makes the best pies in town."

Olivia understood how difficult it was for her mother to deal with change. It wasn't easy for anyone, but the older people got, the harder it was. In her eighties now, Charlotte had coped with the transition from home to the assisted-living complex pretty well. She'd given up the house where she'd lived so many years of her life and surrendered much of her independence. Olivia was exceptionally proud of Charlotte and Ben. Naturally, there'd been doubts along the way, but all in all, the move had been a success.

"Anything else you'd like on the menu?" Olivia asked.

"My homemade applesauce."

"Of course, with the sweet pickles from last summer."

Charlotte rested her hands in her lap. "Those will be the last sweet pickles I put up," she said and, after a short pause, resumed her knitting.

Olivia opened her mouth to reassure her mother that there'd be more pickles and more summers, then realized this was Charlotte's way of telling her she was willing to give up that part of her life. No longer would she maintain a large garden or make applesauce and sauerkraut. The time had come to set all those endeavors aside.

A sharp pang of loss stabbed Olivia, but then she brightened. None of those activities, those special times, were really lost. With a little planning and foresight, they could continue into the next generation, and the one after that, too.

"Justine was talking about your pickle recipe a little while ago," Olivia said, and gently patted her mother's knee. "It wouldn't surprise me if she decided to put up sweet pickles next summer."

Her mother nodded approvingly. "I'll help if she needs advice."

"I know you will." A shift had taken place in their family. It hadn't been apparent at first and the irony of it was that Charlotte had recognized it before anyone else. Olivia felt a burst of joy. The recipes, the special family times, the laughter and the pleasures of being together would re-

main intact. Each generation would take what was pro-
duced and what was passed on by the one before, and then
share it with the next. Eventually other traditions would
be added, too.

"I'll be by to pick you and Ben up at five," she said.
Reaching for her purse, Olivia stood.

"When are James and his family coming?" her mother
asked as her fingers expertly wove the yarn around the
needle. Socks again. Charlotte must have knit more than
a hundred pairs over the years. These, no doubt, were for
one of the great-grandchildren.

"James, Selina and the children will be there in plenty of
time, don't worry." Olivia didn't have the heart to explain
that they'd arrived the night before. Charlotte had spoken
to her grandson on the phone but she'd obviously forgotten.

Unfortunately, these lapses happened more and more
often. Her mother could recall the recipe for sweet pickles
from memory, but a brief conversation the day before completely eluded her. They'd have a more definitive answer
to Charlotte's memory problems when they met with the
specialist in January. Until then, all they could do was wait.

"I love you, Olivia," her mother said softly as Olivia
started out the door.

The comment struck her as odd. Her mother rarely said
those words. She smiled. "I know, Mom, and I love you,
too." She came back and bent over to kiss her mother's
cheek. "I'll see you in a few hours."

For an instant Charlotte regarded her blankly and Olivia knew that her mother had no idea why her daughter would be returning so soon.

Five

Five puppies now had homes. Five to go.

It'd been love at first sight. Jack Griffin had come by with his son, Eric, and Eric's family. The grandsons had each chosen a puppy. They'd fallen to their knees and eight puppies had raced into their arms. It had taken quite a long time for the boys to make their decisions. In the end, they'd selected two males; in fact, they'd already given their puppies names, albeit not very original ones: Baron and Duke. Five were left, since Eddie Cox had picked one up for his parents—three females and two males. Ted had volunteered to watch over whatever puppies didn't have homes when Beth and the girls drove to Whistler, but she hated to burden him with extra animals.

Instead of returning to the house after she'd seen off the Griffins and their puppies, Beth wandered into the back of the yard where she had the heated kennel. She opened the gate and let her dogs run in among the trees. They were happy to exercise and she enjoyed playing with them, enjoyed their boundless energy.

Her whole family had been pet lovers. From her earliest memories, they'd always had a dog. Kent loved animals, too, which was one of the reasons she'd been attracted to him all those years ago…and now. At one time he'd considered entering veterinary college, but the application process was complex and difficult, with only a few candidates accepted each year. He'd tried two years running and was declined both times. Although bitterly disappointed, he'd decided to change his course of study to engineering. In the end, that career choice had suited him well.

Thinking of Kent, Beth was forced to confront his news head-on. He was involved with someone else. Danielle had made a point of telling everyone what "good" friends they were. Although Kent had called her merely a friend, it was obvious that Danielle intended it to be so much more.

After three years, this shouldn't come as such a shock—only it did. Her heart felt weighted down by grief and disappointment. Yet she was the one who'd set him free. Not once had she made an effort to turn the tide of the divorce proceedings. Perhaps this was one of those classic scenarios; she didn't want him but she didn't want anyone else to have him, either.

Still, she had to ask herself: Did she want her ex-husband

back? She couldn't answer that, not with certainty, and in any event the decision had been taken out of her hands. This sense of loss and confusion was probably typical of ex-wives, she reasoned. It must be.

"Mom?" Bailey was calling her.

Pulling herself out of her musing, she shouted and waved. "Over here."

"I saw the Griffins leave and you didn't come back in the house."

Beth didn't feel much like company at the moment. "I thought I'd let the dogs run a bit first," she said.

Sophie joined her sister. It'd started to snow again, thick flakes that drifted lazily down. The wind chilled her through her thick jacket. Because she spent so much time outdoors, she'd learned to ignore the cold. But this particular chill seemed to come from the inside out....

"Are you upset about Dad and Danielle?" Sophie asked, still putting on her gloves. She didn't look at Beth, as though she wanted to hide her own reaction to Kent's "friend."

"You mean because your father has someone else in his life? Oh, heavens, no." She wondered how effective her lie had been.

"We don't like Danielle," Bailey announced for the two of them.

"You have to admit she's beautiful."

Both girls rolled their eyes. "Mom, she's plastic. I can't

imagine what Dad sees in her. Besides, she treats us like we're still in diapers."

"Give her a chance," Beth urged. She didn't know why she was championing the other woman when she agreed with everything her daughters said.

"Tell us again, how did you and Dad meet?" Bailey asked.

Instead of answering their question, she asked one of her own. "Did you know that at one time your father wanted to be a veterinarian?"

"Dad?"

"Get out of here!"

"We met in college," Beth said. "You remember that." They'd heard the story a hundred times. It didn't make sense to repeat it now. "Are you sure you want to hear this?"

Their response was immediate and enthusiastic. "Yes!"

"Okay. We met on campus. A friend-of-a-friend situation. My roommate was dating your father, and I was dating another guy named Steve. I liked your father a whole lot more than Steve, but he was with Melanie and I couldn't very well make a play for him. We dated as a foursome quite a bit and then one day Melanie told me she liked Steve better than Kent and I confessed that I liked Kent better than Steve."

"And the two of you wanted to switch dates," Sophie finished for her.

"That is so cool," Bailey said.

"Well, it would've been if the guys felt the same way about us, but they didn't. Steve claimed he wanted to marry me, but I wasn't interested. Kent, on the other hand, only had eyes for Melanie."

"Oh, brother. Clearly, Dad's needed direction in the girl-friend department for a long time."

"We worked it out. Melanie broke up with Kent and I took the initiative and phoned to console him. What he wanted was for me to convince Melanie to take him back...." She paused and kicked at a pile of snow. "I guess I was always the second choice with your father."

"Oh, Mom, that isn't true!"

Beth smiled, letting her daughters know she wasn't serious. Well, maybe she was, not that it mattered.

"Whatever happened to Melanie? Did she marry Steve?"

"No. She left college in our junior year and dated a guy from France. Eventually she followed him there. We lost contact after a while. I haven't heard from her in years."

Princess raced to Beth's side. Panting, the collie dropped a stick at her feet. "You want to play fetch, do you?" she asked, and bent to pet her thick fur. Princess was a rescue someone had brought her. Her friend had found the collie on the side of the road near the freeway. With some effort she was able to get the large dog into the car. Rather than take her to the animal shelter, Beth's friend had brought her to Beth. Half-starved, Princess was in bad shape, and

Beth had nourished her back to health. She'd tried to find her owner, but the dog had no identification. Now Princess was deeply attached to Beth and was one of the dogs in the Reading with Rover program Grace had instigated at the library.

"Dad still loves you," Bailey insisted.

"Of course he does," Beth said, and meant it. "We were married for twenty-three years. I'm the mother of his children. While we might have opposing opinions on certain issues, when it comes to you girls, we're in total agreement."

"Bailey means he *really* loves you."

Beth threw her arms around her daughters and brought them close. "Listen, you two. I know this is difficult. Maybe you believed that your father's visit to Cedar Cove meant more than he intended it to mean. Maybe you believed he was making a statement about reconciliation." Well, he'd made a statement, all right. He wanted to introduce their daughters to his "friend." "The reason your father's here is because he wanted us all to meet Danielle. He wants us to welcome her into the family."

"I can't do it." Sophie's chin rose defiantly.

"Me, neither."

For that matter, it wasn't going to be any easier for Beth. Nevertheless, she was determined to do her best.

"They'll be coming back here, and I want us all to make an effort, okay?"

Bailey sighed expressively and, after a moment, said, "I'll try...I guess."

"Will Dad be here when we decorate the tree?"

Beth had assumed not. He was with Danielle and it would be awkward to include the other woman. "I...I don't know, but I don't think so."

"Dad used to enjoy that," Sophie said.

Beth had, too. It was their special family tradition. They'd always waited until Christmas Eve to decorate the tree, which went back to her German roots. Her grandparents hadn't put up a tree until the night before Christmas, a tradition that had come from the old country.

"Shouldn't we at least ask Dad about decorating the tree with us?"

"I suppose..." Beth said without much enthusiasm. He would probably assume the invitation included Danielle.

The girls returned to the house, and Beth stayed outside, letting the dogs run until they were tired. She gave them each a healthy snack, then they retreated to their kennel and she went back inside.

Beth had never intended to own six dogs—make that seven with the puppy upstairs. But then she'd never intended to have her children barely a year apart, either. Kent was still in his last year of engineering school and she was working as a teaching assistant to help support them when she discovered she was pregnant with Bailey.

Sophie hadn't been a planned pregnancy, either, and she'd arrived a mere fourteen months after her sister.

Beth had gotten pregnant with Bailey at Christmastime. Christmas Eve, to be exact. Hard to prove, perhaps, but she was sure of it. She'd *felt* it, felt they'd made a baby that night. Beth wondered if Kent remembered and suspected that, after all these years, he'd put it out of his mind.

They could only afford a small tree that year and had waited until Christmas Eve to decorate it. Beth had said it was tradition, and while it hadn't been *his* family's tradition, he'd been a good sport about it. With little money for ornaments, Beth had made their own. Kent had done his part, stringing popcorn and cranberries while she sewed gingerbread men from pieces of felt, decorating them with eyes and a row of tiny buttons down the front. Each was unique, individual. She still had several of the original ones and others, too, that she'd crafted through the years. She kept them carefully packed away in boxes.

It'd snowed that Christmas Eve, too, but their tiny basement apartment was warm and cozy. As a surprise, Kent had purchased two miniature bottles of rum to make hot drinks. After decorating the tree, they sat in front of the woodstove, their only source of heat, and with Beth on Kent's lap and the cat curled up on the ottoman, they'd toasted the holidays. They'd started kissing and then one thing led to another and three weeks later the stick was blue.

That was Bailey.

How excited Kent had been to have a daughter. When they learned Beth was pregnant a second time, he'd hoped for another girl and had gotten his wish.

The early years of their marriage were financially tight. They'd met every crisis, refusing to let their money problems come between them. They were a unit, a couple, determined to beat the odds. And when it was smooth sailing financially, her marriage had fallen apart.

Somewhere, while the girls were in their early teen years, they'd lost the glue that held them together.

Well, good grief, there was no need to analyze the past at this late date. What was done was done. She smiled despite her mood. If ever there was a profound statement, that was it. *What's done is done. Accept it.* Beth found herself humming a Christmas carol as she headed back to the house.

Bailey was on her cell phone in the kitchen. When she saw Beth, she abruptly ended the conversation.

"That was Dad," she explained. "He said he wants to be here when we decorate the tree."

Beth's chest tightened. "Is he... Did he say he was bringing Danielle?"

"I don't know. I didn't ask."

"Where did he take her to lunch yesterday?" she asked conversationally as she considered the situation. Danielle didn't appear to be the sensitive sort who'd recognize that her presence might be uncomfortable for Beth and the girls. Beth decided she needed to brace herself for the inevitable.

"The Lighthouse restaurant, I think."

"Oh." Of course Kent would take Danielle to one of the most expensive places in town.

"What are you making for dinner, Mom?" Bailey asked.

Sophie sent her a pleading look. "*Please* let it be your lasagna."

Beth laughed. "Of course." She'd better add two extra settings to the table.

"With Grandma Carlucci's marinara sauce?"

"Would I use anything else?" The recipe came from Kent's maternal grandmother, who was Italian. Because the dish demanded a lot of time and effort she only served it on special occasions. It was one of Kent's favorites, too. She'd actually made it for him, thinking…well, what she'd thought was irrelevant.

"Did your father tell you when he plans to come over?" she asked, trying to hide how anxious this news made her.

"He's on his way now."

"Okay," she said, rubbing her palms together. "Why don't you girls help me carry down the ornaments and we can have everything ready for when your dad gets here."

"Can we bring Roscoe downstairs?" Bailey pleaded.

"Sure, but you'll need to keep a careful eye on him. He's still a bit weak."

Roscoe was Beau's—the Hardings' puppy's—brother,

and the sickliest of the litter. Ted hadn't held out much hope for his survival, but Beth had given the undernourished puppy plenty of love and attention, bottle-feeding him and carefully administering his medication. At three months he seemed to have turned the corner and she thought he'd survive.

"Can we bring Princess in the house, too?" Sophie asked.

"Of course." Her dogs spent more time inside than out.

For the next few minutes Beth and her daughters carried down boxes from the storage area upstairs. Princess watched from her place by the sofa. Roscoe was in his bed with his chin resting on his paws, still too weak to move about much, although he seemed to enjoy the activity around him. "Did you and Dad ever have birds?" Bailey asked, standing near the canaries' cage.

Beth unsuccessfully hid a smile.

"What's so funny?"

"I did have a canary named Tweetie shortly after we were married, but we had to give her away."

"But why? Dad loves animals, too!"

"Yes, I know, but both your father and I were gone during the day. We had to keep the apartment heated for Tweetie, and after the first heating bill, your father insisted I find her a wealthier owner."

"Did you hate giving her up?"

"A little. She went to an aunt of mine, who had her for

years." She smiled again. "Your father promised me there'd be other birds when we could afford them."

"But you never got another canary until you came to Cedar Cove."

"And now you've got two."

"So they could keep each other company," Beth said. Kent had long ago forgotten his promise and, frankly, so had she. Then one day last year she saw the canaries in a feed store and impulsively purchased them.

They heard a car drive up to the house.

"Dad's back," Bailey said, looking out the living room window.

"Is... Did Danielle come with him?" Beth asked, trying to make the best of this.

Sophie joined her sister and glared out the window.

"Yup. Danielle's with Dad," Bailey said in a stark voice.

Beth didn't know why she'd expected anything else.

Six

"Is that Allison?" Rosie Cox called from the kitchen.

Zach glanced out the window and, sure enough, his daughter's car had just pulled into the drive. "Yes," he called back. She'd gone to pick up her boyfriend, Anson Butler, at the airport, since he'd be spending the holidays with them. Rosie had been cooking and decorating for days in preparation for Christmas. Zach had gotten roped into helping, not that he minded.

Eddie, their son, who was home from college, came out of his bedroom. He'd spent most of the afternoon there, which was unusual. Eddie was tall and lanky, and he'd shot past Zach's six feet by two or three inches. Eddie must be working on some project in his room, but when he heard the commotion in the hallway, he hurried out, earbuds plugged into his ears and his iPod playing. He yanked one plug free. "What did you say?"

"Your sister and Anson are here."

"Cool."

Zach already had the front door open. The decorative lights on the roof flashed on and off, their colors reflecting in the layer of fresh snow. Anson waved. He'd flown in from Washington, D.C., that afternoon.

Anson had entered the army at eighteen and currently worked in Military Intelligence at the Pentagon. Zach was proud of Anson's achievements, although there'd been a time he was convinced the young man was a felon. Zach had done everything he could to keep his daughter away from Anson.

Fortunately, as Zach had discovered, he'd been wrong about his daughter's boyfriend. Anson hadn't been born with many advantages, but he'd risen above those difficulties, thanks in part, Zach believed, to his daughter. The two of them had met in high school, and they'd maintained their relationship all these years.

At this stage, Zach would welcome Anson as his son-in-law. Rosie cautioned him not to rush their daughter into an engagement, and she was right. Allison and Anson were still young and, as Rosie said, these things had to develop on their own. Parents shouldn't involve themselves one way or the other.

Zach opened the screen door for his daughter and

Anson, who set down his bag as he stepped inside and extended his hand. "Mr. Cox, thank you for having me." His handshake was firm and solid.

"My pleasure."

Rosie came forward and hugged Anson. "Merry Christmas!"

"You're bedding down with me," Eddie said, leading Anson down the hallway to his room. "You can have the top bunk."

While Eddie showed Anson where he'd be sleeping, Allison followed her mother into the kitchen. "The traffic was a nightmare," she said. "I can't believe this many people are out on the roads on Christmas Eve."

"Everyone has places to go," Zach said, tagging behind his wife and daughter. "Hey, it smells good in here. What's cooking?"

"Honestly, Zach, I've baked ham every Christmas Eve since we were married. You'd think after twenty-four years you'd remember that."

"Right. Ham." Now that he thought about it, they did seem to have ham every year. Rosie used the bone for a black bean soup she served on New Year's Day, which was some Southern tradition she'd read about and adopted. It was supposed to guarantee good luck for the upcoming year. He doubted anyone believed that, but he liked black bean soup and so did Rosie.

By New Year's, the kids would be heading back to

school, and he and Rosie would be alone again. Zach had to admit he missed his children. Without them, the house seemed too quiet.

"What can I do?" Allison asked, reaching for an apron.

Zach smiled at his daughter's eagerness to help. She was an intelligent, considerate young woman, and one day she'd make a fine attorney. In her first year of law school, Allison had gotten top grades. Zach was proud of her.

"Dinner won't be ready for a while, but if you want to make the salad you can."

"Sure." She went over to the refrigerator, collecting the lettuce, tomatoes and other vegetables.

Normally, Zach would've sat down in front of the television at this point. He and Rosie both enjoyed football and had spent many a lazy Sunday afternoon watching the Seattle Seahawks. At first she hadn't understood much about football, but she was a fast learner. Before long, she knew the players' names and positions and understood the game. Spending Sunday afternoons with his wife was *fun*.

Anson joined him at the breakfast bar, pulling out a stool and sitting down.

"So how does it feel to be back home?" Zach asked him. Anson wore jeans and an army sweatshirt, and his hair was shorn. Very different from his high school days when his hair straggled to his shoulders and he wore a long black raincoat. The difference between then and now was striking.

"I talked to my mother," Anson said. He looked down as if to hide his reaction.

"You're welcome to invite her for dinner, if you'd like," Rosie offered.

Zach wasn't keen to spend Christmas Eve with Cherry Butler, but he certainly wouldn't refuse to entertain her.

"Thanks, Mrs. Cox, but Mom has other plans. She's got a new...friend." Anson's tongue seemed to trip over the word. "She's sure it's love this time and wants to be with him."

"You'll have a chance to see her while you're on leave," Rosie said reassuringly.

"I probably will."

Zach noticed that Anson didn't sound all that confident.

Rosie started into the dining room and paused in the doorway—underneath the mistletoe. Zach couldn't have planned this better had he tried. He'd hung it there earlier and now, taking advantage of the opportunity, he slipped out of his chair and hurried toward his wife.

Rosie gave him an odd look as if she didn't understand what he was doing.

"You're standing under the mistletoe," he told her.

Surprised, Rosie immediately looked up.

Taking her in his arms, he kissed her deeply, and with an exaggerated flourish bent her backward over his arm. He might be middle-aged, but he wasn't dead yet and he loved his wife.

Debbie Macomber

Anson and Allison hooted and cheered, but he didn't need any encouragement.

"Zach." Rosie was breathless by the time he released her. So was he.

She planted her hand over her heart as though to slow its beat.

Zach winked at his son, who'd just joined them.

"I remember when we never used to see you and Mom kiss," Eddie reminded them.

Disbelief on his face, Anson looked from Allison to Eddie.

"My parents were divorced for a while," Allison explained. "I'm sure I told you."

"You did, but…it's hard to believe, seeing them now."

Eddie pulled out a stool on Anson's other side and propped his elbows on the counter. "It wasn't a good year for our family, but it all turned out okay in the end."

Anson shook his head incredulously.

"It was a long time ago," Eddie said.

"Not *that* long," Rosie countered.

"What happened?" Anson asked. "I mean, if you don't mind talking about it."

"Basically the divorce just didn't work out for us," Zach teased, his eyes meeting Rosie's. That had been a difficult period in their marriage, but, as Eddie had said, it'd all turned out in the end, due in large part to…

"The judge… Well, she…" Rosie looked at her husband. "You tell them."

"It was Judge Lockhart. That was her name back then. She's Judge Griffin now. I think she could see that the divorce was a mistake for us, but she didn't have any grounds for denying it the way she did with another couple we heard about."

"Actually, I don't think either of us would have accepted a denial. At the time, we were pretty much at loggerheads."

That was putting it mildly, Zach thought, but kept quiet. No point in mentioning it.

"Mom and Dad wanted joint custody of Allison and me," Eddie said. "If Judge Olivia okayed their parenting plan, it meant Allison and I would've had to change houses every few days. Three days with Dad, four days with Mom—that sort of thing."

"They would've stayed in the same school district," Rosie added. She closed the refrigerator and leaned against the kitchen counter, facing the three of them, all sitting at the breakfast bar. "Zach got an apartment a few miles from the house."

"Judge Olivia told Mom and Dad they weren't the ones who needed a stable life," Allison went on to tell him. "Eddie and I were. The judge didn't want us changing residences every few days, so she gave us the family home. Mom and Dad had to move in and out."

"In other words," Eddie said, "when Dad was with us, Mom stayed at his apartment, and vice versa."

"Zach and I weren't too keen on this plan," Rosie inserted.

Anson grinned. "But apparently it worked."

Zach had to agree. "I remember the night Allison and Eddie brought us together, arranging for us to have a romantic dinner here at the house."

"Our parents needed our help," Eddie said, smiling at his sister. "Actually, that was Allison's idea and it was a good one."

"It was indeed." Zach reached across the counter to take Rosie's hand. He raised it to his lips and kissed her fingers. "And I'm very grateful."

"I am, too," Rosie whispered.

"We owe the judge a big debt of thanks," Allison said.

"And I owe *you* one," Anson said in a low voice, his gaze connecting with hers. "You always had faith in me."

"Oh, Anson, I had my moments. I so badly wanted to believe you didn't have anything to do with the fire that burned down the Lighthouse restaurant."

"The evidence *was* damning," he said, frowning slightly. "I couldn't blame you for doubting me."

"When I learned you'd been at the restaurant that night, and then later, when your mother told me you'd started a number of small fires when you were a kid, my faith wavered."

"Mine would have, too." Again Anson came to her defense. "I looked guilty as sin. I can't blame you, Allie."

"Luckily you saw the man who really started the fire and were able to identify him."

Zach had played a role in determining that Warren Saget, a local builder, was the arsonist. Teaming up with Sheriff Troy Davis, Zach had convinced Anson to come forward and speak to the authorities.

"If it wasn't for your dad, I might still be on the run," Anson said. "Your family's been a lifeline to me," he continued. "Mrs. Cox, Rosie, you've been more of a mother to me than my own. I know Cherry loves me in her way. She never counted on being a single mother, and she didn't have the greatest role model herself. She does the best she can."

Zach admired Anson for defending his mother. He didn't question that she loved her son. Unfortunately, Cherry's life had been a long series of low-paying jobs and living with ne'er-do-wells who used and abused her. Anson had been instructed to refer to these men as "uncle," none of them ever being a father figure of any kind. His father had left Cherry as soon as he discovered she was pregnant. Turned out he already had a wife and family.

"Are we going to play bingo?" Eddie asked, straightening. "It's tradition, you know." He nudged Anson as he said that, and Anson elbowed him back.

"Why don't we set it up while Allison and your mother finish getting dinner ready," Zach suggested. He slid off the stool and headed into the living room. He didn't recall how Christmas Eve bingo had begun, but the kids couldn't have been more than eight and ten. He thought Rosie's parents might've started it and that Rosie had carried it on, since she was big on traditions.

In the living room, Zach took out the game. He handed the cards to Anson to arrange, while Eddie gathered up the small prizes and placed them on the coffee table.

"If you have a few minutes I'd like to speak to you privately," Anson said, sitting next to Zach on the sofa.

Eddie picked up on the "private" part right away and excused himself, mumbling that he needed to make a phone call.

Anson waited until Eddie had left the room. "What I said earlier about you and Mrs. Cox being more of a family to me than my own? I meant that."

"We feel the same way about you, Anson. I'm proud of what you've accomplished."

Anson smiled, as if Zach's words had pleased him. "I never applied myself in school. I didn't really have to. Everything came easily to me, so I got through without trying. I had no real plans, no aspirations. Then I met Allison and she encouraged me to do better—to *be* better. I would've done anything to make her happy."

Zach remembered how he'd separated the two as teenagers. Anson had given his word and broken it, and as a result Zach had refused to allow Anson and Allison to date or even talk to each other. On Valentine's Day, Anson had come to the door and handed Zach a card for Allison. At that moment Zach had begun to see a real sense of honor in the boy.

"I loved Allison when I was seventeen, and I love her now," Anson went on. "It hasn't been easy to maintain a long-distance relationship with me living in D.C. and her going to school here in Seattle."

Zach nodded; he understood the challenges of such a relationship.

"I want you to know I've dated other women, but it's Allison I love."

His daughter had gone out with other young men through the years, but she felt the same way about Anson.

"I believe this conversation is leading up to something," Zach said.

"I'd like to ask your permission to marry Allison," Anson said quickly.

Zach leaned back on the sofa. He'd known this was coming, but hadn't thought it would be so soon. "Allison still has a year of law school left."

"I know. We've talked about that and she's applied to law schools in the Washington, D.C., area."

Zach arched his brows. "She has, has she?" Apparently, this had been an ongoing discussion between them. "So Allison's already accepted your proposal?"

"No, sir," Anson said. Then he nodded. "Well, yes. I realize speaking to you about this is just formality, but it's important to me."

Zach sent him an encouraging smile.

"Allison wanted me to give her the ring when she picked me up at the airport. I told her I wanted to talk to you and Mrs. Cox first."

Zach could bet his daughter hadn't been keen on that. He approved, though. He liked Anson's old-fashioned sense of protocol and his respect for both Allison and her family.

"Rosie!" Zach called his wife. "Could you come here for a minute? Allison, you, too."

"Sure."

Allison came into the other room, holding her mother's hand.

"It seems that Anson here would like our permission to marry our daughter."

Rosie turned to look at Allison. "But you haven't finished school yet and…you're both so young."

"They've taken both matters into account and still want to get married. Allison will continue her schooling in D.C."

"Oh."

"What do you think?" Zach asked Rosie.

"Well…yes, of course. I would welcome Anson into the family with open arms."

"Oh, thank you, Mom." Allison kissed her mother's cheek and then hurried across the room to her father.

"Hold on a minute," Zach said, stopping her. "I haven't given my consent."

"Daddy!"

Wearing a huge grin, Zach stood and hugged his daughter, and then Anson. "I couldn't imagine a son-in-law I'd rather have. You both have our blessing." Zach was confident in the strength of this relationship, despite their age. They'd proven their commitment to each other. He'd miss his daughter, but the family was close and they'd see her frequently.

"What's going on in here?" Eddie asked, returning to the living room.

"Anson and I are engaged."

"Cool," Eddie said.

"We'd like a June wedding, and then I'll move to Washington, D.C., to be with Anson."

Eddie shook his head. "I don't know about Mom and Dad having an empty nest."

"Hey, it hasn't been a problem so far," Zach told him.

"But it could be." Eddie seemed intent on making his case. "Allison's going to be on the other side of the country, and I'll be away at school."

Rosie frowned and looked at Zach. He shrugged, unsure what his son was getting at.

"Mom," Eddie said. "You need someone to mother. And, Dad, who are you going to boss around? Everyone knows Mom won't put up with that for long."

Allison laughed, but Zach was less amused.

"Now, just a minute, young man—"

Eddie interrupted him. "I've come up with the perfect solution."

"You have?"

Eddie nodded. He turned away for a moment and stepped into the hallway, then came back carrying a basket—with a puppy curled up inside, fast asleep.

"Merry Christmas, Mom and Dad."

"A puppy!" Rosie said, lifting the sleeping pup from his warm bed and holding him close. "He's adorable!"

"What a great idea." Zach grinned, delighted at the prospect of taking a dog for long country rambles. He could already picture the three of them—Rosie, the puppy and him—sitting by the fire....

"Actually, you gave me the idea, Dad. A while back you said you missed having a dog around the house. I'm a starving college student and I couldn't afford to buy you guys a big gift. When we went to get the Christmas tree I heard one of the workers say that Beth Morehouse had a houseful of puppies she needed to find good homes for. So...voilà."

"Now, we'll need to come up with a name," he said.

"I've already named him, okay? I had to call him something. I know you like 1940s and '50s movies, so...meet Bogart. Or Humphrey if you prefer."

"Bogie!" Allison said. "That's it."

"Bogie." Rosie smiled. "This is quite the Christmas," she said, cradling the puppy in her arms. "Not only do we gain a son, but we add a dog to the family, as well."

Seven

"I'll start making the hot chocolate," Beth said, turning away from her daughters. A few minutes in the kitchen would help her prepare to deal with her ex and his...friend. Kent kept insisting Danielle was "just a friend," but Beth felt there was more to it. Really, why would he bring "just a friend" to a traditional family occasion?

Although she had no idea what Kent was thinking, Beth couldn't imagine him actually spending the rest of his life with this woman. It was a mistake. Even her daughters could see that. Kent wouldn't appreciate hearing her opinion, so Beth was determined to keep it to herself— although that was a struggle.

From inside the kitchen Beth heard Sophie greeting Kent and Danielle at the front door and ushering them into the family room. The Christmas tree was still bare, surrounded by the boxes they'd carried down.

"Mom's in the kitchen."

This came from Bailey. Kent must have asked where she was. A moment later, he joined her. "Listen, I'd appreciate it if we—"

"Is there anything I can do?" Danielle asked in the sweetest of voices.

"No, thanks. I've got everything under control," she told the other woman. Her eyes connected with Kent's. She wanted to berate him for bringing Danielle to a family function; instead, she bit her tongue and tried to disguise her feelings, although she suspected she'd failed.

She realized she'd need to get used to the fact that Kent was his own man now and made his own decisions. Beth forced a smile and continued stirring the chocolate.

"Dad," Bailey called. "Come and help."

Kent hesitated and it looked as if there was something else he wanted to say. With obvious reluctance, he returned to the family room, Danielle on his heels.

Beth took as long as she dared in the kitchen. Fortunately, Grace phoned while she was there, which kept her occupied for another five minutes. Beth peered into the living room when she'd hung up. From her vantage point, she could see that the girls had opened the boxes of old ornaments and were reminiscing with their father. Danielle sat on the sofa, her expression bored. Eventually she reached for her cell phone and started texting.

"Mom!" Sophie shouted. "Where are you?"

"Coming!" Beth loaded the serving tray with pretty holiday mugs. She'd decorated the top of each mug of cocoa with whipped topping and chocolate sprinkles, which was how Kent and the girls had always liked it. "Here we go," she said, hoping she sounded cheerful. Surely there was a reward in heaven for first wives who were nice to their exes' new girlfriends.

"Remember this one?" Sophie said, and held up a snowman she'd made with a wood-burning kit when she was around ten.

"What I remember is the blister you got on your finger because you weren't careful," Kent teased his daughter.

"I was so proud of this silly snowman. I was sure I'd make a career out of wood-burning."

Danielle gave a saccharine smile. "It's…lovely." The words rang empty as her phone chirped and she returned to texting.

"It's terrible," Sophie said. "In fact, it's downright ugly."

"Well, maybe," Danielle agreed, putting her cell back in her sweater pocket, "but you were just a kid. I'm surprised you kept it, though. If it was me I would've tossed it years ago."

Beth opened her mouth to defend her daughter, then closed it. No need to get into a useless argument.

"If you think it's ugly, why would you put it on the tree?" Danielle asked. "I mean, you're right, it really isn't very attractive." She stood and retrieved an ornament from the box. "There are some darling ones here." She held up one of the felt gingerbread men Beth had sewn the first Christmas she and Kent were married. "Now this is kind of amateurish, but it's...nice. By comparison."

"We put up the wooden snowman," Beth said, carefully handing Danielle her cocoa, "because Sophie made it herself. The decorated tree in the living room is for show. This one is for family, for memories of Christmases past."

"Sort of like that Charles Dickens book," Danielle said. "The one with the ghosts. And Tiny Tim."

"Something like that," Beth murmured as she brought Kent his hot cocoa.

"Do you have one without any chocolate sprinkles?" Danielle asked.

"Sure." Beth retrieved the cup and went back to the kitchen. She dumped the whipped cream in the sink and added a fresh dollop minus the chocolate sprinkles.

"Mom sewed those for her and Dad's first Christmas," Bailey was telling Danielle when Beth came back.

"The hot chocolate is even better than I remember." Kent spoke quickly, breaking into his daughter's reminiscence.

"I make good hot chocolate, too," Danielle said. "I'm an excellent cook. I want you to try my macaroni and cheese."

"Uh, sure." Kent looked decidedly uncomfortable.

Danielle beamed. "I have a special cooking trick. You start with the boxed kind and then you just add stuff. My secret is to put ketchup in the water when I cook the noodles."

"I'll have to try that myself," Beth said politely, trying not to cringe. Difficult as it was, she turned her mind away from Kent and his…friend. She hated to admit this, but she was jealous of Danielle.

Danielle sneezed once, loudly. So loudly, in fact, that it startled Beth and Princess, too. The sneeze sounded like a moose in heat—or what Beth imagined that would sound like.

"Oh, sorry," Danielle said, clearly embarrassed.

"Bless you," Sophie said.

Bailey handed Danielle a tissue.

"Thank you." She noisily blew her nose. "It's that dog," she said, pointing an accusing finger at Princess. "I'm allergic to dogs."

"Oh, you should've said something earlier." Beth immediately collected Princess and took her to the kennel outside. Even with Princess out of the room, there was still Roscoe, sleeping beside the fireplace. While Beth kept a tidy house, there was bound to be dog hair everywhere. It was the perfect excuse to send Kent and Danielle on their merry way.

"Beth."

Kent met her on the back porch as she returned from

the kennel. He kept his hands in his pockets, his arms held close to his body to ward off the cold. He followed Beth inside, to the laundry room. One of the five remaining puppies jumped up, balancing his paws against her calf. Beth automatically reached down and brought him into her arms, resting her cheek against his soft head.

"Listen," Kent said. "I hadn't planned to bring Danielle with me. It's just that—"

"Don't worry about it."

She carefully put the puppy back on the floor. She attempted to brush off his apology because her heart was doing crazy things. With the two of them in such a small space, the atmosphere was intimate, and with both doors closed it was private. All she needed to do was lean forward ever so slightly and their lips would meet…

Where did *that* idea come from? She couldn't give in to the impulse. But it seemed so natural to kiss Kent, to press her mouth to his. Beth immediately opened the door leading into the house.

Unfortunately, she forgot about the puppies. An open door was an opportunity and they took it. They shot out of the room as though fleeing a burning building.

Beth rushed after them and Kent did, too. He trapped one by falling to his knees and had him back inside the laundry room seconds later. Beth wasn't nearly as lucky. Seizing their opportunity, the other four dashed in different directions.

Beth knew the instant one of the puppies made it into the family room because Danielle let out a squeal. "Get that dog," she cried, apparently to one or both of the girls. Her command was followed by another moose-in-heat sneeze.

Beth hurried into the room. "I'm so sorry," she said, and she was. She'd had no intention of freeing the puppies when she'd opened the door. The truth was she'd completely forgotten they were there.

Bailey grabbed one puppy and Sophie another. Beth scooped up the third. The last one made a beeline for the Christmas tree and got tangled in the bottom garland.

"Get those dogs out of here," Danielle shouted between sneezes. "Oh, good grief, there's another one. What is this place—a puppy mill?"

"My mother would *never*—"

"It's all right," Beth said, cutting Bailey off. "Danielle is understandably upset. I apologize, Danielle. I opened the door without realizing—"

"You did that on purpose!"

"Danielle," Kent said, his voice calm and reasonable, unlike hers. "It was an honest mistake."

The other woman sank down on the sofa and held a wad of tissues to her nose before she sneezed three times in quick succession.

"I'm afraid there's dog hair all over the house," Beth said. "Maybe it would be best if—"

Danielle held up one hand, stopping her. The other

clasped a tissue to her face. "I have allergy medication. We will not be leaving on my account." This last part was said in a muffled voice that nonetheless conveyed steadfast determination.

Kent sat next to Danielle, who sneezed again.

It wasn't funny; still, Beth couldn't help it—she had to smother a giggle. Kent caught her eye and knew instantly that she was having trouble hiding her amusement, and that was when Beth lost it. She started laughing and tried desperately to hide her laughter by coughing.

"What's so funny?" Danielle demanded.

"Nothing," Kent said promptly, getting to his feet. "I think, uh, Beth might have swallowed wrong."

"This…isn't funny."

"No, it isn't," Kent said. He bent down and untangled the last puppy from the garland on the tree and brought him back to the laundry room.

In the meantime Beth carried Roscoe upstairs and out of harm's way. Making it through tonight would require a Christmas miracle.

The phone rang as she came down the stairs. Call display told her it was Bob Beldon. They exchanged Christmas greetings, then he said, "I heard you're looking for homes for some puppies."

"Yes, I am."

"Great. Well, I'm interested in taking one."

They chatted for a few more minutes and she'd just replaced the receiver when the phone rang a second time.

"Your mother gets more phone calls than a bookie," Beth heard Danielle comment.

Teri Polgar was inquiring about a puppy for her sister, Christie.

A moment later, another call. This time it was Ted. "How's it going?" he asked.

"About as well as could be expected." She'd mentioned casually that her ex-husband was coming to Cedar Cove for Christmas. Lowering her voice, she said, "Except that Kent arrived with a…friend."

"A friend?" Ted sounded perplexed. "I was asking about the puppies."

"Oh…the puppies." She wanted to roll her eyes. Of course he'd be phoning about the puppies. "Five down and five to go, although I just heard from someone who's a possibility. And if Bob Beldon takes one too, that'll leave three."

"Listen, I know someone else who could be interested. Gloria Ashton—for her parents," he said. "Would it be all right if I stopped by later to say merry Christmas?"

"Sure. That would be nice." Ted was exactly the balm she needed. And, if he came over, Kent would see that she hadn't been twiddling her thumbs for the past three years.

She missed Kent. She missed their life together and it was killing her that he'd found someone else. The divorce wasn't the end, she realized now; his remarriage would be. If he married Danielle—and the other woman had certainly staked her claim on him—it would mean their life together was over. Really over.

"Who just called?" Bailey asked.

"Bob Beldon. And then Teri Polgar. And Ted."

"Bob from the B and B?" Kent looked up at her. "Did he want to speak to me?"

"No, no, he was inquiring about a puppy."

"Oh, dear," Danielle murmured and, for good measure, sneezed again.

Beth had assumed she would've taken one of her allergy pills by now.

"What did Ted want?" Sophie asked.

"He'll be visiting later."

Bailey and Sophie seemed gratified by this bit of news. "That's wonderful," Sophie said as Bailey nodded. "He's a real sweetheart."

"Oh?" Kent asked, turning to his daughters for an explanation.

"Yeah, he reminds me of the vet in those James Herriot books you read us when we were little," Bailey told her father.

Ted? James Herriot? What were her girls up to? Beth sent Bailey a disapproving frown, which her daughter chose to ignore.

They resumed trimming the tree, and when they'd finished, it didn't look half-bad. With its mismatched ornaments collected over the years, it had its own homespun charm. There was the wooden snowman Sophie had made at the age of ten. And a photo of Bailey in the first grade, framed in Popsicle sticks. Another that resembled a pincushion, which Sophie had made when she was in the third grade. Beth's gingerbread men. And a few that she and the girls had constructed through the years with varying degrees of artistic skill.

They stepped back and, hardly aware she was doing it, Beth stood next to Kent. Delighted with their tree, she glanced up at him and smiled. He smiled back and their eyes met. Beth had to force herself to look away; when she did, she saw Danielle watching them both.

The other woman's eyes narrowed, and Beth could tell that Danielle wasn't pleased. Without making an issue of it, Beth moved away from Kent.

Searching for something to do, Beth picked up the empty cocoa mugs and carried them into the kitchen. She was busy placing them in the dishwasher when Danielle joined her.

"I know what you're doing," Danielle said without preamble. She rested her hip against the kitchen counter, crossed her arms and glared at Beth.

"Putting dirty dishes in the dishwasher?" Beth asked.

"You don't like it that Kent brought me here."

Beth straightened and leaned against the counter, too,

crossing her own arms. "And what gives you that impression?"

"I saw the way you looked at him just now."

"Really? And how was that?"

"You're jealous."

"Am I?" Beth asked, striving to sound anything but jealous.

"You want him back."

Beth laughed. "In case you've forgotten, I had him for twenty-three years."

"And you miss him."

Beth faked a short laugh. "I don't know what you think you saw, but let me assure you, you're mistaken."

"No, I'm not," Danielle insisted.

Beth looked into the other room to make sure Kent and the girls couldn't overhear this rather unpleasant conversation. "Well, then, let's agree to disagree," she suggested in a low voice, hoping to avoid a pointless exchange.

"You want him."

Beth disregarded the comment, turned her back on Danielle and continued loading the dishwasher.

"You can deny you're jealous all you want, but if you listen to only one thing, listen to this," Danielle said tightly. "He told me about the divorce and how you wanted out of the marriage. You blew it and now you regret it."

This was too much. If Danielle thought she was helping... Well, she wasn't. "Listen," Beth said, pronouncing each word distinctly. "If you want Kent, he's all yours. You're welcome to him." With that she slammed the dishwasher closed and turned to see Kent standing in the doorway.

Eight

The scent of cinnamon and allspice filled Peggy Beldon's kitchen as she arranged the decorated sugar cookies on colorful plates lining the counter.

The plates of cookies, toffee and hand-rolled chocolates were her and Bob's gift to their friends each year. Peggy enjoyed baking and never more than at Christmas. She began wrapping the plates in red cellophane and tying the ends with a ribbon. She and Bob delivered the plates on Christmas Eve, usually late in the afternoon.

Thyme and Tide, their bed-and-breakfast, did fairly well this time of year and she was grateful that despite a weak economy they continued to be busy. They already had several reservations for the winter months and the summer looked promising.

Currently they had two guests, who seemed to be a couple, although they had their own rooms. Beth Morehouse's ex and...Diana? No, Danielle. It wasn't unusual to have guests over the Christmas holidays, although Peggy would've preferred to close, but as Bob said, they couldn't turn down business. Christmas or not, they had rooms to rent. She could guarantee that the Christmas morning buffet would be something Kent Morehouse and his friend would long remember.

Humming a Christmas carol to herself, Peggy glanced out the kitchen window and saw her husband pull into the driveway. He'd run a few errands for her. A couple of minutes later, she glanced outside again, wondering why he hadn't come in.

Just then the door opened. Bob knocked the snow off his boots as he entered the house, a big grin on his face. By nature her husband was an upbeat, happy person, always sociable, which was one reason their B and B was successful. Peggy tended to remain in the background, creating the meals, while Bob provided the warm welcome and the entertainment.

"What took so long?" she asked, pausing to kiss him and take the bags out of his hands.

"You should see the grocery store. There wasn't a cart to be had."

"Christmas Eve...what did you expect?"

"Everyone seems to leave the shopping until the last

minute—even my wife." He kissed her cheek but not before Peggy saw him swipe a cookie.

Bob reached for a date bar and she returned his sheepish smile with an approving grin. She had plenty to spare and, after his trek to the store, Bob deserved a reward.

"Do you have one for Roy and Corrie?" Bob asked, surveying the kitchen counter and the row of finished plates.

"Of course."

"Troy and Faith Davis?"

"Bob, you know I do. What makes you ask?"

"Just wanted to be sure. I saw Faith shopping and Corrie was coming into the store as I was leaving." Bob poured himself a cup of coffee and sat on the kitchen stool, watching as Peggy put the final touches on the gifts, adding small handmade cards. These cards were another gift. Each included a personal note thanking the recipients for their friendship.

"I'm so thankful to Roy," she said fervently. "Who knows what would've happened if he hadn't been willing to take us on as clients." The private investigator had stepped in at a crucial time in their lives.

"Troy Davis, too," Bob reminded her.

"Oh, yes."

The memory of those painful days took over her thoughts for a moment. A stranger had arrived late one night in the middle of a storm, rain-drenched and seeking a room. Bob hadn't recognized the man but had sensed...something.

He'd had a bad feeling about him. Peggy, however, couldn't turn someone away in the middle of a downpour. In retrospect, she wished she'd listened to her husband, because the next morning the man was dead.

"I know what you're thinking," Bob said, sipping his coffee.

"So now you're a mind reader, too?" she asked with a smile. Her husband did possess multiple talents—including acting and singing—but she had serious doubts regarding his psychic abilities.

"After all these years I can read you like a *People* magazine," he joked right back. "It's about Max Russell, isn't it?"

She could pretend otherwise but didn't. "Yes. I was remembering the night he showed up and how you didn't want to give him a room."

"That night was a turning point for me," Bob admitted. "The start of healing. I was finally able to lay what happened in 'Nam to rest."

Bob and his best friend from high school, Dan Sherman—who'd married Grace—had enlisted in the army together under the buddy program. Following basic training they'd been sent to Vietnam. Max had been part of their unit.

The war changed all three men. An incident involving the deaths of innocent civilians had haunted them.

For years Dan Sherman had struggled with depression.

When he was in that state of mind, he'd block out family and friends, isolating himself from the world.

After the war Bob had turned to alcohol for solace. Their marriage suffered, and more than once Peggy decided to leave him, taking their son and daughter. Each time Bob convinced her he'd give up drinking and be the husband she deserved. He'd tried, but with limited success. After a few weeks of sobriety Bob would return to the bottle. He hit bottom after losing a promising job, and that was when he went into rehab. Thankfully, he came out a different person. He hadn't had a drink since that day more than twenty years ago. Or was it twenty-five? She no longer kept count of the years. Each day was a victory, each day a blessing.

"I mailed Hannah a Christmas card," Peggy confessed. Even now, knowing what she did about the young woman, Peggy had a soft spot for her despite the grief she'd caused them both.

Hannah was the dead man's daughter and, in fact, had been responsible for his murder.

"Did she write back?"

"No." Peggy knew it was highly unlikely that Hannah would acknowledge the card. That was fine. Perhaps it was for the best.

"You really came to care for her, didn't you?"

"Well, yes, but…" Peggy had mixed feelings about the woman. Hannah had attempted to steer blame for the murder toward Bob, and that was unforgivable in Peggy's eyes. Still, the poor girl had lived a hard life with a father tortured by the past. Max took his self-hatred out on Hannah and her mother. Hannah's mind became as twisted as her father's, and as far as she was concerned, he deserved to die.

She'd tried to kill him once before and, to Hannah's horror, her beloved mother had died instead. Her father had survived the car accident, which made Hannah's hatred of him even greater. She had deeply loved her mother and to lose her when she'd so carefully planned to kill Max had nearly destroyed her. Hannah redoubled her efforts to make her father pay.

Again Bob's instincts had been on target. From the first he hadn't trusted Max's daughter, who'd shown up at their home after her father's death. Although he wasn't able to identify exactly what he disliked about Hannah, he'd made his feelings clear. Hannah had avoided him as much as possible. It wasn't until much later that they understood why.

"I'll be forever grateful those days are gone," Bob murmured, still sipping his coffee.

"Me, too," Peggy agreed. "You're free now. The past is over and the future is bright."

"I'm a lucky man," Bob said.

Nevertheless, those memories were all too vivid, all too real.

"Hey, why so melancholy?" Bob said, tipping up her

chin with his index finger. "We have a lot to celebrate. Hollie and Marc will be here this afternoon and we'll have a real family Christmas."

Peggy instantly brightened. Their children were coming for the holidays and spending a few days. To have both of them there was a rare treat. Their family had healed in the past few years.

Hollie and Marc had grown up in the volatile atmosphere created by their father's problems with alcohol. As much as possible, Peggy had shielded them. It'd taken her years of Al Anon meetings to straighten out her own thinking. Without realizing what she was doing, Peggy had enabled Bob in his drinking. Once she'd stepped aside and allowed him to deal with the consequences of his actions, he was forced to admit that he had a problem.

Those years of struggle had taken a heavy toll. It was only since the move to Cedar Cove that Hollie and Marc were willing to have a relationship with their father. Both were professionals, married but without children. Peggy envied her friends their grandchildren but, so far, her own kids had shown no interest in starting families. Peggy had accepted the situation and was content to lavish affection on her friends' grandchildren, especially those of her best friend, Corrie McAfee.

"We'd better head out with those gift plates soon, don't you think?" Peggy said. She wanted to be home when the children arrived with their spouses.

"Anytime now."

"Everything's just about ready," she said, and finished the last of the gift cards with a flourish.

Bob put his cup in the sink and walked into the large family room, where they'd set up the Christmas tree. "I have an early present for you."

"Oh?" she asked, her curiosity piqued.

He looked pleased with himself. "Actually, your gift's in the garage."

"Bob," Peggy breathed. They'd discussed buying her a new vehicle, but she'd assumed she'd be making the choice. "You bought me a car?"

Bob laughed. "Sorry. That's a natural assumption but no, it isn't a car. I hope you aren't disappointed."

"Of course not, but I am somewhat curious as to why this can't wait until morning."

"Well… This is the type of gift we'd generally talk about in advance."

She couldn't imagine what he was talking about. "Give me a clue."

"Remember the other day when we were at the library?"

"Of course…but what's that got to do with anything?" Peggy couldn't recall anything special taking place. They'd dropped off books and picked up others. Both were big readers and loyal library patrons.

"Remember the children reading to the dogs?"

"Well, yes, Grace told me about the program. It seems to be doing well."

"Largely thanks to Beth Morehouse, the woman who owns the Christmas tree farm."

"Where we bought our tree," she said, certain Bob would clarify everything in a moment. Her husband had a flair for drama, which was one reason he volunteered at the local theater. Over the years Bob had appeared in a number of productions, everything from musicals to *Death of a Salesman*. It was his creative outlet the same way gardening and cooking were hers.

"I'm sure there's a point to all this," she said, urging him to explain.

"There is."

"Wonderful. Might I suggest you get back to my Christmas gift that's currently being stored in the garage?"

"You'll see."

"I'm waiting with bated breath," she returned, smiling.

"Stay here."

"Okay," Peggy said. "Do you want me to close my eyes?"

Bob paused at the back door and nodded. "Good idea. Close your eyes."

Peggy sat at the kitchen table with one hand on her coffee mug and the other in her lap and squeezed her eyes shut. She wondered if her gift was what had kept Bob in the garage so long after he'd driven home. After a couple of minutes she heard him come in.

"Can I open my eyes yet?"

"Just a second."

Her husband's footsteps echoed as he moved toward the Christmas tree. "All right," he called out. "You can open your eyes now."

Peggy did, and then blinked. Beneath the tree, surrounded by wrapped gifts, sat a basket, one she kept in the garage and often took into the garden. Bedded down inside was…a puppy. A small black puppy.

Peggy didn't know if she should laugh or cry. "You got me a *puppy?*"

"I was thinking we could use a dog," Bob said.

"But a puppy?" she said, unsure of her feelings.

"Look at her, Peggy, she's so cute. I couldn't resist. We need a dog, and Beth Morehouse has a litter of ten she needs to find homes for."

"So *that* was the connection with Beth and the library. You volunteered," she said. "Obviously."

"Well, yes…"

"You'll train her?"

"If you want, but she's your dog. You're happy about this, aren't you?"

The puppy raised her head and regarded Peggy with large doleful eyes.

"What do you want to name her?" Bob asked, lifting

the tiny squirming creature out of the basket and bringing her to Peggy.

The puppy immediately made herself at home in Peggy's arms. "Let's name her...Millie."

"Millie, it is," Bob said. "Merry Christmas, sweetheart."

"Merry Christmas, darling. And Merry Christmas, Millie."

Millie barked, adding her own greetings.

Nine

"Let's go for a sleigh ride," Bailey said excitedly, as if this was the most brilliant idea of the century. "Can we, Mom?" She clasped both hands. "I mean, now that Gloria and Chad have picked up the puppy…"

"Ah…" Beth hesitated as a sense of dread filled her. Every minute with Kent and Danielle felt more awkward than the one before.

"Mom, we should. Dad's never seen the Christmas tree farm." Sophie was as animated as her sister.

"You want to, don't you, Dad?" Bailey asked, hurrying to her father's side and slipping her arm through his.

"That way Danielle can breathe some fresh air and not have to worry about sneezing," Sophie said in a solicitous voice.

Beth didn't dare look at her ex-husband. She had to believe he was as miserable as she was. This entire family Christmas was a disaster. She'd seen the expression on his face when she'd so vehemently declared Danielle was welcome to him. Shock and pain had flashed in his eyes so quickly she wasn't even sure she'd read his feelings correctly. Everything inside her cried out to take the words back, swear that none of it was true. But she couldn't do that. Not with Danielle standing right there.

"Danielle probably isn't up to this," Kent said with an unmistakable lack of enthusiasm.

Beth figured the other woman would willingly return to the Thyme and Tide. She couldn't be enjoying the afternoon any more than Beth was. The only ones who seemed to derive any pleasure from this fiasco were Bailey and Sophie, who were apparently oblivious to the tension in the room.

"A sleigh ride *might* be fun," Danielle said with a half-hearted shrug.

Bailey and Sophie leaped up and down and clapped their hands. Their behavior reminded Beth of when they were youngsters and were told they could stay up past their bedtime.

"I didn't know you had a sleigh," Kent said as he reached for his coat and gloves. His scarf, Beth noticed, was one she'd knit him years earlier for Christmas. It warmed her to know that he still wore it. Did he think of her every time he put it on?

"The sleigh, which is pretty old, is in one of the out-buildings," she said. "It came with the property. We don't use it much."

"A sleigh ride is perfect after a snowfall, though. Right, Mom?" Sophie asked.

Perfect wasn't exactly the word she'd use.

"You don't have any horses." Kent seemed to be look-ing for excuses to get out of this. Beth didn't blame him; she'd rather avoid a cozy ride herself. She'd had about all the togetherness she could handle.

"Mom's neighbors. The Nelsons," Bailey explained. "They have horses and said we can borrow them any time we want." Without waiting for the go-ahead, Bailey picked up the phone and grabbed the personal directory Beth kept in a kitchen drawer.

"We'll go have a great time," Sophie told Kent.

"The Nelsons said no problem." Bailey replaced the re-ceiver, her eyes shining with glee.

"I'll go get a few blankets," Beth muttered, eager to make an escape. She rushed up the stairs and into her bed-room. Slumping on the edge of her bed, she brought her hands to her heated face. She wasn't sure how much lon-ger she'd be able to pull this off.

"Get a grip," she ordered herself. She walked into the master bath and splashed cold water on her cheeks. Her reflection in the mirror revealed that her face was flushed.

She looked feverish. This wasn't due to illness, though, but acute embarrassment.

"Mom," Sophie called her from the foot of the stairs. "The Nelsons said they'd bring over the horses."

Beth came out of her bedroom. "Okay," she called down. "I'll be there in a minute." Collecting warm blankets from the hall closet, she returned to the main floor.

By the time she got her hat, coat and gloves, Kent and the girls had opened the doors to the storage shed where the sleigh was kept. The large white uncovered sleigh had two red velvet benches, one of them for the driver.

John Nelson, who lived next door, walked over, leading two large geldings. Kent introduced himself. Danielle was still in the house, refreshing her makeup or so Beth assumed.

"When you're finished, would you mind if we took the sleigh out for a ride?" John asked.

"Of course not," Beth told him. She glanced up at the sky. "I can't imagine we'll be out long. When we're finished, I'll take the sleigh over to your place."

"I appreciate it, Beth. You're a good neighbor."

"So are you."

The harnesses were in the storage shed, and John helped Beth hitch the two horses to the sleigh.

Danielle had come out of the house but remained on the porch until that was done. John left, and the girls climbed on board the sleigh to arrange the blankets.

Danielle looked uncertain, as if she wasn't sure a sleigh ride was something she wanted, after all. "It's cold out here." She squinted at the sky. "And it looks like it's going to snow. Plus, I'm expecting a phone call."

"Snow! Isn't that *wonderful?*" Bailey sounded as if snow was the most magical thing that could possibly happen.

"I'm not used to the cold."

"Then you need to sit between us," Sophie said. "Bailey and I will keep you snug and warm."

Kent helped Danielle into the sleigh, and Bailey and Sophie immediately covered her lap with blankets and wrapped an extra one about her shoulders. By the time they'd finished, all that showed was Danielle's pinched face.

Not until Beth climbed into the worn front seat did she realize that the only place left for Kent to sit was next to her. He seemed to realize that at the same time she did. They stared at each other until Kent got into the sleigh. They sat as far apart on the bench as humanly possible.

"Would you like me to take the reins?" he asked, refusing to look at her.

"If you'd like." She handed them over, knowing he was capable of managing the horses and sleigh.

They started off with a jolt and Danielle let out a cry of alarm. After the initial jerk, the ride went smoothly. The horses' hooves made muted clopping sounds as the sleigh glided over the snowy road.

"You going to be my navigator?" Kent asked.

"Sure."

Kent had moved toward the middle of the seat and she did, too, for fear of falling off if the sleigh hit bumpy ground.

Kent seemed willing to overlook her earlier comment. She was grateful and wished she could take back the lie. "Go left at the fork in the road," she told him, pointing in that direction.

"How many acres do you have here?" he asked, sounding genuinely interested. The trees had been trimmed and shaped until they were the perfect size for Christmas. Now they glistened with bright, fresh snow.

"Forty acres in total, but only twenty are planted in trees. I'm planting another five acres each year and replacing the ones we've cut."

Kent held the reins loosely. "I assumed most families bought artificial trees these days."

"Certainly that's the trend, but there are still plenty of people who prefer a fresh tree, especially if they can chop it down themselves. It makes for wonderful memories. And after Christmas, people cut them up for compost, so ecologically speaking, you could argue that they're superior."

"That's good."

"In addition, a lot of my trees are shipped overseas."

"Really."

She chatted easily, explaining what she'd learned in the

past three seasons and her hopes for the future. After a while, she paused, embarrassed that she'd talked for so long. "I apologize. I didn't mean to drone on like that."

He gave her a quick smile. "You really love it here, don't you?"

"It's a very different lifestyle from California, but I needed a change. I was in a horrible rut." The instant the words were out, she regretted being so honest. "I didn't mean that the way it sounded. What I said earlier, it… isn't— I wish…"

"Don't worry about it," he murmured.

Kent had always been ready to forgive and forget; she admired that about him. She was the one who held on to hurts far longer than she should.

"We should sing Christmas carols," Bailey suggested, and then broke into "Silent Night." Sophie joined in and so did Kent. Beth added her own voice. The last one to sing was Danielle. Unfortunately, she was off-key and sounded terrible.

Beth chanced a look at Kent and found him glancing at her at the same time. They broke into giggles, which they did their best to hide.

The group's enthusiasm faded after two or three songs, and their voices gradually dwindled away.

"Remember our first Christmas?" Kent asked, keeping his voice low.

"I thought about it…recently. It was a magical time for

us, wasn't it?" He met her eyes for several seconds until she forced herself to look down. The intensity of the attraction she felt confused her. Disconcerted her. Oh, dear. It was happening again and this time Danielle was with them.

As the sleigh glided through the snow, she pointed to another turn in the road, one that cut through the property.

"Right or left?"

"Left." She was so caught up in the moment that she'd said *left* when she meant *right*.

Kent turned right. "Sorry," he said, sounding flustered. "You said left, didn't you?"

"No, this is fine," she told him. She clenched her gloved hands in her lap, grateful that the wind and cold were a convenient excuse for the color splotching her face.

"Oh, look," Sophie cried. "It's snowing again."

Thick, fat flakes drifted lazily from a slate-gray sky.

"It'll probably melt by morning," Danielle said, "and everything will be mud and slush."

"But for now it's beautiful," Beth countered. This was the coldest winter on record in the Pacific Northwest. The weatherperson broadcasting from the Seattle TV station had been effusive about the unusual amount of snow in the area, especially this early in the winter.

"I'm cold," Danielle complained. "And I can't move my arms."

"Let me help you," Bailey said.

"Ouch! You're pulling the blankets tighter. I feel like a sausage."

"I thought you said you were cold."

"I am, but I want to breathe, too," Danielle snapped. "Take this ridiculous thing off me."

"Girls," Beth said, twisting around. Danielle was right; she did resemble a sausage. "Make her comfortable."

"Can we go back to the house soon?" Danielle pleaded.

"I'll head over there now," Kent told her. He glanced at Beth and grinned boyishly. "Okay, navigator, which way?"

"Recalculating, recalculating," she said, using the tinny voice of her car's navigational system.

Kent laughed and turned the sleigh around when he came to a place where that was possible.

"Do you ever think back to those early years?" he asked with his attention focused on the road ahead. "When we were first married…"

The snow was coming down thicker and faster, making for limited visibility.

"I…try not to, but yes, I do." She hadn't wanted to admit that, but it seemed senseless to deny the truth. "You?"

"Sometimes." He paused. "What happened to us, Beth?"

"I…wish I knew."

"Me, too."

"Are we there yet?" Danielle asked plaintively.

A question hovered on the end of Beth's tongue but she refused to ask it. If Kent was looking for a second wife who was completely her opposite, he'd found that woman in Danielle. She and Beth were about as dissimilar as any two women could be. Perhaps that was what he wanted. The thought depressed her.... Unless he was telling the truth and Danielle really *was* just a friend. But in that case, why did she stick to Kent like glue? Why had he even brought her to Cedar Cove?

"Mom?" Bailey asked. "My birthday's in September—when did you get pregnant with me?"

"Bailey!" Beth was shocked that her daughter would ask such a question, especially in front of Danielle.

"Christmas Eve," Kent answered.

"Really? Wow. You're sure?"

"Yup."

"So tonight's more of a celebration than I realized."

"What about me?" Sophie wanted to know.

"Easter," Beth said. "It was an early Easter that year. We were at your parents'. Remember, Kent?"

His eyes widened as the memory drifted back. He caught her eye and they both struggled to contain their amusement. They'd slept in the guest bedroom, which was just down the hall from his parents' room. Their bed squeaked...so they'd rolled onto the floor and Kent's foot had become tangled in the lamp cord and the lamp came crashing down on him. On hearing the crash, his mother had knocked on the door to make sure everything was all right. It'd been a comedy of errors.

"What's so funny?" Danielle demanded.

Beth felt guilty for being so rude as to exclude everyone else from their private conversation. "I apologize, Danielle," she said, turning around. "Kent and I were… just remembering something that happened years ago."

"I was the result," Sophie announced proudly.

"Can we talk about something different?" Danielle said, clearly not amused.

"Of course," Beth assured her.

"I always wanted a brother," Bailey said. "An older brother."

"You got your sister instead."

"Yeah. And not only that, she's younger."

"I never had a sister," Danielle said. "And *my* brother was younger and a real nuisance. He used to spy on me and my friends."

"Sophie used to spy on me."

"Did not."

"Did, too."

"Girls," Beth said, annoyed by their behavior. "You're out of grade school. Please act like it."

They broke into peals of laughter.

"What?" Beth turned again to see what her daughters were laughing about now.

"Mom, you're so predictable. That's exactly what we told Danielle you'd say."

Kent pulled the sleigh over to the shed and handed the

reins to Beth while he jumped down. He helped Sophie out first, then Danielle and Bailey.

"I'll take the sled over to the Nelsons'," Beth said, but before she could set off, Kent leaped back into place beside her.

"I'll go with you."

"That isn't necessary," she told him, thinking he'd want to be inside with the others.

"Yes, it is. You aren't going to argue with me, are you?"

"I...no."

"Good, because it would be very tempting to stop you the way I used to once upon a time."

Beth swallowed hard. She'd forgotten. In the early days of their marriage, anytime she disagreed with him, Kent would take her in his arms and kiss her.

Ten

"Honey, can you get the door?" Corrie called from the back bedroom. She swore that if Roy didn't get his hearing checked soon, she'd start ignoring every word he said. That would give him a little demonstration of what she put up with every day.

"Okay," he yelled from the living room.

With an exasperated sigh Corrie went back to her wrapping paper and ribbon. She was almost finished with Noelle's birthday gift, the one they'd take to Grace Harding's party. She still needed to arrange the last of the Christmas presents under the tree before their children arrived for dinner, which would be followed by Christmas Eve church services. After that, they'd go to Noelle's first-birthday celebration at the Hardings'. Gloria, Roy and

Corrie's eldest daughter, would be coming tonight. Corrie hoped Gloria would bring Chad Timmons.

She couldn't help worrying about Gloria, who was single, pregnant and determined to manage on her own. What disturbed Corrie most was the fact that there was no reason for Gloria to be so stubborn. Chad loved her; Corrie was convinced of that. She'd invited him to dinner and hoped Gloria wouldn't be upset with her. Oh, she hadn't made a secret of it, but she hadn't talked it over with Gloria, either.

Mack and Mary Jo would be with them and of course little Noelle, too. She'd been born on Christmas Eve one year ago, at the Harding ranch; Mack had delivered her. Corrie had a lovely birthday cake ready for her adopted granddaughter, not to mention a pile of gifts. Corrie couldn't wait to watch Noelle open them. There was nothing like a baby to bring excitement and joy back to Christmas.

"Corrie," Roy shouted. "It's the Beldons."

"I'll be right there," she shouted back as she finished tying the ribbon on the gift she'd just wrapped.

Corrie had been expecting Peggy and Bob to stop by at some point that afternoon. It was tradition. Every Christmas Eve the Beldons came over with a plate of Peggy's homemade cookies and specialty candies.

"Merry Christmas," Corrie said, hurrying into the room and opening her arms. She hugged Bob and then, after taking the plate from Peggy, embraced her, too.

"I hope we aren't interrupting your day."

"Nonsense," Corrie told her. "You know you're welcome anytime."

"Especially when you come bearing gifts," Roy joked.

"Sit down, please. I've got eggnog and coffee, whichever you prefer."

"We can only stay a few minutes," Bob said, claiming the corner of the sofa. "Hollie and Marc are driving over from Spokane."

"Wonderful! I'm glad they can make it." Corrie hadn't met the Beldons' daughter and son, but she'd heard lots about them. She and Peggy often met for lunch and had a strong friendship.

"It'll be good to have them here for Christmas."

"We'll have a full house ourselves," Roy said. "Mack and Mary Jo are coming for dinner tonight and they'll be here on Christmas Day, as well."

"Gloria will be here tonight, too, and she'll attend church services with us," Corrie added.

"And Christmas Day?" Peggy asked.

Corrie shrugged. "She didn't say. I imagine she'll come for dinner, unless…"

"Unless?"

"Unless she plans to spend it with Chad."

"Ah, yes. How are things going between her and Chad?"

"Fine, I think. Gloria hasn't said much, but she seems happier these days, less…confused. I know they're seeing each other regularly. If they have any wedding plans, however, they haven't shared them with us."

"Chad put the crib together," Roy said. "I volunteered and so did Mack, but Gloria said Chad would do it."

"That sounds positive," Peggy murmured.

"I just wish those two would get married," Corrie responded. "I know the world's different these days. So many young women choose to be single mothers, but it's hard work."

"A baby needs a father," Roy inserted. "I wanted to tell Gloria that, but Corrie wouldn't let me."

"When has that stopped you in the past?" Corrie retorted as she headed into the kitchen to get their drinks. It still annoyed her that her husband had gone against her wishes and informed Chad of Gloria's pregnancy. After she and Chad had broken up, Gloria had wanted to keep the information from him.

The irony of her daughter's situation astonished her. This was history repeating itself. Well, almost...

Years ago, in college, Corrie had discovered she was pregnant after Roy had ended their relationship. Instead of letting him know, she'd returned home and given her daughter up for adoption. Not until they'd reunited a couple of years later did Roy learn about his baby. And not for more than three decades did they actually meet her. Her husband had been determined that the same thing not happen to Chad Timmons.

Peggy helped her prepare the coffee. Roy and Bob had both requested eggnog, which Corrie poured into festive glasses decorated with green holly leaves and red berries. They'd once belonged to her mother and Corrie reserved them for this special season and for special friends.

"What have you heard from Linnette?" Peggy asked when they were all seated again.

"She and Pete will be in North Dakota over Christmas."

"Was it just a year ago that Pete drove her to Cedar Cove for Christmas?" Roy asked, shaking his head.

Corrie felt the same way. So much had taken place this past year.... During the holidays, Linnette, their younger daughter, had brought home a man she'd met, a farmer named Pete Mason. They'd liked him, but at the time Peggy hadn't thought the relationship was going anywhere. Pete farmed with his brothers near Buffalo Valley, where Linnette had recently accepted a position as a physician assistant. Although Linnette hadn't been in Buffalo Valley long, she seemed genuinely happy for the first time since Cal Washburn had broken her heart. Soon after that, she'd packed up her car and set off with no destination in mind. Peggy had worried endlessly, sure this was a formula for disaster. Then Linnette had phoned from this small prairie town where she'd ended up and sounded... content. She'd sounded more like herself than she had in a very long while.

Corrie hated that her younger daughter lived so far from

the family. But she loved Linnette enough to realize she had to make her own decisions. Pete had fallen in love with her first and initially Corrie feared Linnette might have married on the rebound. Those concerns had been laid to rest. On Corrie's recent trip to Buffalo Valley, after the birth of Linnette and Pete's son, she had all the reassurance she'd ever need. It was abundantly clear that Linnette loved her husband and the life she'd created in this small North Dakota community.

"We had quite a Christmas last year," Roy commented, chuckling. "Mack had just been hired by the fire department and he was at the Hardings' to deliver Mary Jo's baby."

Bob grinned. "What I remember was Mary Jo's three brothers racing around town looking for her."

"And not a one of them had any sense of direction."

"Hey, be fair. They'd never been on this side of the sound before."

"And now Linc lives here, too."

"And married to the Bellamy girl."

"They are the sweetest couple," Peggy said with the hint of a sigh. "I saw them in the grocery store the other day. It was positively romantic just seeing the two of them together. We spoke for a few minutes and apparently Linc and Lori are spending Christmas with her family."

"Well," Bob said, "that's an improvement. Bellamy was

trying to ruin Linc's business. Until you and Troy intervened…"

Roy shrugged off Bob's comment. "I'm glad they reconciled with Lori's family, but I don't know why Bellamy couldn't just accept the fact that they're married. End of story."

"It wasn't the only wedding this past year, either," Bob said. "Faith and Troy tied the knot, and of course so did Mack and Mary Jo."

"I do love a wedding," Corrie said. To her way of thinking, there should be one more, and preferably soon. She'd feel so much better about Gloria's situation if she was married to Chad.

"Well…" Bob lowered his empty glass. "I hate to cut this short, but we've got a few other stops to make."

Corrie and Roy walked their friends to the front door and thanked them again.

"This is one small way of repaying you for all you've done for us," Peggy said.

"How can you say that?" Corrie asked. Their friendship had been one of her biggest blessings since moving to Cedar Cove. "You've done so much for *us*."

"You kept me out of prison," Bob reminded them, referring to the death at the B and B. "Believe me, I'll be forever grateful for that."

"Ancient history," Roy insisted, standing on the front porch. He wrapped his arm around Corrie's shoulders.

"Ancient history to you, perhaps," Bob said, "but it's something I'll never forget."

They got into their vehicle, and Corrie and Roy returned to the warmth of the house.

"I really didn't do that much," Roy protested. "Bob was so obviously innocent...."

"Are you complaining about the cookies and candy they brought?" she asked, half-joking.

"No way!"

"Then enjoy and quit your muttering."

He laughed. "You're right. Have you tasted that English toffee yet? It's good stuff."

"Don't tell me how good it is, I'm resisting."

"Why?"

Corrie rolled her eyes. "Because it's hard enough not to overindulge during the holidays without you telling me how good everything tastes."

"Fine. Leaves more for me."

Sighing, Corrie brought the tray into the kitchen and covered it with a towel. Out of sight, out of mind. She returned to the back bedroom and resumed wrapping gifts.

Fifteen minutes later, Roy poked his head in. "You about done?"

"Yup. I'm putting the final touches on the last package. Why?"

"Anything here for Gloria?"

"Of course."

"Well, she just parked outside the house."

"Oh." Corrie felt a bit flustered.

"She isn't alone."

"Did Chad come with her?" Corrie couldn't hide the excitement in her voice.

Roy nodded. "Only they don't seem to be in any big hurry to come inside. They've been sitting in the car chatting for the past ten minutes."

Corrie arched her eyebrows. "Can you tell if they're arguing?" She certainly hoped not!

"I didn't want it to be obvious that I saw them."

"Good point." Still, one might think that Roy, a private investigator, would know how to watch without being seen.

"Besides, this is *their* business."

Another good point, although that hadn't troubled him earlier when he'd gone to see Chad, which she restrained herself from mentioning.

The doorbell chimed.

"I'll get it," Roy said.

Corrie made her way into the kitchen and brewed a fresh pot of coffee. She heard Roy greet their daughter and Chad, and she quickly joined them.

"I know we're early," Gloria said. She held hands with Chad—a positive sign. "Chad thought we should all talk before everyone came for dinner tonight."

"Sure," Roy said, sitting down in his recliner.

Gloria and Chad took the sofa, huddled close to each other.

Corrie slid onto her favorite chair, her heart in her throat.

A tense silence pervaded the room as both she and Roy waited for whatever announcement was about to be made.

Gloria looked at Chad as if she wanted him to do the talking.

"Gloria and I wanted you to know we decided to get married," he blurted out. "She agreed to marry me a couple of weeks ago but we wanted to keep it to ourselves until Christmas, and—"

Corrie was instantly on her feet. "That's wonderful news!" she said, interrupting him and clasping her hands together. Her mind was whirling. While she hoped it would be soon, for the baby's sake, she'd love a June wedding. That would give her enough time to plan. She'd get started first thing after Christmas. They'd need someplace special for the reception and, of course, there were the invitations, which they'd want to send out immediately. They'd have to find a dress; at this stage of her pregnancy, Gloria probably wouldn't fit into Corrie's wedding gown, which was a shame.

"When's the happy date?" Roy asked.

"Actually…we're already married," Chad said.

Corrie blinked, assuming she'd misunderstood. "Already married?" she repeated. That wasn't possible!

"When?" Roy asked, following the first question with a second. "Where?"

Again it was Chad who explained. "I'm afraid I'm responsible. Gloria said she'd marry me but we couldn't agree on a date."

"I wanted to wait until after the baby's born and have a summer wedding," she told them.

Corrie nodded, understanding.

"And I wanted us to be married *before* the baby's born," Chad said.

Ah, yes, Corrie thought, seeing the problem.

"So we decided to simply go ahead and get married right away and then, this summer, have another ceremony and a reception."

"Makes sense to me," Roy said, obviously pleased by this unexpected turn of events.

"Why didn't you let us know?" Corrie asked, feeling a twinge of hurt despite her happiness. Even if it was a quick affair, she would've liked to be there.

"I agree we should have asked you to attend," Gloria said. "But if you were there and Chad's parents weren't, they would've felt cheated. So we just did it. We applied for the license and were married a couple of days later."

"By whom?"

"Judge Griffin," Chad said. "At the courthouse. Mack and Mary Jo stood up with us." He paused. "I don't blame you for being upset."

"We're not upset," Roy told him, and Corrie nodded.

"As Gloria mentioned, we plan to have another ceremony later, with friends and family from both sides."

"This way we *all* get what we want," Corrie said happily. A marriage and a baby—another grandchild for her and Roy—and a wedding.

Roy stood, extending his hand to Chad. "Welcome to the family."

"Thank you." The two men shook hands.

Corrie hugged her daughter and Chad. She'd spend the next few months getting ready for the wedding and reception, and the thought filled her with anticipation.

"Mom and Dad, there's another reason we stopped by early."

"Oh?" Corrie murmured.

"You're not pregnant with twins, are you?" Roy asked, half-joking.

"No. We wanted to get your okay before we had one of your gifts delivered."

"All right…." Roy glanced at Corrie, clearly wondering if she knew what this was about; she shook her head, as confused as he was.

"Did you hear someone left ten puppies on Beth Morehouse's porch?"

"We did," Corrie confirmed. "In fact, Bob was just telling us he got one of those pups for Peggy."

"And we chose one for you," Gloria said.

Their daughter had gotten them a puppy?

Corrie stared at her.

"Not long ago, Dad talked about a Labrador he had while he was growing up and he got a nostalgic look in his eyes. I heard about these puppies from Ted Reynolds, and Chad and I went to Beth's house today to pick one up."

"If you don't want the dog," Chad said, moving toward the edge of the sofa, "Gloria and I will take her. She's cute as a bug and has personality to boot."

"Where is she now?" Corrie asked.

"At my place," Gloria replied. "We thought we'd bring her over tomorrow."

"A puppy." Roy wore a silly grin, as if the prospect delighted him. "What about a name?" he asked.

"I know—Asta. That's the dog in the *Thin Man* movies, remember?" Corrie suggested.

"Perfect for a detective's dog." Roy smiled. "Even if the original Asta was a boy."

"Asta it is," Corrie said, adding, "We need a puppy in the house again."

This was going to be the most wonderful Christmas in recent memory. Weddings, grandchildren—and now a puppy.

Eleven

"Come in out of the cold," Danielle said as Kent and Beth returned to the house after delivering the sleigh to the Nelsons'. It might have been Beth's imagination, but she suspected Danielle had been standing by the door waiting for them. She had her cell phone in her hand again.

She immediately ran up to Kent and spoke urgently in his ear. Kent looked decidedly uncomfortable as she hugged him, but put his arms lightly around her. Beth saw Danielle's hug as a claim of ownership. Unable to watch, she stepped around the embracing couple and hurried into the kitchen, grateful for the escape.

Bailey and Sophie were standing in a corner of the family room, whispering heatedly.

"Girls?" Beth said, wondering what they were up to. They didn't seem to be arguing, but clearly had different opinions on something or other. "Is everything all right?" she asked.

Bailey turned around so quickly, she nearly stumbled. "Ah...sure. Why wouldn't it be?"

Sophie narrowed her eyes as Danielle and Kent stepped into the room.

"It was a...lovely afternoon, but it's time I...we left," Danielle said, and then inclined her head as if to say the decision was final.

"You're *leaving?*" Bailey cried in apparent shock.

"You're not staying for dinner?" Sophie sounded equally shocked.

"I thought you came to Cedar Cove so you could spend Christmas with us," Bailey reminded her father.

Frankly, Beth was just as glad to see them go. She didn't understand exactly what had happened between her and Kent in the sleigh, but whatever it was had made her feel confused and a bit panicky. She'd actually *wanted* him to kiss her. Her ex-husband had brought another woman to spend Christmas with the family, and yet Beth could hardly stop herself from leaning into him....

"Kent will be back on Christmas Day," Danielle said to the girls, as if they were small children in need of reassurance. "Christmas Eve is a time for family and—"

"Our father *is* family," Bailey protested as she curled her hands into tight fists. She seemed to be on the verge of tears.

Sophie cast a pleading glance at her father. "Daddy?" she implored.

Kent hesitated.

Danielle tugged him over to the door. "I need to go. Don't worry, your father will be back in the morning." She turned to him, hissing, "The girls need to spend time with their mother, too."

"I'll stay," Kent said decisively. "That is, if you're sure it's what you want." The question was directed at Beth.

Holding her breath, she realized she didn't have a choice. Which meant that her Christmas Eve dinner would be shared with Kent and…Danielle. What she wouldn't give for a peaceful evening alone with her daughters. Instead, she was forced to watch her husband—er, *ex*-husband— with another woman.

"Mom?" Bailey whispered.

"Of course you should stay," Beth said, just a little too brightly.

"Mom's making lasagna," Sophie said, and then added, apparently to enlighten Danielle, "It's a family tradition. The recipe comes from Grandma Carlucci."

Danielle pursed her lips in a pout, then squared her shoulders, coming to some decision. "In that case, I insist on helping."

The last thing Beth wanted was this woman in *her* kitchen. "All I need to do is get the lasagna in the oven," she said. "It's already put together—just needs to bake."

"Well, then, I'll make a salad," Danielle said.

"Mom always makes Caesar salad and garlic bread," Bailey told her.

"I can make a Caesar salad." Danielle pushed up the sleeves of her sweater and grabbed an apron off the countertop, staking out her territory.

Beth felt as though the other woman had declared war. Fine. In that case, she was prepared to surrender without a fight. This was Christmas, and if Danielle wanted to plant her flag in Beth's kitchen, she was welcome to it. Only Beth wouldn't be there.

"Are you sure you don't mind making the salad?" she asked.

"I offered, didn't I?" Danielle placed one hand on her hip.

"Okay, then, there's no reason for me to stay. I'll use the time to deliver one of the puppies." She'd drive the Randalls' puppy over to Grace Harding's place.

Danielle cast her a triumphant look, as if to say she'd taken great satisfaction in maneuvering Beth out of her own kitchen.

Sophie smiled; Beth could tell this was precisely what she'd hoped would happen. "Dad, you should go with Mom."

"Kent!" Danielle said sharply. "I might...you know, need you."

"Dad," Bailey challenged, "do you want Mom driving on treacherous roads *alone?* What if she had an accident?"

Beth tried to remember whether her daughter had ever taken drama. If so, she'd had a good teacher. The kid was ready for Broadway.

"It's fine, Kent," Beth assured him, trying to hide her laughter and not quite succeeding. "I've driven these roads alone any number of times."

"But not when there's *snow* on the ground," Sophie wailed, as if she'd attended the same drama class.

"Your mother knows what she's doing," Danielle tossed in casually. "She'll be perfectly fine *by herself.*" The last two words were given heavy emphasis.

Again Bailey and Sophie turned to their father with wide eyes even Scrooge couldn't have ignored.

"Dad? Are you really going to let Mom go out all on her own?"

"Would you ever forgive yourself if anything happened to the mother of your children?" Sophie wailed.

Unwilling to be part of this ridiculous conversation any longer, Beth grabbed her coat, gloves and scarf and headed for the back door. She was outside and halfway to the car with the puppy in its carrier when Kent jogged up behind her.

"Hey, wait up," he called.

"Kent, really, this isn't necessary."

"According to our daughters, it is."

Beth rolled her eyes. "I don't remember you being manipulated quite this easily when we were married." She opened the rear passenger door and placed the puppy's carrier inside.

Kent climbed into the front passenger seat and waited until Beth joined him before he responded. "Did you ever stop to think I might actually *want* to accompany you?"

She hadn't. For the life of her, Beth couldn't manage a single word. In fact, it was all she could do to breathe. All at once the interior of her SUV seemed to shrink until it felt as if the two of them were trapped inside a box the size of a milk crate. Her mouth went dry and she concentrated on driving rather than the man she'd loved and married and… left. Oh, how she wished she could turn back the clock.

Risking a look at Kent, she wondered if he was thinking the same thing.

The silence that stretched between them threatened to snap.

"I…" She started to say something—although what, she wasn't sure.

"I was—"

They both spoke at the same time.

"You first," she said.

"No, you."

She laughed. "Please, you go first."

"Well," he murmured after a few awkward seconds, "I

was just thinking back to all the animals you rescued while we were married. Remember Ugly Arnie?"

Like she'd ever forget the injured raccoon she'd found at their back door. "How could I forget him?"

"Vicious, ungrateful—"

"Kent, he was in pain! As I recall, you aren't exactly Prince Charming when you aren't feeling well."

"Prince Charming? So is that how you remember me when…I was feeling good?"

She doubted that he expected an answer, but she gave him one, anyway. "You had your moments."

"So did you."

"Thank you." They could play nice, she realized. It hadn't always been this silent battle of wills.

"I kind of thought you'd remarry," he said, frowning as he spoke.

"Really?" She, on the other hand, hadn't even considered the possibility that Kent might marry someone else— well, other than in some vague, abstract way. Certainly not someone like Danielle. Beth was astonished that Kent would find this hard, brusque woman appealing. Yes, superficially Danielle was attractive—okay, gorgeous—but she seemed to lack all the qualities Beth had expected him to value.

"If you did remarry, I assumed you'd choose a vet."

"Oh, my goodness…" Without thinking, Beth eased her

foot off the brake and the car swerved on the icy road and went sideways. "Hold on," she cried.

Kent braced his arms against the dashboard until the car came to a complete stop on the side of the road. "You okay?" he demanded.

"I'm fine...what about you?"

"My heart is somewhere in my throat," he said, "but other than that I'll survive. What just happened? I didn't see anything in the road."

"It's Ted."

"Ted? Who's Ted?"

"The local vet... He said he'd stop by this afternoon and I need to be there."

"Give him a call," Kent muttered, as if it was of little concern.

"I will." She reached across for her handbag and grabbed her cell, pushing the button that would connect her with him.

"You have him on speed dial?" Kent asked with raised eyebrows.

Beth ignored the question and waited impatiently for Ted to answer. After four long rings, the phone went to voice mail. She exhaled loudly, then carefully put the car in Reverse and turned around.

"Where are you going now?" Kent asked.

She would've thought the answer was obvious. "To Ted's

place. He's probably with an animal, so he couldn't get the phone."

"You could've left a message."

He was right, she could have, but that seemed rather unfriendly. Besides, she wanted to explain. "His place isn't far from here," she said, instead of responding to his comment.

The silence returned.

Again it was Kent who broke it. "Do you see a lot of this Tim fellow?"

"Ted," she corrected. "About once or twice a week, I guess." She downplayed the veterinarian's role in her life, which had taken on more significance in the past three or four months. There'd been a shift in their relationship, beginning in late September, when he'd come over after caring for a sick goat nearby. He'd stayed for a glass of wine, followed by a leisurely dinner.

A week later they'd met in town, and Ted had insisted he owed her dinner. That was how it had started, almost innocently. Recently, however, it'd become more. Ted had kissed her, and that had been a turning point. Lately, Ted had taken to dropping in during the evenings, and Beth looked forward to his visits.

"Any particular reason Ted was coming to the house?" Kent asked nonchalantly.

"Nothing formal, if that's what you mean. To wish us a merry Christmas. And I want him to meet the girls. He has a line on someone who wants a puppy, too."

"So it's serious? Between you and him?"

"We have a lot in common," she said, well aware that she hadn't really answered the question.

Ted's driveway came into view, and she signaled, then drove down the long gravel road that led to his home and his veterinary clinic.

Ted was in the yard clearing snow. When he saw her car, he smiled and waved, then leaned his shovel against a tree.

Beth parked and turned off the engine, slipping out of the car.

Walking over to meet her, Ted grinned from ear to ear. "Good to see you, Beth," he said. He didn't kiss her, no doubt because he'd noticed there was a man with her.

Beth tried to see the veterinarian as Kent might. Ted was a few years older, a big man with large, strong hands and an easy smile. He had a receding hairline, visible despite his wool hat. His gentle nature comforted animals— and people.

"Kent Morehouse," Kent said, stepping forward, his hand extended.

Ted pulled off his glove to shake hands but his gaze immediately shot to Beth.

"Kent is my ex-husband. He's here to spend Christmas with the girls," Beth said, feeling uncomfortable saying anything more.

"Oh, yes. You mentioned that Kent was planning to visit," Ted commented.

"I was just driving to the Hardings' to drop off a puppy when I recalled that you were coming over today," she said quickly.

"Well, seeing that you've got visitors, perhaps I shouldn't—"

"No, please, I want you to," Beth said, eager to reassure him. "In fact, I was hoping you'd stay for dinner."

"Dinner?" Kent repeated, frowning.

"Yes, dinner," she said pointedly. "I'm making lasagna. A family recipe."

"My grandmother was Italian," Kent added in a meaningful voice, essentially explaining that this was *his* family's recipe.

"Kent's, uh, friend is with the girls, preparing a Caesar salad and garlic bread."

"That sounds wonderful."

"It will be," Beth said. "*Please* say you'll join us."

Ignoring Kent, Ted stared at her for a long moment. "You're sure?"

"I'm positive."

Ted nodded decisively. "Then I accept. Thank you. What time would you like me there?"

Beth was about to suggest as soon as possible, but before she could, Kent spoke.

"I believe Beth mentioned something about dinner being ready around five."

"Yes, five. We're eating early so we won't be late for church," she murmured.

"Can I bring anything? Wine? Dessert?"

"I've got everything covered, but thanks." She wanted to visit longer, but Kent had already walked back to the car and stood with the door open, waiting for her.

"I'll see you soon," Ted promised. "And I've got a couple bottles of a nice red. To go with the lasagna."

"Thank you," she whispered, and hoped Ted understood how much she appreciated his willingness to show, once again, what a good friend he was. As good a friend as Danielle....

Twelve

Justine Gunderson busied herself in the kitchen, enjoying an afternoon free from the responsibility of managing the Victorian Tea Room. She'd given the staff an extra day off so they could celebrate Christmas Eve with their own families.

The holiday season at the tearoom had been hectic, with a number of special high teas. Her favorite had been Tea with Santa. The children had been so excited, and Santa, a theater friend of Bob Beldon's, had played the role with verve and charm.

In a few years Livvy would be able to go, but for now the toddler, at nearly eighteen months, was too young for Santa in his frightening red suit.

The back door opened, and her husband entered the house. Seth was a blond Swede who towered well over six feet. Just seeing him made Justine's heart react with a surge of love. She'd never expected to marry, let alone have a family of her own. In fact, she'd gone out of her way to avoid serious relationships…until she'd worked on her ten-year high school reunion. That was when she'd run into Seth Gunderson, who was also on the reunion committee.

She'd known Seth nearly her entire life. He'd been her twin brother's best friend. As irrational as it sounded, after the accident that claimed Jordan's life, Justine had wanted to blame Seth. If he'd been with her brother at the lake that day, Jordan might not have died. Seth would have noticed that her brother hadn't surfaced after diving off the floating dock. He would've gone after him. If only Seth had been there.…

But he hadn't. It'd been Justine who'd held her brother's lifeless body on the dock until the paramedics showed up.

That fateful summer afternoon had forever changed her world.

Seth smiled at her as he stripped off his coat.

She smiled back and felt, as she so often had in the past, that Jordan would have approved of her marrying Seth Gunderson. Through the years, at various times, Justine had sensed her twin's presence. During those indescribable moments of connection, she hadn't felt the horrific loss of her brother; instead, she'd felt his blessing. Jordan seemed to be standing right beside her, smiling and happy, teasing her the way he'd once done, full of life and boyish humor.

The first time it'd happened was shortly after she'd given birth to Leif. Still in the hospital, exhausted and woozy from the drugs, she'd closed her eyes. Suddenly, Jordan was there before her, and he wore the biggest, goofiest grin she'd ever seen. He was telling her how happy he was for her and Seth; she was sure of it. She could almost hear him saying how excited he was that they'd decided to name their son after him: Leif Jordan Gunderson.

"Daddy, Daddy." Leif shot across the room, dropping his handheld computer game on the way, with Penny barking at his heels. "Santa's coming tonight!"

"He sure is." Lifting the boy high above his head, Seth nuzzled Leif's tummy while the little boy squealed in delight.

Hearing her brother, Livvy toddled out, clutching her teddy bear under her left arm, pressing its face against her side. Livvy and that silly bear were inseparable. She'd be getting her first doll from Santa this Christmas. Justine sincerely hoped Livvy would enjoy the doll as much as she did her teddy bear.

"How's my girl?" Seth asked, setting Leif down and reaching for his daughter. He planted a noisy kiss on her cheek. She, too, squealed with delight.

"Hey, don't I get one of those kisses?" Justine teased.

"You bet." He came to her in the kitchen and slipped his arms around her from behind, planting his hands over her still-flat stomach. "How long have you been working in here?"

"A while." The family cookbook her grandmother, Charlotte Jefferson Rhodes, had compiled, lay open in front of her. Various ingredients, organized according to the recipes, were spread along the counter.

"Seems to me you were in the kitchen when I left for work this morning. Are you sure you're up to this?"

"Stop worrying, okay?" Hosting the family for Christmas Eve dinner required a lot of extra preparation, but Justine never turned away from a challenge.

"Did you bake those homemade rolls I like so much?" Seth asked, eyeing the covered breadbasket.

"I did that first thing this morning."

Seth grinned. "I hope you doubled the batch."

"I did."

"That's my girl."

Justine reached up and kissed him. "I promise you can have as many as you want."

"How are you feeling?" Seth asked.

"I feel wonderful. I always do when I'm pregnant."

Seth closed his eyes. "I don't know how we let this happen," he said as he feathered kisses down the side of her neck.

Justine giggled and put her arms around her husband's neck. "You'd think by now we'd know how babies are made."

"If it was up to you, we'd live in a shoe and have a dozen children."

"Three suits me just fine," she assured him, although she'd be the first to admit she loved being a mother. She could hardly believe that at one time she'd been willing to give all of this up without even knowing what she'd be missing.

The pregnancy would be this year's Christmas surprise for her family. Keeping it secret had been far more difficult than she'd expected. At least a dozen times she'd been tempted to tell her mother and her grandmother. Both would be thrilled.

"Can I help with anything?" Seth asked.

"You could check Livvy's diaper," she said.

Seth swept his daughter into his arms and carried her to her room. When he returned a few minutes later, Livvy's head lolled against his shoulder.

"Did you have a chance to get the mail?" he asked.

"Not yet."

"I'll do it." Seth set Livvy down on the carpet. She leaned her head against the sofa cushion. She'd woken late that morning and hadn't been interested in a nap. Now her eyes drooped as her thumb found its way into her mouth.

Justine had sucked her thumb, too; so had Jordan. After washing her hands, Justine picked up her sweet baby girl and brought her back to her crib. She gently placed her inside and covered her with the blanket Charlotte had knit for her.

Seth came into their daughter's bedroom as she sat beside the crib, watching Livvy's deep, even breaths.

He stood beside her. "It's difficult to fathom how much love we can have for children, isn't it?" he whispered.

"Impossible to believe until we become parents ourselves," she whispered back.

They left the bedroom and Seth closed the door.

"Anything interesting in the mail?" Justine asked as he sat down, flipping through the envelopes. She poured her husband a cup of tea and joined him at the kitchen table.

"The usual Christmas cards—and one rather interesting letter."

"Oh? Who from?"

Seth leafed through the holiday cards until he came across a plain, business-size white envelope. He glanced at it again, then handed it to her.

Justine saw that the envelope held her name—and only hers. The return address made her catch her breath. After taking a moment to compose herself, she raised her eyes to meet Seth's. "It's stamped prison mail. The postmark is Shelton, Washington—that's where the state prison is. One of them, anyway."

"I noticed that, too."

"There's only one person who could be writing me from there." The paper seemed to grow hot in her hands.

"Warren Saget," Seth muttered.

Justine dropped the letter on the table and avoided looking at it.

"Aren't you going to open it?" her husband asked.

"I...I don't know." She'd once had a deep affection for Warren, a successful local builder, although he was old enough to be her father. They'd dated for a while. He'd liked having a tall, beautiful woman on his arm, and she'd liked the fact that he was rich and powerful and made no physical demands on her.

He couldn't. That was their little secret. With Warren she was safe from emotional—and physical—entanglements. Safe, until she'd agreed to work on the class reunion project and Seth had shown up. Justine hadn't wanted to become involved with Seth, yet he was all she thought about. Warren had offered her a huge diamond engagement ring. He was willing to do anything not to lose her. But even that diamond hadn't enticed her. All she wanted, all she *needed,* was Seth.

"I wonder if Warren has any idea of everything he did for us," Seth commented.

Her husband's words jarred Justine from her reverie. "You mean what he did *to* us, don't you?" Warren had tried to destroy them.

"But in the end that's what saved our marriage."

"You're right," she said slowly. "Ironic, isn't it?"

"We were killing ourselves with the restaurant, working all hours of the day and night...."

"You don't need to remind me," Justine said, shaking her head at the memory. It'd been a difficult period in their marriage. They'd been working impossibly long hours with no time as a couple or a family.

The restaurant had been Seth's dream. For nearly ten years he'd saved his money from fishing the crab-rich Alaskan waters. He'd lived on a sailboat in the marina while in town, and spent every waking moment studying restaurant management. He'd dreamed of one day opening an elegant seafood restaurant in Cedar Cove. Together they'd made his dream come true, and the Lighthouse had been the success he'd always planned.

But Seth had worked far too hard. Justine shared his dream, and they'd redoubled their efforts until it all became too much. By then Leif had been born, which meant Justine was torn between being with her son and working at the restaurant.

Their marriage had started to show the stress of too many demands and too few hours. For the first time Seth and Justine had been at odds.

Then, one night, the restaurant had burned down. All their dreams, all their hard work, their blood, sweat and tears, had gone up in smoke.

Even now, memories of that night were surreal. After being contacted by the authorities, they'd rushed to the scene and walked around in a stupor, shocked and bereft. It wasn't long before the fire inspector declared it'd been arson.

Someone had purposely set their restaurant on fire. The police had what they called "a person of interest," a high school kid who'd worked there briefly before Seth let him go. Anson Butler had a history of being in trouble and had started fires when he was younger. Someone had seen him inside the restaurant that night. Then Anson disappeared.... Meanwhile, Justine and Seth were left to pick up the charred remains of their life. The stress on their marriage brought them close to the breaking point.

It didn't help that Warren took every opportunity to talk about how good things had been between them. Justine didn't believe it, not for a minute; still, it was comforting to have someone pay her that kind of attention.

Not working and depressed, Seth had struggled emotionally. He'd given up fishing in Alaska, and she was grateful. She wanted her husband with her. Leif needed him. So did she.

It was during this time that she'd come up with the idea of building a tearoom and giving it the ambience of England's Victorian era. The plans were already in motion when Seth was approached by a family friend who owned a boatyard and offered him a job in sales. Seth took it and turned out to be a natural.

Later, thanks to Sheriff Troy Davis, Warren Saget was

arrested, tried and convicted of arson. Currently, he was serving time in prison.

Justine poked at the envelope with her finger. She expected to feel *something*. Some emotion. Regret. Anger. Something. Instead, she felt nothing. Only a sadness that Warren could have been this vindictive, this desperate. He'd never forgiven her for leaving him and he'd wanted to punish Seth for stealing away the one woman who understood him, understood his needs.

"Are you going to read it?" Seth asked.

"Do you want me to?"

He thought about it, then nodded.

Personally, Justine would be content to toss the letter. Yet a part of her wanted to know what Warren had to say. Taking a deep breath, she opened the envelope and pulled out a single sheet of paper. She read it, then crumpled it in one hand.

"What did he say?"

"Just that he'll be up for parole in a few years and wondered if I'd be waiting for him when he's released."

"You're joking!"

"The man is delusional," she groaned. Even now, Warren seemed to be living in a dreamworld. He'd convinced himself that she was pining for him, anticipating his release. Needless to say, she had no interest in the man who'd done his best to ruin her and Seth's lives.

Taking the letter, she threw it inside the recycling bin, among the unwanted flyers and empty cereal boxes.

Seth grinned, and she grinned in reply. "Merry Christmas, my dear husband."

"Merry Christmas, my darling wife."

Thirteen

"What are we going to do?" Sophie whispered to her older sister. "Nothing's turning out like we planned."

"You're telling me?" Bailey muttered back. Dinner was on the table. The lasagna, with the salad next to it, sat in the center. Wooden serving utensils leaned against the side of the large salad bowl. The bread was out of the oven, and the warm pungent scent of butter and garlic wafted through the house.

Peering out the swinging kitchen door into the formal dining room, Bailey saw that the situation was even worse than she'd realized. Mom was in one corner of the room, deep in conversation with Ted Reynolds. Danielle and Dad stood on the opposite side. Danielle appeared to be talking Kent's ears off, no doubt regaling him with horror stories of the time she'd spent alone with his daughters. She was clutching her cell phone—again. While Kent and Beth were away, she'd made repeated calls but hadn't connected, growing more and more frustrated. Her impatience with Bailey and Sophie had increased just as quickly.

Okay, so that part of their plan had worked perfectly. Danielle had been stuck with the two of them, and she hadn't liked it one bit. She'd been outsmarted by Beth and wasn't in any mood to be friendly with Bailey and Sophie. Besides, she was distracted, frequently calling and texting some unknown person.

Not long after their parents left, Bailey and Sophie had learned that Danielle knew next to nothing about making a Caesar salad. She assumed all salad dressing came out of a bottle. When Bailey informed her their mother made her own, Danielle snarled that she could make her own, too, only she needed a recipe. Tearing through Beth's cookbooks, she finally came up with one but was disgusted by half the ingredients. No way was she using anchovies! In the end, she'd opted for the bottled Italian dressing she'd found in the fridge.

"Your mother makes her own dressing. Oh, yeah, I can tell!" Danielle had brandished the half-full bottle. "That's the most ridiculous thing I've ever heard," she'd raged. "You're just saying that so I'll feel inferior." Danielle fumed until Kent returned. Her cell phone was in her hands constantly, and her thumbs worked at sending text messages.

Bailey and Sophie had several whispered conversations about it, wondering who she was trying so hard to reach.

Danielle had cornered Kent in the dining room, her mouth moving at warp speed. It didn't look as if Dad had an opportunity to say much of anything.

Bailey refused to believe he was dumb enough to actually fall for Danielle. It contradicted everything she knew about her father.

The instant their parents had walked in the house, Bailey sensed something was wrong. She'd quickly discovered the cause. Mom had invited Ted Reynolds to dinner. Oh, great. Based on what she'd heard from Beth, Bailey had suspected for a month or two that Ted was interested in their mother. The invitation had probably been a defensive move on Beth's part; unfortunately, it'd sent the wrong message to Dad.

Now Bailey and Sophie were battling on two fronts. They certainly could've done without this additional complication.

"Look at them," Sophie muttered as the sisters peeked out the door. Mom was still talking to Ted, with her back to Dad, who also had his back to her. If that wasn't bad enough, Danielle chattered at their father like a noisy crow. Her parents couldn't even look at each other. Communication, what little there was of it, had come to a complete standstill.

"This isn't going to work." Bailey felt like dumping the

so-called Caesar salad over her parents' heads. "We need to figure out what to do next."

Sophie nodded. "We've got to think of something fast."

"This divorce should never have happened," Bailey moaned—not for the first time. If she or Sophie had guessed their parents were planning to split up, the girls would've stepped in much earlier. Now the situation was much more difficult, and there were other people involved. Now she and her sister were stuck cleaning up the mess.

Bailey shrugged. She brought the salad plates into the dining room and said, "Dinner's ready if you'd like to sit down." She did her best to sound cheerful and festive.

They took the chairs closest to where they stood. That put Danielle beside their father, and Ted and their mother across from them, leaving the two end chairs for Bailey and Sophie.

"Mom made the lasagna," Bailey said, although everyone already knew that. Before she could mention Danielle's role in their dinner, the other woman broke in.

"And I made the salad and the bread, which I'm sure you'll find delicious."

Both men smiled, apparently impressed with the woman who'd managed to spread garlic butter on a sliced baguette. From their admiring gazes, one would think Danielle was qualified to open her own restaurant.

Bailey wanted to point out that the lasagna had required a great deal more expertise than buttering bread.

She opened her mouth, but before she could utter a word, she caught her mother's look. Funny how much Mom could communicate in a single glance. Bailey snapped her mouth shut.

Beth served generous slices of lasagna. The salad and bread were passed around the table to sighs of appreciation. Ted poured the wine he'd brought with him. After filling the glasses, he looked around the table. "A toast?"

They all raised their goblets, but before Ted could speak, their father beat him to it. "To a wonderful meal shared with family and friends."

"Hear, hear," Ted added. They all touched the rims of their glasses, then tasted the wine.

"This is excellent," Beth said, praising Ted's choice.

"Very good," Kent agreed.

Wine, Bailey mused. That was it. A common link—her parents were both interested in wine. Well, so was Ted, but she was going to ignore that.

"It's a pinot noir," Ted was saying, "from Oregon."

"Ted and I discovered it a couple of weeks ago at a fund-raising event," Beth said. "I generally prefer the rich, deep reds, so this one took me by surprise."

Oh, yes, life was full of surprises, Bailey thought. Some of them weren't pleasant, either—her mother and father being a prime example.

Dinner became less awkward as they enjoyed the wine and the meal. Conversation revolved around the holidays.

Beth talked about the ski trip to Whistler, and the girls chimed in, excited at the prospect of an entire week on the slopes. In the past it had been a family trip, with their father included.

As soon as everyone had finished, Bailey and Sophie jumped up, eager for an excuse to leave.

Bailey carried two dinner plates into the kitchen and set them in the sink. Sophie followed with two more.

"Why didn't you *do* something?" her sister hissed. "Getting Mom and Dad back together was your idea."

"That doesn't mean I have to do everything, does it?" she returned in a heated whisper. A few suggestions from her younger sister certainly would've helped.

Back in the dining room, Bailey could see that Danielle was texting on her cell phone again, keeping it hidden below the table, although everyone knew what she was doing.

"I'm afraid we'll have to leave early," Kent said reluctantly. "Unfortunately, Danielle isn't feeling well."

"Can I get you anything?" Beth asked, sounding concerned.

Bailey wanted to suggest a broom, but her little joke was unlikely to be appreciated, so she said nothing.

"I apologize," Danielle murmured, pressing her fingertips to her temple. "I have a terrible headache that won't go away."

A headache? That was the weakest excuse in the book.

A regular ol' headache? Couldn't she be a bit more imaginative? Perhaps a sprained thumb from all that texting?

"So you won't be able to come to church services with us?" Sophie asked with such a lack of sincerity it was embarrassing.

"I think I should get Danielle back to the bed-and-breakfast," their father said.

Mom didn't waste any time retrieving their coats. Standing at the front door, their dad loitered a moment, as if he wanted to say something else. "It was a lovely day," he finally said.

"Thank you," Beth said simply.

"Kent?" Danielle insisted.

"When will I see you again?" Kent asked, directing the question to Beth. His eyes held hers.

"Ah…"

"Mom." Bailey jabbed her elbow into her mother's side.

"Tomorrow?" Beth suggested, poking her right back. "Christmas morning. You and Danielle are welcome to join us."

Danielle shook her head. "I doubt—"

Kent cut her off. "What time?"

"Anytime you want, Dad," Bailey threw in. "Early, though. You should be here when we open gifts."

"I have a *really* bad headache," Danielle reminded him.

"Why don't we wait until morning and see how Danielle feels," Beth said.

Their mother was being far too congenial. In fact, she was ruining everything. Bailey had hoped it would be just the four of them. If her parents could be together, remember Christmases past and enjoy each other's company, then maybe they'd finally figure things out....

Their father shook Ted's hand. Why did everyone have to be so darned polite? The two men locked eyes for an instant. Bailey hoped her father was staking claim to Beth, but she couldn't read his expression.

"Bailey and I'll do dishes," Sophie offered.

Bailey stared at Sophie. What was her sister doing? The last thing they needed was to give their mother time alone with the local vet. She was half-smitten with him already. *Smitten.* That was an old-fashioned word, one their grandmother might have used, but Bailey had always been fond of it.

She followed her sister into the kitchen. "Why'd you do that?" she cried.

"I thought you wanted to discuss ideas about getting Mom and Dad together."

"By leaving her alone with *Ted?*"

"Oh...yeah. I guess I didn't think about that."

"No kidding! Well, you keep an eye on them," commanded Bailey. "If they get too close, tell me." Sophie obediently pushed the door open a crack and looked out. Bailey started loading the dishwasher. Thankfully, their mother had emptied it earlier, so all Bailey had to do was put the rinsed dishes inside.

"You ready to go back out?" she asked five minutes later.

Sophie shook her head. "No," she said flatly. "Go ahead without me."

"No." It was important to Bailey that they present a united front.

Her sister took her time transferring the leftover salad to another bowl and wrapping up the bread, which Bailey noticed had barely been touched. She didn't want to be catty but Danielle had been a little too generous with the garlic. Their father hadn't tasted more than a bite or two. And Bailey was convinced he'd only eaten that to be polite.

To her credit, Danielle had created a halfway decent salad using the bottled dressing. But then who could go wrong with store-bought dressing?

"What are Mom and Ted doing now?" Sophie asked.

Bailey peeked out the swinging door, stepping around her sister. She saw that her mother and Ted had returned to the dining room table and were finishing their coffee. The atmosphere was almost…intimate, vastly different from what it'd been earlier. His arm across the back of an empty chair, Ted was leaning back, speaking animatedly about one thing or another. Whatever he was saying obviously amused Beth, who laughed more than once. She looked relaxed and at ease.

This wasn't how it was supposed to be! It should be Dad

in that chair. It should be Kent laughing with Mom. Not Ted Reynolds. Bailey didn't have anything against him; he was a decent guy. But he wasn't their father.

"Well?" Sophie said from behind her.

"They're getting along just fine," Bailey muttered.

"We should break it up," Sophie said, drying her hands on a kitchen towel. Everything was inside the refrigerator and the counters were wiped clean.

Bailey swung open the door. "Okay if we join you?" she asked, feigning cheerfulness.

"By all means." Ted removed his arm from the back of the chair, straightened and set his cup on the table.

"How long have you two known each other?" Sophie asked.

"A while." Beth was the one who answered. "I've brought more than one dog to Ted. He helps me with the rescues, too."

"You must like animals," Sophie went on.

Bailey thought that was a dumb remark. The guy was a vet; obviously he liked animals.

"I do." Ted hesitated. He must've thought it was a dumb remark, too. But then he added, "And I like your mother."

His announcement fell like bricks from the sky.

"What about my dad?" Bailey asked.

"Yeah, our dad," Sophie echoed plaintively.

"Oh, dear," Beth whispered. "If you two have any hopes that your father and I are getting back together, you need to forget them. It's much too late for that."

Fourteen

"Who'd be calling on Christmas Eve?" Bobby Polgar asked when Teri hung up the phone. It was after dinner, and the children were—finally—all snug in their beds.

"Beth Morehouse," Teri said. "She wants to know if it would be all right if she dropped the puppy off tonight instead of in the morning." Actually, it sounded as though Beth needed to get out of the house.

"What did you tell her?"

"I said come on over."

Bobby glanced into the family room, where he had three scooter-riders out of the boxes ready for assembling. The triplets were eight months old now and crawling. Robbie, the firstborn, was already standing on his own. Teri figured he'd be walking soon; the boy was fearless. Little Jimmy, the middle child and the smallest, was content to continue crawling, and Christopher, the youngest by a couple of minutes, loved sitting on the floor, banging pots and pans. Bobby felt sure their son was destined to be a drummer.

"I asked James to give me a hand assembling these," Bobby admitted a bit sheepishly.

"You'll do fine." Her husband might be a chess genius, but he didn't excel in certain other areas—like household repairs. Or "assembly required" toys.

"Are the boys down for the night?" Bobby asked.

Teri nodded, too exhausted for a detailed description of what it took to get all three to fall asleep at roughly the same time. Their nanny had the next two days off to spend the holidays with her family, and it felt like she'd been gone for a month. Teri's sister, Christie, had agreed to help make Christmas dinner and look after the triplets.

"Come and sit with me," Bobby said, holding his arm out to Teri.

She sat beside him on the sofa and laid her head on his shoulder. Bobby was semi-retired these days, following the birth of his sons, and Teri was grateful. Bobby and his best friend, James, had developed a chess-based computer game that consumed a great deal of their time, since they were now working on the second version. Still, Teri was glad to have her husband at home instead of on the road.

Closing her eyes, she remembered how she'd met Bobby Polgar. It had definitely been an unusual introduction.... He was in a championship chess match in Seattle and to everyone's shock he was losing. The chess world was aghast that the great Bobby Polgar could be toppled. One look at the chess player on the TV screen told Teri what his problem was. Bobby was distracted by his hair, which was too long and kept flopping in his eyes. He needed a cut.

In retrospect she was astonished that Security had let her through to see him. When she explained why she'd come, Bobby had stared at her as if she was some kind of lunatic, but he'd allowed her to trim his hair. Then she'd quietly left. Bobby had gone on to win the match and afterward he'd sought her out. Crazy as it sounded, that was how it all began.

She wasn't quite sure when she fell in love with him. In the beginning, she'd fought against having any feelings for this man. Really, what could come of it? She was a hairdresser from a little backwater town and Bobby Polgar was a champion chess player admired by the whole world. He might be infatuated with her for a while, but his affection would quickly wane. She'd bore him, and Bobby would soon grow tired of her.

Talk about an odd couple! But fall in love with him she did, despite her efforts not to. And when she fell, she fell hard.

She'd questioned why an intellectual like him—a celebrity to boot—would love someone like her. He'd said that she brought emotion into his life, that he liked her practical and intuitive approach, that she'd taught him how to *feel*.

Before that tournament in Seattle, every minute of Bobby's life had been involved with chess. He lived, breathed and slept chess. It was all he thought about, all he cared about...until he fell in love with her.

"You're smiling," Bobby said now, brushing the hair off her forehead almost as if she were a child.

"I was remembering our honeymoon." They got married in Las Vegas. Bobby had been in a chess competition there, and they were given the most luxurious penthouse suite in the hotel. The morning after their wedding night, Bobby had to leave for a chess match. Teri had stayed in bed and turned on the television to watch her husband play.

She knew from the first move he made that his mind wasn't on the game. He was thinking about *her,* thinking about coming back to the room and making love to her again. Then something happened; she could almost see the transformation taking place.... His expression changed. Even his posture changed. Bobby had realized that the sooner he won, the sooner he could return to their room. His focus, his attention, went straight into the game. His opponent didn't stand a chance. The poor man lost in record time. A second later, Bobby popped out of his seat and raced for the elevator, the camera crew on his heels.

Teri had been waiting for him....

The doorbell chimed and Teri sighed, not wanting to leave the comfort of her husband's arms and the warm memories that had wrapped themselves around her. She started to get up, but Bobby stopped her.

"I'll get it."

As Bobby was rising to his feet she slipped her hand around his neck and brought his mouth down to hers for a lengthy kiss. They broke it off when the doorbell chimed again.

Bobby's glasses were askew and his face flushed by the time he moved away from her. He cleared his throat. "You need to warn me before you do that," he muttered.

"Okay, I will," she said, smiling up at him. "That was just to say how much I love you."

Bobby cleared his throat again and gave her a small, crooked smile. He never quite knew how to respond when she mentioned love. "Thank you," he whispered, then hurried to the door.

In a minute he was back with Christie and James. They were another odd couple, Teri mused. When she'd first met James Wilbur, she hadn't known what to think of the tall, exceptionally thin man who served as Bobby's driver. It wasn't until much later that she discovered James was Bobby's dearest friend. He'd been a chess prodigy like Bobby, but James had suffered a breakdown caused by all the pressure. He'd disappeared from the public eye and been forgotten by everyone except Bobby. Her husband refused to abandon his friend, so he'd hired James as his driver. For years no one had recognized Bobby's chauffeur as the teenager who'd made chess history along with Bobby Polgar.

As soon as James met Christie, he fell for her. Teri hated to be the one to tell him, but her younger sister came with plenty of baggage, just like she had. To her complete surprise, Christie had fallen in love with James. Their relationship had been a series of stops and starts, had taken a number of unexpected turns. But in the end Christie had dumped the losers who'd taken advantage of her, gone back to school and straightened out her life.

A year ago, over Christmas, she'd split up with James. A story in the press had identified him as James Gardner, the prodigy who'd disappeared. It might not have been such a big news item if not for the fact that he'd still been part of the chess world all that time. He hadn't played in years, not since his collapse, but he enjoyed belonging to that world. Christie hadn't been able to tolerate his deception, his inability to trust her with his secret. Eventually, however, they'd reconciled and their estrangement had led them to a greater understanding of each other.

Teri realized James was like Bobby, in that chess was all he knew. He'd acknowledged he no longer wanted to play high-pressure big-money chess, but liked being close to the game—and close to the one friend he could count on, Bobby Polgar.

"We're here to help with the kids' Christmas gifts," Christie announced.

"Wonderful." Teri patted the empty space next to her on the sofa. "We'll let the men put together these toys while you and I visit."

"Sounds like a great idea to me," Christie said. "By the way, the house looks gorgeous." She gestured at the candles arranged on the fireplace mantel and at the Christmas tree, its lights reflected in the picture window overlooking Puget Sound.

Falling in love had changed Christie, just as it'd changed Teri. The hard edges of her personality had softened. She'd proven to herself she could get whatever she wanted as long as she worked hard and persevered. Christie had recently graduated from Olympic Community College, and she planned to start her own business, photographing the contents of houses for insurance purposes. Teri was proud of her little sister.

"I heard from Johnny this afternoon," she told Christie. Johnny was their younger brother. He was in school, attending the University of Washington. "He'll come over for dinner tomorrow. With his new girlfriend." Johnny never lacked for girlfriends, but he hadn't met anyone who was going to change *his* life. Not yet.

Teri had been more of a mother to him than their own. Another memory floated into Teri's mind. Soon after she'd married Bobby, Teri had made a huge dinner and invited her family to the house to meet her husband.

Sadly, her mother had arrived half-drunk, and from the

moment Ruth stepped through the door, she did nothing but find fault with Teri.

Bobby wasn't about to let his mother-in-law insult his wife and had handled the situation in a firm, yet subtle way. He'd wordlessly picked up Ruth's purse and set it by the front door, indicating it was time for her to leave. Ruth had immediately taken offense and, dragging her fourth— or was it fifth?—husband, she'd stomped out.

"James, what do they mean by a flat-head screwdriver?" Bobby and James sat on the family room floor with the pieces of one scooter scattered about the room. Bobby held out the instruction sheet, frowning at the diagrams. Then he turned it upside down before turning it right side up again.

"I didn't know there was more than one kind of screwdriver," James confessed.

"You learn something new every day, right?"

"Right," James agreed.

"I'll get a flat-head screwdriver for you," Teri said, sliding off the sofa.

Bobby gazed up at her as if she were the most brilliant woman who'd ever lived. "You have one?"

"That and a Phillips and a square tip…" She went to the kitchen drawer and returned with the required screwdriver.

"Do you need anything else?" she asked, handing it to him.

"Uh…" He showed her the instruction sheet. "Can you

tell me what I'm supposed to do with that?" He pointed to the drawing of a part.

"Teri," Christie said, getting up from the sofa. "It looks like these two are going to need a bit of assistance."

"Looks that way," she concurred.

"We can do this," Bobby insisted.

"Yeah," James echoed, but without much conviction.

"Do you want them to help us?" Bobby asked his friend.

James regarded Christie, and then Teri. "I don't think it would hurt. What about you?"

"I don't need help," Bobby said, "but if Teri wants to volunteer I won't stop her."

Teri and Christie exchanged an eye-rolling glance.

All of them were on the floor when the doorbell chimed yet again.

"That'll be Beth Morehouse," Teri said.

"Oh, were you expecting her?" Christie asked. "Why's she here?"

"Delivering a puppy," she said on her way to the door.

"Teri, don't tell me you and Bobby are getting a puppy!" Christie called after her.

"No," James answered on her behalf. "We are."

"James!" Christie yelped. "Isn't this something you should've discussed with me first?"

"Well…"

Before he could respond, Teri walked into the living room, followed by her guest. Beth held a basket—with a small black puppy staring out. The little creature wore a pink bow that contrasted with its glossy fur.

"Oh, she's adorable."

"Yes, and she's all yours," James told her. "Merry Christmas, darling."

"Merry Christmas," Christie said, her voice choked.

"Why are you crying?" James asked, drawing his wife into his arms.

"I...I always wanted a...dog."

"I know."

Christie threw her arms around James's neck.

Teri took the basket out of Beth's arms. "Thank you so much for bringing over the puppy."

"I was happy to," Beth said. "I know this little girl will have a wonderful home, so thank *you*."

"Our pleasure," Christie murmured.

James kissed her forehead. "Merry Christmas, my love," he said again. "I thought we could name her Chessie."

"Chessie! Of course." Christie laughed.

"You'll get your gift later," she promised in a husky voice.

James turned three shades of red. "I'll hold you to that," he said. "Now come and meet your dog."

Fifteen

After dropping off the puppy at the Polgars', Beth headed back to her house on Christmas Tree Lane. She'd enjoyed her brief visit with Bobby and Teri and James and Christie. The two couples were obviously devoted to one another. Watching them all working together, assembling toys for the triplets, reminded Beth of those early years with Kent. Finances had been tight back then, but they'd managed; their happiness had more than compensated for the luxuries they'd done without. She missed those times, and yes, she missed Kent, too.

On the way home Beth felt empty inside. For three years she'd pretended she was happy. Pretended she'd rather live her life without Kent. It'd all been a lie.

And now it was too late.

The girls would be getting ready for evening services

at the church and the three of them would arrive together. Kent had said he might attend, as well, but she knew he'd sit with Danielle, not with Beth and the girls. That made sense, but it was another blow she wasn't ready to deal with.

While waiting at a red light, she saw the open sign at Mocha Mama's. Because she didn't want to return home until she'd regained control of her emotions, she decided to go in. Stopping for a quick cup of coffee would give her a chance to sort through her feelings, to better understand what was happening and accept the reality that she had lost Kent for good. The life they'd once had was truly over.

She pulled into a parking space and turned off the engine. Sitting in the car, she pressed her hand over her eyes as unfamiliar and unwelcome emotions swirled through her. This Christmas was nothing like she'd anticipated. For weeks she'd looked forward to her children's visit. She'd carefully planned events, shopped, wrapped gifts, cooked their favorite meals. What she realized now was that she'd done it for Kent, too. Since he was coming to Cedar Cove for the holiday, she'd wanted to remind him of what they'd had. Of everything that was gone now, but could…perhaps…be recovered. She hadn't even acknowledged this to herself. Not really.

What made it all so impossible was Danielle. Facing the ghosts of Christmas past, back when she and Kent were so much in love, only depressed her now.

When Beth entered the coffee shop, she saw that it was nearly deserted. A teenager stood behind the counter, playing a handheld game. He didn't seem to notice he had a customer.

"Hello! I'd like a decaf Americano," she said briskly.

Startled, the kid glanced up. He blinked and reluctantly set aside his game. "Anything else?"

"No, thanks." She paid, adding a nice Christmas tip, and waited for her coffee.

A couple of minutes later he delivered it in a to-go cup, which was fine, although she wasn't in any rush to leave. Carrying it with her, she chose a table by the window, one that overlooked Harbor Street.

She gazed out at the serene and yet festive view of the town's main street. Garlands were strung across it. Silver bells dangled from the lampposts, and the town had never seemed more inviting. A light dusting of snow glistened on the large Christmas tree, which blinked red and green lights, outside city hall, while Christmas carols were broadcast from the bell tower.

"I wondered if that was your car outside."

Stunned by the familiar voice, Beth turned. Kent stood next to her small table, although she hadn't seen him come in.

"What are you doing here?" she asked breathlessly.

"I decided to take a drive—"

"Where's your friend? Danielle?" she interrupted.

"At the Thyme and Tide. Resting. And, Beth, she really is a friend."

Sure she was. Ex-husbands usually traveled with *friends*. But apparently the headache was real.

"She took a couple of aspirin and is lying down."

Beth cupped her hands around the paper cup, the heat of the coffee stinging her palms. "I hope she feels better soon."

"She'll be fine." Without waiting for an invitation, Kent pulled out a chair and sat down across from her.

"You want a coffee, sir?" the kid behind the counter called out.

"Sure. I'll have whatever she's having," he said.

"You got it," Mr. Gameboy said with a promptness he hadn't demonstrated earlier. Maybe her generous tip had something to do with it.

"You looked deep in thought when I walked in," Kent said, relaxing against the back of the chair. He extended his legs into the aisle, crossing them at the ankles. He seemed so comfortable, so calm, as if he hadn't a care in the world.

Beth stared at her ex-husband, unable to grasp how he could remain so unaffected by what had happened between them.

Perhaps Beth was the only one who had regrets, who wanted to examine the reasons their marriage had failed. What did it matter, anyway? she reflected darkly. Kent was with Danielle. He'd moved on, and she should, too.

"Beth?" he said, breaking into her thoughts.

She looked over at him, wondering what he'd just said.

"You worried about something?"

"Of course not," she said, forcing a brightness into her voice. "Why would you think that?"

"You never were much of a liar."

Beth shrugged, knowing it was true.

"Why are you out here, anyway?"

"I dropped off a puppy. A Christmas gift."

He seemed to be waiting for her to explain why she hadn't gone directly home. If she knew the answer to that question, she wouldn't be sipping blistering hot coffee and feeling as if the entire world was against her.

"So, how long have you and Ted been…friends?"

"Oh, for some time now."

"Is it serious?"

"No." She managed a nonchalant smile. "Perhaps I should've clarified that. I routinely see Ted on a professional basis—and yes, we've been out socially." She didn't mention the few kisses they'd shared because, frankly, it wasn't any of his business. When it came to *his* friend, she'd rather not know.

"But it could develop into something serious?" he asked.

This was even more difficult to answer. "I suppose. If we both wanted it to."

"And do you?"

She stared down into her coffee to avoid looking at him.

"No." Then she quickly shook her head. "Well, maybe."

"Maybe," he repeated slowly.

"It depends."

"On what?" he prodded.

Beth straightened. "I'd rather not talk about Ted and me. I didn't ask you about Danielle."

"True." He nodded. "All right, what *do* you want to talk about?"

"Do we need to talk about anything?"

He hesitated. "I guess not."

The kid brought over Kent's coffee and he paid for it. He was about to take his first sip when Beth warned him, "Careful, it's hot."

Kent sipped his coffee guardedly and grimaced. "You're right."

Beth took another sip of her own coffee, which had cooled slightly. "The puppy I delivered—it was to the Polgars."

"Polgar. That's an unusual name. As in Bobby Polgar, the chess champion?"

"Yes, he lives in Cedar Cove."

"Bobby Polgar lives here?" Kent arched his brows, clearly impressed.

"His wife is, or rather was, a local hairdresser. She's a wonderful, wonderful person."

"You mean to tell me Bobby Polgar married a beautician?" Kent grinned, as if the idea amused him.

"Don't say it like that. Teri's perfect for Bobby and now they have triplet sons...."

"And they took a puppy?"

"Actually, no. The puppy was for Teri's sister."

"What did you want to say about the Polgars?" Kent asked.

"I...I was remembering how it was with us when the girls were little."

"We talked about that earlier."

"We did," she agreed. "Those early Christmases, the basement apartment, those silly gingerbread decorations I sewed."

"What you're really saying is that you wonder what happened to us."

So Kent was the one brave enough to lay it on the table, the subject neither of them had been willing to broach until now.

Beth suppressed the urge to say it was too late. All of a sudden, she didn't want to dig up the past anymore, a past that was full of hurts and slights committed on both sides. If they dug too deep, she didn't know what they might uncover. Anyway, what was the point? They weren't together anymore. He had a new life and so did she.

Another part of her, the more rational part, recognized that unless she knew why her relationship with Kent had dissolved, history might repeat itself. If she did fall in love with Ted, she could revert to the same pattern that had destroyed her marriage to Kent.

"I don't think we can or should assign blame," Kent said, sitting up. He leaned forward and extended his arms, cupping his coffee between his hands. "So...I guess we should figure out what went wrong."

Beth swallowed hard, unsure where to start. She couldn't.

"Do you want to go first?" he asked. Kent, too, apparently found it difficult.

"No. You go."

"All right." He took a breath. "Once the girls got their driver's licenses, they didn't seem to need me anymore. They had their own lives. And that's the way it should be."

"A father's more than a chauffeur," she said with the glimmer of a smile. "But I know what you mean. They were becoming adults, so our role as parents changed."

He nodded. "And you had your career, while I had mine."

"At some point, without even being aware of it, we lost sight of what's important," Beth said. "And then it became a matter of pride, as if the most vital thing was proving how little we needed each other."

He nodded again.

"You stopped attending college social functions with me, and I retaliated by not attending your business dinners."

He lowered his gaze. "I'm sorry, but I found them boring."

"They were." She'd be the first to admit it.

"You always made them fun, though—in a slightly scandalous way," he said, grinning. "I got all the gossip. We'd stand in a corner and you'd tell me the most inappropriate stories."

"And you'd embarrass me by laughing at the most inappropriate times," she reminded him, and had trouble not breaking into giggles right then.

They looked at each other in silence.

"We both got absorbed in our lives, apart from each other," he finally said.

"We became strangers who happened to be married."

"I can't think of a single defining incident, an event that triggered the end of our marriage. Can you?"

"Not really." It was more an accumulation of grudges, of minor slights and careless acts. Oh, there were plenty of small decisions Beth had made through the years. Decisions that seemed inconsequential, insignificant. For some reason she thought of the morning Kent had asked her to drop off a letter at the post office. It was on her way to the college, while he was driving in the opposite direction. She told him she couldn't because she was running late. Really, how much time would it have taken? A minute? Two? Kent hadn't complained. He'd dropped off the letter himself.

Then there was the night she'd phoned and asked Kent to pick up bread and milk on his way home from work and he forgot. Such a little thing, but it had annoyed her no end.

At some stage she must have decided to ask nothing more of Kent. Was that when the pettiness began? When they turned to a silent battle of wills? How ridiculous they'd been. How silly and selfish and juvenile. No wonder their marriage had crumbled into pieces....

Beth visualized the slights, the put-downs, the irritations on both sides as pebbles, each a small stone in the growing pile that eventually crushed their marriage. Kent was right; it hadn't been any one thing. Nothing big. No infidelity. No drugs or alcohol abuse. No money problems.

"Folks," the teenager said. He stood in front of their table with a tray and a white rag. "We're closing now."

"Oh." Feeling disjointed, Beth looked up.

"Normally I wouldn't mind staying while you finished your coffee, but it's Christmas Eve and my grandma's at the house."

"No problem," Kent said. He took one last drink of his coffee and left the cup on the table. "Thanks, and merry Christmas."

"Merry Christmas," Beth echoed. She left her cup behind, too.

Kent walked her to her car. He seemed to have more he wanted to say. Beth knew she did. Perhaps later...

"I'll see you at the church in twenty minutes," Kent said.

He tucked his hands inside his pockets. "Bob at the B and B told me where it is."

"I'm going to pick up Bailey and Sophie. We'll see you there."

He started to turn away, but Beth stopped him.

"Kent..."

"Yes?"

"Would you mind sitting with the girls and me?"

He smiled. "I'd be happy to," he said.

Beth smiled back. Even if that meant Danielle joined them—well, she could tolerate that. It was the season of goodwill, after all. The important thing was for their family to be together.

Sixteen

Emily Flemming blew out the last candle after the seven o'clock Christmas Eve service at the Methodist church where her husband, Dave, was pastor. Every pew had been filled and the choir had sounded glorious. Both of their sons had gone back to the house with her parents. Emily appreciated the fact that the service was relatively early. Some churches waited until after nine, and the Catholic church always had a midnight mass.

Dave finished greeting the last of his parishioners, Bible in hand, as Emily joined him in the vestibule.

"That was lovely, sweetheart," she told her husband. Dave worked hard on his sermons, heading over to the church two hours before the first service in order to practice and pray. He took his responsibilities seriously and looked after his flock.

"Thank you." Dave slipped his arm around Emily's waist. "Did you see the man with Beth Morehouse?"

Emily had noticed him, and it wasn't the local veterinarian. Emily had suspected for some time that a romance between Beth and Ted Reynolds was in the offing. But when she'd seen Beth with this other man, she'd changed her mind. Judging by the electricity that sizzled between them, they were more than acquaintances or even friends. "I saw him."

"That's her ex-husband. His name is Kent."

"Her ex-husband?" They sure didn't act like exes, Emily thought. They'd exchanged frequent looks throughout the service and seemed keenly aware of each other. At first, Beth's glances had been shy, but as the service progressed, she'd grown bolder. Several times their eyes had met, and neither seemed inclined to look away.

The two girls had been sitting on one side of Beth, with Kent on the other, closest to the aisle. The girls hadn't exactly hidden their delight.

"On her way out of church, Beth mentioned a litter of part-Labrador puppies that were left on her doorstep. Ten in all."

"Ten? But I thought she was leaving for a short vacation with her daughters."

"She is, so she needs to find homes for these puppies quickly. She's only got two left and wanted to know if we're interested."

"Are we?" Emily asked, almost afraid of the answer.

"I was thinking a couple of puppies would help teach Mark and Matthew a sense of responsibility."

"Mark's been asking for a dog," Emily added with some reluctance. Her fear was that her son would lose interest and she'd be the one taking care of his dog. She had no concerns about Matthew; he was the dependable one.

"I was thinking—"

"Dave, before you say anything, we need to consider this very carefully. A puppy, let alone two, is a lot of work and—"

"Mark's old enough to understand that. Besides, Beth sounded desperate to find a good home for these dogs. Especially at this late date."

Emily could feel herself weakening. Especially when her husband was regarding her with a puppy-dog look of his own....

"I had a Lab while I was growing up," Dave said.

Emily nodded, remembering his fond stories about the family pet.

"We named him Blackie," David went on. "Not very original, but, oh, how I loved that dog."

"In other words, you'd like our sons to have the same wonderful experience with a dog that you did?"

Dave smiled sheepishly. "But only if you agree."

While she wasn't one hundred percent sold, Emily was willing to take a chance.

"Can we at least look at them?" Dave asked, his eyes alight with excitement.

"Tonight?"

"Well, yes. It would be perfect. The boys are with your parents and we can drive out to Beth's place. By the time we get back, Matthew and Mark will be asleep. When they wake up in the morning, the puppies will be there—the best Christmas gift ever."

Clearly, her husband had worked this all out.

"All right," she said, holding back a smile. "We can go see the puppies, but there are no guarantees. Understand?"

"Definitely," he assured her. "We'll go to Beth's and look at them, and if you don't think it'll work, or you take an instant dislike to either dog or whatever, then we'll leave."

She raised her eyebrows. Dave knew her far too well. The minute she laid eyes on those puppies she'd be lost. She couldn't possibly say no. Especially since he wanted to provide his sons with the same childhood experience that he'd enjoyed.

During a quick phone call to the house, Emily told her mother that she and Dave had an errand to run. She explained what it was, and her mother promised that the boys would be in bed when Emily and Dave returned.

While Emily was talking to her mother, Dave contacted Beth, who said it would be fine to stop by the house that evening. In fact, she wished he would, because she planned to leave with the girls early on the morning of the twenty-sixth, so the sooner these last two puppies found homes, the better.

In the car on the way to Beth's house, Emily gazed out at the sky. The night was clear, with a million stars twinkling like jewels, but far more precious than any stone she'd ever seen. Her eyes fell to the wedding ring on her left hand. She'd almost removed it when she believed Dave was having an affair. Those had been dark days in their marriage and she'd been so sure, so completely convinced, that her husband was seeing another woman. It wasn't as if pastors were exempt from temptation.

In retrospect, she felt embarrassed that she'd suspected Dave of anything so underhanded. Yet what else was she to believe? He was gone almost every night and, well... thankfully those days were over. Probably every marriage went through at least one rocky period.

"Dave?"

"Yes, love?"

"I think Beth and her ex-husband still have feelings for each other."

Dave didn't speak for several minutes. "I had the same impression," he finally said.

"What do you suppose went wrong between them?" Emily asked.

"Probably the same thing that went wrong with us."

"Lack of communication," she murmured. "I guess it almost always comes down to that."

They pulled into Beth's yard and saw another vehicle parked next to hers.

"Maybe Kent's still with her," Dave commented.

Emily had heard Kent was staying at the Beldons' B and B. Rumor had it that he hadn't arrived alone, but if so, whoever he'd brought hadn't been at the church.

The front door opened and Beth stepped onto the porch to greet them. "Welcome, welcome! Please, come inside."

Dave held Emily's hand as they walked into the gaily decorated house.

"The girls have hot cocoa on the stove. I hope we'll be able to interest you in a mug."

"With whipped cream," Kent added, joining Beth.

He extended his hand to Dave. "We met in church earlier. Kent Morehouse."

"Dave Flemming, and my wife, Emily."

"Hi, Emily. Good to see you again, Dave."

Beth led the way into the kitchen. She opened the door leading to the laundry room and returned a moment later with two beautiful black puppies. They wore the saddest, most forlorn looks Emily could imagine.

"These two are the last of the litter, both males." Beth handed one to Emily.

"They're gorgeous," Emily said, falling hard and fast. All it had taken was one look, and she was convinced these puppies needed to be part of their family.

She sat on one of the kitchen chairs, holding the puppy

on her lap. The little creature licked her hand, then immediately curled up and went to sleep. Yup, Emily was lost. Mark would love this dog and she felt confident he'd do a good job of feeding, training and caring for this puppy. Matthew, too, would love and train his dog.

When Emily glanced up she saw that Dave was holding the other puppy, all the while engaged in conversation with Kent Morehouse.

"The sermon tonight really touched me," Beth said. "I've heard the Christmas story all my life. But I'd never really considered the role Joseph played. How he must have loved Mary."

Emily agreed. "It's a beautiful love story and one that's often overlooked." This was Dave's gift. He looked at Biblical stories in ways that stirred people's hearts and brought them closer to God. He could take familiar passages and study them from a different point of view, bringing contemporary relevance and new insight.

Beth returned to the stove, and removed the pan from the burner. Bailey and Sophie, who'd poked their heads in to say hello, were playing a computer game in the family room.

"Girls! Cocoa," Beth called out.

Neither seemed to hear her, too engrossed in their game. Shaking her head, Beth finished filling the mugs and brought two of them to Emily and Dave, both sitting at the kitchen table.

Kent picked up the other two, then he and Beth sat down with her guests.

"I see they've taken a liking to us," Dave said, motioning to the puppy on his lap. The second one was asleep, too, chin now resting on Emily's arm.

"You know what a soft touch I am," she complained laughingly.

"Yeah, I guess we're a two-dog family now."

"Dave was telling me he likes to golf," Kent said to Beth a moment later.

"It's a prerequisite for pastors," Dave joked. "A lot of men bond over the sport."

"There was a time not so long ago when Dave gave it up, though," Emily said. "We were going through a difficult financial period and he didn't want me to know how bad things were. The idiot let me think he was out golfing when he was actually working at a second job." Emily wasn't sure about confiding anything so personal, but she felt this was something Beth and Kent might benefit from hearing.

"How did you find out?" Beth asked.

"Peggy Beldon casually mentioned that Bob missed seeing Dave on the golf course."

"Of course, Emily didn't say anything at the time. She just waited for me to come back to the house. She was cool as a cucumber—until I walked in the front door."

"Was that before or after I dyed my hair blond?"

Beth stared at her. "You went blond?"

"It was stupid, but we do stupid things when we're desperate."

"We do," Kent agreed far too quickly.

"In the end we worked everything out, thank God," Dave said. "I made such a mess of my marriage. I nearly destroyed my wife's faith in me."

"And then there were those missing jewels," Emily added. There was far more to the story.

"Oh, yes, the jewels." Dave sighed, lifting his mug of cocoa.

"Missing jewels?" Kent asked, looking from one to the other.

"It's a long story, so allow me to condense it. One of the older ladies in the church, Martha Evans, died and several pieces of her jewelry turned up missing."

"Dave was the last person to see her alive," Emily said. "Which immediately threw suspicion on him."

"So everyone assumed I was the one who took the jewelry—even my wife," Dave said, grinning at Emily.

She smiled back. "What else was I supposed to believe?" she murmured. "Besides, I found Martha's earring in his suit pocket. Only I didn't know it belonged to Martha or that someone had purposely placed it there. At the time, I imagined my husband was having an affair."

"My goodness, you two had quite a few troubles, didn't you?" Kent glanced at Beth.

"What saved your marriage?" she asked.

"Prayer," Emily said, "and the two of us talking honestly. Dave finally admitted we had more bills at the end of the month than money, and that he was doing two jobs."

"And Sheriff Davis was instrumental in capturing the man responsible for the theft of Martha's jewelry," Dave explained, "with Roy McAfee's help."

"What an incredible story!"

"It really is, and I'll fill in the missing pieces the next time we see you," Emily promised. She took a last swallow of her cocoa and stood, the puppy in her arms. "We need to head home. My parents are looking after the boys."

"Wait," Kent said. "I want to know who actually took the jewelry?"

"Someone who worked on Martha's will, a paralegal," Dave explained. "His name is Geoff Duncan. He's serving prison time now. He was trying to impress his fiancée's family, so he stole the jewelry, pawned it all and spent the money."

"Lori Bellamy, the fiancée, didn't have a clue what Geoff had done," Emily said. "She's Lori Wyse now. She got married not long ago to Lincoln Wyse, who opened a body shop in town earlier this year. They seem to be a good match, although they had a few problems with Lori's family. But apparently that's all settled now."

"This Geoff guy. Did he have a grudge against you?" Kent asked.

"Not that I know of. I was just the perfect candidate for him to frame because, as Martha's pastor, I spent a lot of time with her. Like I said, I seemed to be the last person to see her alive, and I was also the one who found the body. The obvious suspect." He shook his head. "Thank goodness Sheriff Davis and Roy McAfee looked beyond the obvious."

"It must've been a terrible time for you," Beth said sympathetically.

"The worst, but we made it through and I'm so grateful we did."

"I can imagine."

"Some people are far too willing to give up on…" She let the rest fade once she realized what she was about to say. Emily didn't want to embarrass the divorced couple.

Kent moved closer to Beth. "I agree."

"So do I," Beth said, almost before the words had left Kent's mouth.

They looked at each other, but the moment was broken by the sharp peal of Kent's cell phone.

He answered it on the second ring, and although Emily couldn't make out what was being said, the person calling him was clearly female—and clearly upset.

"Yes, of course," he said. "Yes, I know." He closed his cell with a snap. "I apologize, but I need to leave."

He reached for his coat and, after a few words of farewell, was out the door.

"I know it's none of my business, but who was that?" Dave asked Beth.

"His...friend," Beth said.

Emily looked at Dave just as he turned to look at her. So the rumors of a female companion had been correct, and for some reason this woman had stayed back at the B and B. There were more obstacles to a reconciliation between Beth and her ex-husband than either of them had guessed.

Seventeen

"Did you see the way Dad looked at Mom during the service?" Bailey whispered to her sister in the darkened bedroom. Sophie was in the twin bed next to hers. Although she'd turned out the lights several minutes ago, Bailey was too excited to sleep.

"Yes, I know but—"

"They're falling in love all over again," Bailey broke in. "I can *feel* it."

"Well, maybe, but..."

"But what?" Bailey muttered. Sometimes her sister could be so...negative. Well, she refused to allow Sophie's skeptical remarks to dampen her good feelings. For a time it seemed that everything they'd planned was about to fall apart. Then, at the very last minute, their father had shown up at the church...alone. It'd been perfect. Just perfect.

Bailey hadn't asked about Danielle and neither had Sophie. Their dad had slipped into the pew next to Beth, and their mother had smiled over at him and…

Oh, it'd been sheer bliss. Love radiated between them. If this were a movie, a crescendo of music would have burst forth, and there would've been joyful singing in the background. Actually, there *was* music, but it had come from the church choir. Still, the effect was pretty satisfying.

"Can I talk now?" Sophie asked impatiently.

"Oh, all right."

"I have a question."

"Ask away." Bailey sighed, suspecting that Sophie was going to ruin Bailey's Christmas Eve by casting doubt on the likelihood of their parents reuniting. Her father had introduced Danielle as a "friend." *They* were the ones who'd made the assumption that she was more than that.

"What about when Danielle phoned? Dad left in a mighty big hurry after that."

"Yeah, I know," Bailey admitted with more than a little reluctance.

"He's still at Danielle's beck and call."

"But we can't be sure of all the circumstances and—"

"There are no *buts* here," Sophie fumed. "I don't know what Dad sees in Danielle, but there's obviously something."

"Whatever it is, I trust Dad to do the right thing." Bailey rolled onto her back and stared up at the ceiling. Leave it to Sophie.... Now she was worried again. Their father was smart—she hoped. Deep down, she couldn't believe he was involved with Danielle. In fact, the more she thought about it, the more certain she was. He might have brought Danielle with him, but from the moment he arrived Kent only seemed interested in Beth. Danielle was far more attached to her cell phone than she was to their father.

"Mark my words, Dad doesn't care about Danielle," Bailey insisted in a confident voice.

Sophie sighed loudly. "I wish I could believe that."

"Maybe we should help him along."

"Bailey, no!"

"No?"

"No," she repeated. "If we step in now, it'll just complicate everything. Dad has to do this on his own. Otherwise, we'll sabotage the whole reconciliation."

Bailey slowly absorbed her sister's words. Although Sophie was younger—and not studying psychology—she could occasionally be really smart. "Have you ever thought of going into diplomacy? You'd be great."

"You think so?" Sophie loved getting compliments.

Well, everyone did, but her sister was so transparent. She made no effort to hide how much she enjoyed hearing nice things about herself. Bailey could almost see Sophie's self-congratulatory little smile.

"Trust me," Bailey said, returning to the subject at hand. "Mom and Dad are going to remarry. I can feel it."

"Well…we can wish."

"Oh, come on," Bailey urged. "*Believe* it."

"You really buy into that positive thinking idea, don't you?"

"Yes," Bailey concurred. "And you should, too." In her opinion, it would go a long way toward raising Sophie's spirits.

"I'll consider it," Sophie said.

Pulling the sheet and blanket up over her shoulder, Bailey shifted onto her right side, her back to her sister. Despite Sophie's pessimism, Bailey believed with all her heart. She remembered the look her parents had exchanged in church that night. The look of love, of regret and the promise of reconciliation.

Tomorrow morning, when it was Christmas, the biggest and best present wouldn't be under the tree. It would be the fact that her parents still loved each other and wanted to remarry.

On Christmas Day, they'd finally acknowledge their feelings, and the rest of their lives would begin.

Bailey was sure of it.

Eighteen

"Merry Christmas," Bruce Peyton whispered as he drew Rachel into his arms.

Smiling, Rachel arched her back and yawned. "Is it morning already?"

"It sure is. I've got coffee brewing and Jolene's up."

Rachel turned her head to look at the clock. "Bruce, it isn't even eight." She could easily have slept another hour. Or two.

"I know, but Jolene's anxious to get to the presents."

With some effort, Rachel sat up. She was noticeably pregnant now and the baby was more active every day. Thankfully the worst of the morning sickness had passed.

The pregnancy had been unplanned and Jolene, her thirteen-year-old stepdaughter, hadn't yet adjusted to her father's remarriage when she was forced to deal with the news about the baby. The marriage itself had resulted in a difficult transition for the girl, but the pregnancy complicated everything that much more.

Her relationship with Jolene had grown tense. The stress became too much for Rachel and eventually she felt she had no choice but to move out of the family home. Only recently—just weeks ago—had she returned.

The counseling sessions had helped a great deal and they were learning to coexist and work together as a family. Rachel was excited about spending Christmas with her husband and stepdaughter. She and Jolene had planned the dinner menu together and they'd spent most of yesterday in the kitchen, preparing vegetables and side dishes and dessert.

During the afternoon they'd also made a breakfast casserole to put in the oven Christmas morning while they opened gifts. And Jolene had baked her first cinnamon rolls from scratch. Rachel hadn't told her, but this was her first experience, too. The rolls had turned out well, if Bruce's lavish praise was anything to go by.

All the while, Poppy, their new dog, had lounged in the warm kitchen, with occasional bursts of activity and escorted trips to the backyard.

"Would you like tea in bed?" her husband asked her.

"I'd love some."

"And I'd love to bring you some," he said, grinning. "In fact, I'll do anything. I'd stand on my head in the middle of the street in a snowstorm if it meant you'd be with me every Christmas morning for the rest of my life." Leaning forward, he pressed his lips to hers. "Merry Christmas, my beautiful wife."

"Merry Christmas, my silly husband."

"I'll be back in a minute with your tea." Bruce kissed her again, and then he was gone.

Rachel sat up in bed and rearranged her pillows. She held one hand over her stomach, letting her unborn daughter know how much she was loved. Next Christmas, this little one would be crawling around, eager to tear open packages. Rachel closed her eyes, savoring the vision of all the wonderful things the next year would hold.

Bruce returned with a steaming cup of tea, which he handed her just as Jolene burst into the master bedroom, carrying Poppy.

"Rachel, you're awake, aren't you?"

"I'm getting there."

"Hurry up," the girl said, holding the puppy close to Rachel. "There are gifts out there just waiting to be opened."

"Okay, okay," Rachel said, squinting as Poppy licked her face. "Give me five minutes."

"That long?" Jolene whined, and then laughed out loud, sounding young and carefree.

"You're certainly in a good mood," Bruce teased, hugging his daughter.

"Daddy, it's Christmas. Everyone's in a good mood on Christmas Day."

If only that was true. Memories of her childhood drifted into Rachel's mind. After her mother's death, she'd gone to live with an unmarried aunt who'd seen Christmas as a commercial wasteland and refused to partake in anything so frivolous. There'd been no tree, no presents. It was just like every other day, except that Rachel didn't have to go to school.

She'd listened attentively as her friends told of their wonderful holidays and longed for the time when she'd celebrate Christmas with a family of her own. And here it was, unfolding right before her eyes.

Setting her mug aside, she tossed back the covers and slid out of bed. "Did someone say something about presents?" she asked.

Jolene placed Poppy on the floor, grabbed Rachel's hand and led her into the living room. "I put the casserole in the oven."

"Great. Did you preheat it to three hundred and fifty degrees first?"

"Yes, I did."

"You're going to be a terrific cook."

"I already am," Jolene said. "I made dinner the whole time you were gone and I did a good job, didn't I, Dad?"

"Yup." Bruce joined Rachel on the sofa. "Unfortunately, I didn't have much of an appetite."

Jolene sighed. "All he could think about was you and the baby."

"But Rachel's with us now, and that's what matters."

"Hey," Rachel said, "are we going to sit around all morning discussing the past or are we going to open gifts?"

Her question got the desired results. "Open gifts!" Jolene said with renewed energy.

Rachel went back to the bedroom for her robe and tied it loosely about her waist as she slipped her feet into fuzzy slippers.

Bruce had a nice fire going in the fireplace, and Poppy lay stretched out in front of it, snuffling in her sleep. The radio was tuned to a station that played Christmas music without any commercial interruptions. The casserole was baking in the oven, and the scent of bacon and cheese wafted into the room. This was as idyllic a picture as Rachel could ever have conjured up in some blissful fantasy.

"Who gets to open a gift first?" she asked, settling onto the sofa with her husband.

"I have to sort through them all before we open any," Jolene said. "I'll hand everything out and *then* we open them. One at a time," she ordered.

"Then get to it, girl," Bruce said with a laugh, reaching for Rachel's hand.

Jolene walked over to the lighted tree, which they'd just finished decorating yesterday, and got down on all fours, rooting through the gifts. She pulled one out and sat back, checking the name tag.

"This one's for Dad," she said and, stretching forward, passed it to Bruce.

He held the rectangular package close to his ear and shook it. "Who's it from?"

"Rachel," Jolene said. "Looks like a shirt to me."

"Don't spoil the surprise."

"Dad, it's obvious." Jolene grinned from ear to ear.

She disappeared again, foraging under the tree.

"What are you looking for now?" Bruce asked, setting the box at his feet.

"A special gift," Jolene said, her voice muffled.

"Who's it for?"

"Rachel, from me."

"Oh, I love getting gifts." Rachel smiled at Bruce. Considering the months of tension between her and Jolene, she was pleased that her stepdaughter was so eager to give her presents. She leaned her head against her husband's shoulder. This was what she'd always hoped Christmas would be like, surrounded by people she loved and who loved her.

"Here it is," Jolene announced, scooting out backward from beneath the huge tree.

Rachel took the package from her. It was the size and shape of a shoe box.

"Can Rachel open it now?" Jolene asked her father. "Even though that's not the rules."

"That's up to Rachel."

Jolene looked at her, eyes dark and serious. "Will you, Rach?"

"If you want me to."

"I do." She sat on the floor as she waited for Rachel to unwrap her gift.

"I made it myself," Jolene said, her eyes bright as she bit her lower lip. "I hope you like it."

"I'm sure I will." Rachel carefully slid the ribbon off and peeled back the decorative paper. The box had, indeed, held Jolene's new gym shoes. Rachel lifted the lid and stared down at a white hand-knit baby blanket, enfolded in pink tissue. Rachel hardly knew what to say. "You...you knit this yourself?" She drew it out, marveling at the complexity of the design.

Jolene nodded. "We learned how to knit in an after-school class. I bought the pattern and the yarn at that craft shop downtown, the one where Mrs. Flemming works. I worked on it every day. I made a lot of mistakes," she admitted. She hurried to Rachel's side, kneeling in front of her. "See? Here's one."

It was so small Rachel had to squint to see it.

"There are other mistakes, too."

"Oh, Jolene, it's *perfect.*" Rachel struggled to hold back tears. "I'll bring your sister home from the hospital in it."

"You will?"

Rachel leaned forward and brought Jolene toward her, kissing her hair. "I'll always treasure it, because you made it for me and the baby."

"Don't tell me you're both going to get all weepy on me," Bruce groaned.

"I might," she said, struggling to hold back the tears.

Jolene raised her arms and wrapped Rachel in a big hug.

"I love you, Jolene," Rachel whispered.

"I love you, too... You're going to be a great mother."

Bruce put his arms around them both. "She already *is* a great mom," he said.

Jolene nodded and met Rachel's eyes. "Yes, she is."

Nineteen

This was Sheriff Troy Davis's first Christmas with his wife, Faith. It was a second marriage for both. Each of them had been blessed with a long and happy first marriage and each had suffered the loss of their beloved partner. Recently, they'd found a renewed sense of purpose and love with each other.

As it was their first major holiday together, they'd divided the time between his daughter, Megan, and her family and Faith's son, Scott. Christmas Eve had been spent with Megan, her husband, Craig, and their infant daughter, Cassandra.

Today, Troy and Faith were headed for Scott's home. Late Christmas morning, Troy loaded up the car with the Christmas gifts and treats Faith had prepared for her son's family. They'd delivered a carload of presents and homemade sweets to Megan the night before, as well. Faith had been baking for weeks, not that Troy was complaining. He hadn't enjoyed the holidays this much in a very long while. During the last years of her life, Sandy had been in a nursing home, and Troy hadn't bothered with decorating their house or putting up a tree. For the first time since Sandy went into the care facility, it actually felt like Christmas to him. He hadn't realized how much he'd missed all the fuss and bother.

"Can we make one stop?" Faith asked as she climbed into the front seat beside him.

"Sure," he said. "Where?"

"The Beldons'. Peggy and Bob were so kind to bring us that plate of goodies. I'd like to reciprocate."

"The Beldons probably have more than their fair share of candy and cookies."

"This is a peach-and-raspberry cobbler. They can eat it now or put it in the freezer. Peggy's always thinking of others, and I wanted to do something nice for her."

"Then of course we'll drop by."

"It'll just take a moment," Faith promised. "In fact, you don't even need to get out of the car."

Troy reached for his wife's hand and gave it a gentle squeeze. He loved Faith. He'd loved her when they were in high school, and he loved her now. After Sandy died, Troy had never expected to marry again. And then…Faith came back into his life. Their courtship had had its ups and downs, but despite some confused and difficult times, Troy wouldn't change a thing. Faith was with him now. Nothing else mattered.

The Beldons' Thyme and Tide Bed-and-Breakfast on Cranberry Point was en route to Scott's house, so it really wasn't out of their way. Troy entered the long driveway and noticed three vehicles parked in the area reserved for guests. He remembered that Bob had mentioned that their children would be visiting from Spokane, which accounted for two cars. The other must be a guest.

"I'll be right back," Faith assured him as he eased to a stop.

She got out of the car, opened the rear passenger door and took out the cobbler in its lidded plastic container. She'd put a bow on top, giving it a festive look. He hoped she'd tucked one in their freezer for him—and he didn't need the bow!

Bob Beldon answered the door and Faith went inside. Troy listened to Christmas music and sang along with Burl Ives on the car radio. Two or three minutes later, Faith reappeared and motioned for him.

Troy turned off the engine and started toward the house. Something was definitely wrong. He could see it in Faith's stance as she stood in the doorway, waiting for him.

When he approached, Faith said, "Oh, Troy, I'm afraid there's a bit of a…situation here. I think you might be able to help."

"What kind of situation?"

She moved aside and he walked into the house. The instant he did, he heard a woman shrieking and crying uncontrollably in the background. She seemed to be having some sort of temper tantrum. Troy heard things being thrown against the walls.

"It's one of our guests," Bob said, coming toward him. "She arrived with Kent Morehouse, Beth's ex-husband. We thought they were a couple—but apparently not. Seems she was supposed to meet up with a sailor from the navy base, but something happened. She hasn't been able to tell us what."

"So what's her relationship with Kent?"

"Friends, I guess. She works for him."

Kent wandered into the foyer with his hands in his pockets. He looked completely baffled. "I'm sorry," he said. "I tried talking to Danielle, but she's too upset to make much sense. As far as I can tell, the young man she came to see has decided to dump her."

"On Christmas Day?" Troy wasn't impressed with the sailor's timing.

"She hasn't stopped crying.…"

"For hours," Peggy inserted. "And throwing stuff. I don't know if she's broken anything but…"

"She refuses to answer the door," Bob added. "She must have blocked it with a chair or something, because we can't get in."

Troy could well imagine what this was doing to the family's celebration.

"I think all Danielle wants to do now is get back to California. I went on the internet to find a flight, but talking to her is impossible." Kent shook his head.

Troy moved down the hallway to the guest bedrooms and knocked on the door. It wasn't hard to tell which room was Danielle's.

"Sheriff Troy Davis," he announced authoritatively.

Silence followed, which was a blessing after the racket of the past several minutes. Then they heard the unmistakable sound of furniture being moved.

"What seems to be the problem here?" he asked when Danielle slowly opened the bedroom door.

"I have to get out of here," Danielle said, dabbing her eyes with a wadded tissue. "I *hate* this place."

"I found a flight that can get you to LAX, leaving Sea-Tac in a few hours," Kent rushed to say. This was obviously the information he'd been wanting to tell her for some time.

"Fine," she said, slamming her suitcase shut. It was on her bed, although little else was. In fact, the room looked as if it'd been hit by a hurricane. Bedding lay on the floor. So did a potted poinsettia, with dirt scattered everywhere, and a framed picture, its glass now broken. And that wasn't all....

"I'm really sorry about this," Kent said, apologizing to the Beldons.

Danielle seemed to think he was talking to her. "Why didn't Hunter tell me sooner?" she wailed. "It worked out so well that I could come here for Christmas…. He said he'd be tied up, but I said that was fine because my boss invited me to visit his family until Christmas Day and then…then…" She broke into a fresh bout of tears. Angrily, she grabbed the tissue box from the floor and jerked out three. "Then Hunter waited until this morning to tell me…. He didn't even do it to my face. Instead, he sent me a text message and said he was seeing someone else. He let me come all this way and make a fool of myself." She dabbed at her eyes again. "Now all I want is to get away from this horrible town…."

"We'll need to get her to the airport."

Kent shifted uncomfortably. "I had plans with my family but I feel responsible for her. I'll drive her to the airport."

"I want to go home!" Danielle screamed. "I don't care who takes me to the airport. Isn't there a taxi or something?"

"I have a friend who owns a car service," Troy offered. "He can drive you to the airport."

"Fine!" Danielle shouted. "I want to leave *now*."

"Please call your friend," Kent said. "And I'll pay whatever it costs."

The small group watched as Danielle finished gathering up the last of her things, stuffing them in her carry-on. Kent seemed relieved not to be taking her to the airport.

She swung the suitcase off the bed, and it landed on the floor with a loud thump. Straightening her shoulders, she wheeled her bag out of the room, ignoring everyone.

As soon as she'd left, Kent slumped on the edge of the bed and heaved a sigh. He lowered his head and plowed his fingers through his hair.

"You all right?" Troy asked.

Kent nodded. "I've made a big mess of things."

"It's not your fault the sailor broke it off."

"No," Kent said. "My mistake was taking her out to meet Beth and the girls. I let them assume Danielle and I were romantically involved. It was a stupid thing to do and I regretted it almost immediately." He looked disgusted with himself. "Danielle went along with it, since she knows I still love my ex-wife and she wanted to do me a favor. But she totally overplayed her role." He sighed again. "I wanted to tell Beth last night, but before I had a chance Danielle phoned in hysterics because she couldn't get hold of her boyfriend. After that, the situation went from bad to worse." He gestured around him. "I've botched everything."

"Don't be so sure," Faith said, coming to stand next to Troy.

"Do you think there's a way to salvage this?" Kent asked hopefully.

"Troy and I were in the pew behind you and Beth at the

service last night. I believe if you speak to Beth honestly, you'll discover she feels the same way."

Kent's eyes brightened. "Really?"

Faith nodded.

"First let me see if I can arrange this airport ride," Troy said, reaching for his cell. He punched in the appropriate number and waited. Logan, the son of a friend, had recently started a car service, focusing on airport transportation. He was hungry enough to take the fare, even if it was Christmas Day.

After a short conversation, Troy closed his cell. "He'll be here within thirty minutes."

"Have you ever done anything so stupid you wonder what you could possibly have been thinking?" Kent asked Troy.

The sheriff wasn't sure whether this was a real question or a rhetorical one. He decided to answer it anyway. "We all have, at one time or other. All you can do is learn from it—and you've certainly done that. And like Faith says, things will probably turn out okay."

Kent looked up and gave a slight nod. "I appreciate the encouraging words."

After a few minutes, Troy returned to the kitchen. The Beldons had gathered there. Danielle sat in the living room next to her suitcase, crying quietly. He did feel sorry for her. This couldn't be easy; no broken relationship was.

Kent wanted to pay for the damages, but the Beldons

refused. And at their insistence, no charges would be laid. They, too, sympathized with Danielle, despite their exasperation with her out-of-control behavior.

To be on the safe side Troy and Faith remained at the B and B until Logan arrived and Danielle departed.

They left a few minutes later. Faith sighed as Troy turned out of the driveway.

"Well, that was an unexpected interlude," she said in a good-humored voice. "I don't know what would've happened to that poor girl—and Kent—if we hadn't got there when we did. You're my hero, Troy Davis."

"And you're my sweetheart," he returned, smiling in her direction.

Twenty

"Now what?" Will Jefferson asked. He held his gloved hands upright like a surgeon about to enter the operating theater.

"It's a turkey," Miranda Sullivan teased, "not an appendectomy."

Will lowered his arms.

"We're going to stuff it," Miranda said.

"You mean I'm actually going to put my hands *inside* that bird?" His look was incredulous.

"Yes." It was difficult to keep a straight face when Will took everything so seriously.

"I've never done this before."

Miranda rolled her eyes. "Really? You could've fooled me."

"Are you making fun of me?" he asked, eyebrows raised.

"I'm doing my best not to."

Will grinned. "Well, this is hard work. First time in my life that I've cooked a turkey."

"We'll do fine."

"I'm glad you're with me," he said, "and not just because of the turkey."

"I'm happy to be here."

Quite unexpectedly, Will had invited Miranda to spend Christmas Day with him. They'd worked together at the Harbor Street Art Gallery for the past several months. She'd started as part-time help, working a couple of days a week. Gradually, Will had increased her hours.

In the beginning they hadn't gotten along. He thought she was too opinionated; she thought he was stubborn and dictatorial. But as the weeks progressed they'd formed a strong friendship. She'd taken a step toward compromise and he'd taken one, too, and they'd met in the middle.

Recently...well, *very* recently, that friendship took another turn. Miranda wasn't ready to put a name to it; she wasn't sure it was safe for her heart to define it. Not yet. But...there was definitely a sense of excitement that sizzled between them.

They'd kissed. She'd kissed him once, shocking herself far more than she'd shocked Will. And he'd kissed her. More than once.

Will had moved into his childhood home a few weeks earlier, purchasing the residence on Eagle Crest Avenue from his mother. This made it possible for Charlotte and Ben to move into the Sanford assisted-living complex without the additional worry of what would happen to their home.

Will and his sister, Olivia, had come up with the idea and coincidentally the move had benefited Miranda, too. She lived near Gig Harbor, a twenty-minute drive from Cedar Cove. The lease on her apartment was up, and she'd been hoping to move closer to the art gallery when Will approached her about living in his apartment on the premises. He'd had it remodeled and she could move in whenever she wished.

It was an offer too good to refuse. Her best friend, Shirley Bliss, had urged her to accept. Miranda grew a bit sad as she thought about Shirley. They'd become close after they'd both lost their husbands. Miranda had been married to an artist and Shirley was one herself. They'd helped each other adjust to widowhood.

Shirley had remarried a couple of months ago, and as soon as Tanni, her daughter, graduated from high school, Shirley planned to move to California with her new husband, Larry Knight, who was a nationally known and highly respected artist.

It would be hard to see Shirley leave the area and yet Miranda couldn't begrudge her friend this happiness. They'd stay in touch, of course, but…it wasn't the same.

Will had been attracted to Shirley. His ego had taken

a beating when she chose Larry Knight over him. The fact that he'd introduced Shirley to Larry had made the whole situation especially galling for Will; Miranda understood that. When he'd first started paying attention to *her*, Miranda had reason to think he was trying to make Shirley jealous. She wouldn't stand for that and made sure Will knew it.

Lately, however, there'd been a shift in the way he treated her. But his first tentative attempts to deepen their relationship didn't work, mainly because Miranda didn't trust him. He'd invited her to dinner and she'd refused. Later, she felt bad about that and she'd taken him a store-bought chicken. So they'd ended up having dinner together, after all. That was the night he'd invited her to spend Christmas Day with him.

"Now what?" Will asked. He was pushing the homemade stuffing into the cavity.

"Keep going until you can't get any more inside."

"Okay. Although this is kind of a revolting activity."

She laughed. "Will, why did you buy a twenty-three-pound bird for just the two of us?" she asked.

"I don't know... At least there'll be plenty of leftovers."

"Enough to feed an army," she muttered.

"And a navy," he added.

He finished with the stuffing, and washed his hands while Miranda basted the turkey and placed an aluminum-foil tent over top. "Okay, it's ready for the oven," she said.

She held open the oven door and Will slid the turkey inside. "How long will it take?" he asked.

"Twenty minutes a pound, so do the math."

"Seven and a half *hours?*"

"You'll build up an appetite," she said. "And we can have some crackers and cheese while we wait."

"And a nice glass of wine..." Will pulled off his oven mitts. "Any other suggestions?"

"As a matter of fact, yes." She left the kitchen and went into the living room to collect her bag. Reaching inside, she took out a wrapped gift. "For you," she said playfully, handing him the large square box.

Will looked a bit uneasy, which told her what she already suspected. He hadn't purchased her a gift. She hadn't really expected him to. Besides, this was more of a thank-you for having her over.

"It's small, just a token," she said. She didn't want to embarrass him or make him feel guilty for not reciprocating.

"Go ahead and open it," she urged.

"You shouldn't have," he said theatrically. He sat down on the sofa and tore away the paper. When he saw the jigsaw puzzle, he grinned. The picture was a seascape, with dolphins and tropical fish swimming in a blue, blue ocean. "Hey, good idea! We can put it together this afternoon."

Miranda stood and started to clear off the table. "I used to enjoy doing puzzles," she told him. "This table's big enough to lay out all the pieces."

"Here. Now you open my gift," Will said.

Miranda turned around, leaning against the table's edge. She frowned as Will gave her the small, beautifully wrapped gift. The shape and size hinted that it'd come from a jewelry store.

"Is this a marriage proposal?" she joked, and then laughed nervously, wondering how she could have asked something so idiotic.

"Not yet," he returned quite seriously.

Miranda stared at the package, almost afraid to remove the wrapping.

"Open it," he said.

Reluctantly, she untied the ribbon. "You didn't wrap this yourself."

"You're right, the store did." He stood next to her and nudged her to continue unwrapping.

"I...wasn't expecting anything like this," she said. "All I got you is a puzzle."

"I know you'll be surprised, which makes it all the more special."

Her hand trembled as she carefully slipped off the paper. Holding her breath, Miranda lifted the lid of the small blue box. Inside was a gold coin, a very old one, she guessed, framed by a gold bezel.

"It's from a sunken treasure ship found off the Florida coast," Will explained.

Taking it from the box, she saw that the coin was attached to a fine gold chain. Will took it out of her fingers, placed it around her neck and secured the clasp. She could feel the coin resting at the base of her throat, the metal smooth and cool. Automatically, she pressed her hand over it.

"It's treasure, Miranda," Will whispered. "Just like you are to me."

She blinked a couple of times, hardly able to fathom that Will Jefferson would do this for her. Or that he'd say such a thing.

"I…" Speaking seemed impossible, and whatever she said, whatever words of appreciation she managed to form, would never be enough. "I don't know how to…thank you."

"You're kidding. You, speechless? I don't believe it."

"Don't joke, Will. I mean it. I don't think anyone's ever done anything like this for me."

Will kissed her then. Really kissed her. He was gentle and loving, and when he raised his head, his eyes were filled with promise.

Twenty-One

"Mom, what time will Dad get here?" Sophie asked, as she and Bailey hurried into the kitchen. "Is Danielle coming, too?"

Beth had expected them long before now. She was clearing away the last of their brunch dishes, irritated that she hadn't heard from Kent. She was determined not to contact him, although she considered it bad manners to keep his family waiting on Christmas Day. "I don't think your father actually gave us a time," she said with more generosity than she felt. He'd certainly implied it would be that morning.

"Oh," Sophie murmured.

"It's already afternoon," Bailey said. "We've never opened our gifts this late."

That seemed like a minor complaint to Beth. The thought

of spending Christmas Day with Kent's…friend was enough to make her feel like going back to bed. Playing hostess to Danielle was above and beyond the call of duty.

It hadn't bothered her nearly as much until she'd realized how deeply she still loved Kent. For the past three years, she'd been able to live with a degree of contentment, refusing to acknowledge how lonely she was.

"Mom, call Dad and ask when he's going to be here," Bailey said.

"Why don't *you* phone him?" Beth suggested. She purposely banished the picture of Kent and Danielle cuddled together while their daughters impatiently awaited his arrival.

"Okay."

Cell phone in hand, Bailey sat down, propping her elbows on the kitchen table.

Beth tuned out her daughter's conversation as she silently prayed for the strength to get through the day. Depression weighed heavily on her. If she managed to survive this Christmas, she'd tell Kent she'd made a mistake. She loved him and wanted him back in her life. Only she couldn't tell him that in Danielle's presence.

No, she might as well forget any hope of a reconciliation, she told herself. Danielle was young and beautiful and competitive. She wouldn't give Kent up easily. Beth had made the mistake, and now she had to live with the consequences.

"Mom? Mom?"

"Yes," Beth said, turning her thoughts away from her ex-husband.

"Did you hear what I said?"

"Sorry, no."

"Are you feeling all right?" Sophie asked, joining her sister at the table.

"I...don't know." What Beth really wanted was to escape to her room with a fake flu bug and leave the girls to celebrate Christmas with Kent and Danielle. But she couldn't do that to her daughters. She'd muddle through and somehow find the strength to pretend all was well.

"Dad's on his way," Bailey told her.

"Good." She forced a smile. Turning from the sink, she grabbed a dish towel and wiped her hands dry. Needing fortification, she went to freshen her makeup.

Upstairs in her bathroom, she stared at her reflection in the mirror. Sad. Sad. Sad. She straightened her shoulders, saying, "You can do this. You can do this."

When she walked down the stairs she found Kent standing by the front door. She stopped abruptly before she reached the bottom. He looked up at her; their eyes met, and her heart immediately reacted. She gave him a tentative smile.

Kent smiled back.

He spoke first. "Merry Christmas," he said.

"Thank you." Her voice sounded wispy. "Merry Christmas."

"Dad," Bailey said excitedly, rushing over to him. She paused and looked around. "Where's Danielle?"

Kent broke eye contact with her. "She isn't here."

"Isn't here? Did she stay at the B and B?"

"Not…exactly." He bent down to take off his boots.

"Then where is she?"

Kent glanced at his watch. "I imagine she's at the airport about now."

"The airport?" Sophie repeated. "I thought she was spending Christmas in Cedar Cove."

"That was her original plan. She came with me, hoping to meet up with a sailor she'd met when he was on leave in California. Apparently, she read more into the relationship than she should have."

"What?" Beth asked in shock. "She came to meet up with a sailor? But…"

"Danielle was hoping to see this guy, Hunter. She and I were talking about that, and I told her I still had feelings for you, but wasn't sure what to do when you asked me to come here for Christmas. She offered to come with me and—"

"Wait." Beth's hand flew to her chest. "I asked *you?* I think there's been some misunderstanding." Beth noticed that the girls had skittered off as she spoke.

Kent frowned. "You mean you didn't?"

Beth frowned, too. "Are you saying you *weren't* the one who wanted to spend Christmas as a family?"

"Bailey! Sophie!" Beth and Kent shouted at the same time.

"Bailey Madison. Sophie Lynn," Beth threw in for good measure.

Their two daughters reappeared, looking sheepish.

"Okay, we admit it," Bailey said, hands in her back hip pockets. "The thing is, Sophie and I think this whole divorce is wrong. We thought if the two of you were together at Christmas, you'd realize what a terrible mistake you made. Then Dad had to go and ruin everything by bringing Danielle."

"I didn't exactly bring her," he clarified. "Danielle told me she intended to visit the area at the same time, and we discovered we'd be on the same flight and had booked rooms at the same bed-and-breakfast."

"Just a minute," Beth said in confusion. "But she works with you, right? That's all true?"

"Yes. She works in the accounting department."

"Are...are you... Have you ever been involved?"

"Good heavens, no."

"But..."

Kent broke eye contact. "While we were at the airport waiting for the plane, we started talking. Just like I already told you, I explained that I wasn't sure how I felt about being here this Christmas. I missed my wife, but the girls had hinted that you were seeing the local vet and I didn't want to be a fifth wheel. So Danielle said what you needed was some competition and I...agreed. I felt it was worth a shot, anyway. So she put on this ridiculous act and—" He shrugged, glancing up the staircase at Beth. "I regretted the entire charade immediately, but by then it seemed too late. The whole thing had taken on a momentum of its own...." He shrugged. "I just hope you can forgive me."

The girls sent each other a triumphant smile, as if they were personally responsible for this turn of events.

Kent continued to hold Beth's look.

She bit her lip and started down the remaining steps.

"Problem is," he told his daughters, "I don't know how your mother feels about me. It's been three years."

"Mom's crazy about you," Bailey said.

"Of *course* Mom loves you," Sophie added her voice to her sister's. "She'd be a fool not to."

"What about Ted Reynolds?" Kent asked.

"What about him?" Bailey returned. "Mom loves you, not Ted."

"I'd rather have your mother tell me so herself." Kent stood with one foot braced against the bottom step. He stretched out his arm to Beth.

She placed her hand in his. "Oh, Kent, I've never stopped loving you. I never will."

He grabbed her by the waist and lifted her down the last two stairs, setting her feet on the ground.

As Beth slipped her arms around his neck, she buried her face in his shoulder. "We've both been so foolish."

He kissed her again and then again, as if he couldn't get enough of her.

Cradling his face with her hands, Beth gazed into his eyes, aware of their daughters grinning from the sidelines.

"These girls have a lot of 'splainin' to do," Kent said in a stage whisper.

"It was Bailey's idea," Sophie maintained.

"Both of you were being ridiculous about this stupid divorce," Bailey said quickly. "We felt we had to do something." She obviously intended to share the blame—or the praise.

"So you conspired to bring us together," Kent muttered.

"You aren't mad, are you?" Bailey asked, moving closer to her sister.

Kent brought his attention back to Beth and kissed the tip of her nose. "Are *you* upset?" he asked.

With her husband's arms around her and the Christmas tree lights shining in the background, Beth had to admit she wasn't. "Not in the least. Actually, I think it was a brilliant idea."

"Okay, if you must know," Sophie said, "I did help Bailey a little."

"Isn't this the best Christmas ever?" Bailey exclaimed, hugging her sister. "And we haven't even opened our gifts yet."

Beth had to agree. This was the best Christmas of her life.

Epilogue

Valentine's Day

"This is so romantic," Bailey said to her sister. "I'm so happy, I want to cry." They left the kitchen, ready to set out the plates and forks to serve cake to their parents' guests.

"We did it," Sophie said, almost giddy with happiness. "I don't know *how,* but it worked. Mom and Dad are back together."

"Just like they were meant to be."

Their parents were remarried and their dad was now living at 1225 Christmas Tree Lane, where he planned to take on the business aspects of the farm.

Beth came down the stairs and into the living room, with Kent directly behind her. "Oh, girls, the table looks lovely."

"Thanks, Mom."

The coffee- and teapots were filled and the cake sliced. This wasn't a wedding reception, Beth had explained to her daughters. It was an opportunity to introduce Kent to her friends and neighbors in Cedar Cove.

Bailey thought her father had never looked handsomer or her mother more beautiful. They were constantly together now. It had started while they were all in Whistler during Christmas break. Bailey couldn't remember a time they'd had more fun as a family. After their short vacation, Kent had returned to California. Before he could move north to Washington State, he needed to make some decisions and changes.

Within six weeks he'd sold his engineering company to his partner, packed up his house and found responsible tenants. In between all those negotiations and all that packing, Kent flew up to Cedar Cove practically every weekend to be with their mother. It was the most romantic thing.

They'd remarried in a private ceremony on January twenty-eighth. Only the girls and Kent's brother Michael, who'd come in from California to act as best man, had been in attendance. Afterward, their parents had sent out announcements to family and friends. From the comments Bailey heard, everyone seemed to think this remarriage was wonderful. To Bailey and Sophie it was just plain... right.

"We have our first guests," Sophie called out, standing by the living room window. "It's Grace, the lady who has Beau."

"Grace Harding," Beth said. "And her husband, Cliff." She headed for the door.

"There are four of them," Sophie added.

"The other two are Olivia and Jack Griffin."

Their mother ushered their guests in out of the rain. Grace and Olivia stepped inside the house and were warmly greeted by Beth and Kent.

"I think we might have met earlier," Kent said, shaking hands with the two men. "Didn't I see you at the Christmas Eve service?"

Both men nodded.

"Would you like some coffee and cake?" Bailey asked politely.

"Sure! Thanks." The two men eagerly accepted her offer while the women raised their hands to decline. "We're driving to Seattle for a Valentine's treat," Grace said. "I'm saving my calories for that."

"Me, too," Olivia chimed in. "By the way," she told Beth, "my mother sent you a small gift. The ladies in her knitting group made you several cotton dishrags. Not very romantic, perhaps, but Mom says everyone can use extras."

Beth took the package gratefully. "Charlotte is always so thoughtful."

"Oh, Ben and Mom both send their very best wishes. She wanted me to tell you that bringing the dogs to Sanford

Suites has been a real blessing to everyone. They all just love working with those dogs."

"It's a help to me, too."

Bailey smiled. Apparently, her mother was using the senior citizens to help her with dog training. Beth claimed this provided two benefits in one: not only did the older people get a form of therapy spending time with the dogs, they also got a sense of purpose from it. The Reading with Rover program at the library was another of her successes.

Beth slipped an arm around Kent's waist. "I have to admit that getting those dogs to Sanford Suites can be a bit of an ordeal."

"You won't need to do it alone anymore," Kent told her and, leaning over, gave her a quick kiss.

Seeing her parents like this, so openly in love, Bailey almost forgot her job.

"Since Olivia isn't having cake, you can give me a bigger slice," Jack whispered. Bailey threw him a conspirator's smile and willingly complied.

"I heard that, Jack Griffin," the judge said from the other side of the room.

"How's Beau?" Sophie asked.

"I believe he's the smartest dog I've ever owned," Grace said, beaming with pride. She entertained them all for several minutes with stories of the puppy's antics.

The sound of another car pulling into the driveway attracted everyone's attention. "Oh, good," Sophie said, peering out the window. "It's the couple who owns the bed-and-breakfast where Dad stayed during Christmas," she announced. "Oh, and look! They brought their dog."

"They named her Millie," Beth said. "I've been doing dog obedience classes with her and four of her siblings over the past two months."

Bob and Peggy Beldon sat down for cake and coffee just as the Griffins and Hardings left. Millie lay contentedly at Peggy's feet.

Bailey hurried into the kitchen for a doggie treat, returning just in time to hear Bob Beldon say to her father, "Welcome back to Cedar Cove." Bob dug into the white cake with raspberry filling.

"You'll never guess who we heard from," Peggy said conversationally and then, before anyone could guess, she answered her own question. "Danielle!"

Bailey was all ears. Sophie, too. Her sister set down the coffeepot and waited for the punch line.

"And?" Their dad frowned; clearly, Danielle wasn't a good memory.

"She sent a check to pay for the damage she did and wrote a letter of apology."

"I'm glad she apologized," Kent said. "She caused quite a scene."

"I'll say," Bob muttered between bites of cake. "I've been in theater for twenty years, and I've never seen more of a drama queen than that woman."

"But she had a broken heart," Sophie said, looking at Bailey. "Right?"

Her younger sister was far more charitable than Bailey was inclined to be. She had a point, though. They could afford to be generous. Their parents were together again, and, after all, Danielle's plan to make their mother jealous had started out as a misguided favor to their dad.

"In my opinion, the sailor who dumped her made a lucky escape."

"Bob," Peggy said pointedly. "Be kind."

"Okay, okay. At least she was responsible enough to pay for the damages and send us a note of apology."

"I still feel bad about all of that," Kent said. "I had no idea she'd react the way she did."

"It wasn't your fault," Bob told him. "We appreciated your offer to pay for the damages, but you weren't the one who created the mess. We mailed Danielle a letter after the first of the year, and three weeks later the check arrived." They chatted for another twenty minutes, and then the Beldons went home, with Millie heeling very nicely.

The Flemmings and their two sons stopped by next, passing the Beldons in the driveway. The dogs were at home, but Matthew and Mark spoke animatedly about their puppies whom they'd named Charlie and Sam. It was obvious that the boys had taken very successfully to dog ownership. Bailey remembered when she and Sophie had become dog owners for the first time. Watching the two brothers reminded her of the summer their parents had allowed them each to choose a puppy at the local animal shelter. Bailey got a beagle and Sophie had an Australian shepherd. They'd named them Barney and Fi Fi, and those dogs had been their companions for more than ten years.

Over the course of the next two hours, more people than Bailey could keep track of came and went. Bruce and Rachel Peyton arrived with their newborn daughter, Corinna. Jolene had gotten one of the puppies for Christmas, too, and bragged equally about Corinna and Poppy, her dog.

Troy and Faith Davis came by for cake and to chat with their parents. So did the McAfees, who were full of compliments about *their* puppy, Asta—as smart and charming as the dog in those movies, Roy bragged. Everyone was so friendly. Bailey was in charge of serving cake and Sophie busied herself with coffee and tea.

Soon after, Teri and Bobby Polgar, plus Christie and James Wilbur—proud owners of Chessie—dropped over with a bottle of champagne. Then Will Jefferson and Miranda Sullivan, sporting an engagement ring, brought *another* bottle.

By the end of the afternoon it seemed as if everyone their mother knew in town had made the effort to welcome Kent to Cedar Cove.

Everyone, that is, except Ted Reynolds, the veterinarian.

Briefly, Bailey had wondered if her mother's friend

would stop by. No one said anything, but Sophie noticed and so did Bailey. That saddened her a little because she knew that Ted and her mother were fond of each other.

"Well, that looks like everyone," Beth said, carrying the leftover cake into the kitchen.

"You girls did a great job."

"Wait!" Sophie cried out. "I see a car coming down the driveway."

"It's Ted," Bailey said excitedly.

"Ted?" Beth pushed open the kitchen door and stuck her head out. "Oh, I was hoping he'd have a chance to come." She brought out a piece of cake and set it on the table, as if it'd been there all along just waiting for Ted's arrival.

Kent opened the front door and extended his hand. "Good to see you, Ted."

"You, too. I'd like you to meet my friend Lana."

Ted had a female friend? Bailey met her sister's eyes.

"Ted," Beth said, holding out her hand to him. "I'm so glad you brought Lana. I've been wanting to meet her."

Mom knew about this? Bailey thought that was a good sign. Lana was a petite attractive blonde who seemed as effervescent as Ted was low-key.

Ted stood with his hand protectively around Lana's waist. "Everyone, this is Lana Carr."

Bailey and Sophie introduced themselves after their parents did.

"Sit down, please," Beth said and gestured Ted and Lana

toward the chairs. While they took their seats, Bailey and Sophie handed them plates with cake and took drink orders.

"You know, your mother and I haven't had any cake yet," their father said. "I don't suppose we could get a slice, too?"

"Sure thing, Dad."

Bailey cut two additional slices and brought them in while Sophie prepared coffee for their guests.

Bailey went back to the kitchen to start cleaning up, and Sophie joined her there a couple of minutes later. When she opened the kitchen door, the sound of their parents' laughter drifted toward her.

"Everyone seems to be getting along," Bailey commented.

"They are. I think Mom and Dad and Ted and Lana are going to be good friends. Did you hear how they met?"

"Mom and Dad?"

"No, Ted and Lana, silly."

"Tell me."

"She brought in a dog who'd been hit by a car. She used to work for a vet in Tacoma, a friend of Ted's, until she moved to Cedar Cove. His friend had mentioned Lana was single and wanted to introduce them, but Ted said the timing was bad."

"Yeah, he had his eye on our mother," Bailey murmured.

"Lana saw his picture and thought he looked like a nice

guy, but let it go. She figured he'd contact her if he was interested."

"But he didn't."

"No. And then Lana found the injured dog and brought him to the nearest vet, not even knowing it was Ted until she got there. She helped him operate on the dog and did such a good job that he offered her a job at the animal hospital."

"And she accepted."

"That's such a romantic story," Sophie said.

Bailey nodded. "This is a romantic town."

Her sister gave a contented sigh.

"You know, I like Cedar Cove," Bailey said. "I like it a lot."

"I do, too."

It was the kind of town anyone would love to call home.

* * * * *

5-B Poppy Lane

To my parents
Ted and Connie Adler
who married July 25, 1942
before my father headed off to war

Prologue

It was early afternoon, Christmas Eve. Snow was falling
lightly, adding to the festive atmosphere inside and out.
Helen Shelton fussed with the decorations in her small
Cedar Cove duplex, making sure everything was in place.
The tree, a real one, featured the ornaments she'd started
acquiring when she'd married Sam in 1946. He'd bought
her many of these, and as she hung them carefully on the
branches she'd relived their history, hers and Sam's. He'd
died almost thirty years ago but she remembered every
Christmas they'd spent together.

The Nativity pieces were arranged on her coffee table
with the Infant Jesus nestled in the manger, surrounded
by the other familiar figurines. A large evergreen wreath
hung on her front door. The house was redolent with the
scents of spruce and spice—ready for Christmas.

Helen wanted everything perfect when her only grand-daughter and her husband arrived. In preparation she'd mulled cider and baked Ruth's favorite Christmas cook-ies from an old gingerbread recipe; they'd first made it together when Ruth was a child. Even now, after all these years, Helen remembered the thrill she'd felt when her granddaughter was born. Oh, she loved her grandsons, but for a grandmother there was something special about a girl.

The doorbell chimed and Helen peeked outside to see her dear friend Charlotte Rhodes standing on the porch. Delighted, she opened the door and quickly ushered Charlotte inside. They were both getting on in years, and Helen suspected neither of them had many Christmases left. She didn't have a fatalistic view of life by any means, but she was a practical woman. Helen knew what it was to face death. She had no fear of dying.

"Merry Christmas," Charlotte said, unwrapping a hand-knit lace scarf from around her neck. Her friend was the most exquisite knitter. Many a time she'd assisted Helen with her knitting projects. She gave her the confidence to try new things. Why, with Charlotte's help a few years back, Helen had completed a complicated Fair Isle sweater. She still felt a bit of pride whenever she wore that sweater. She was a competent knitter in her own right; she didn't mean to discount her skills. But Charlotte had such an encouraging way about her, and not just when it came to knitting. Helen had confided in Charlotte about what had happened to her during the war, and Charlotte had urged her to share it with her family. Eventually, she had…

"Merry Christmas," Helen said, taking Charlotte's coat and scarf and hanging them up. She led her friend into the kitchen. "This is such a pleasant surprise."

"I knew your granddaughter and her husband were stopping by, so I brought some of my green tomato mincemeat." She removed two beribboned jars from her ever-present knitting bag.

"Oh, Charlotte, *thank* you." Helen accepted the jars and put them on the counter to admire. Charlotte was well aware that Helen had a weakness for her homemade green tomato mincemeat.

"Consider this a small Christmas gift," Charlotte said, looking pleased at Helen's reaction.

"Didn't you say it was too much work this year?" Helen could swear Charlotte had claimed she was finished with canning. And who would blame her?

"I did say that, and then I took a look at all those green tomatoes and I couldn't help myself. Besides, Ben swears mincemeat is his favorite pie."

"I thought your peach pie was his favorite."

Charlotte actually blushed. Those two had been married for several years now but they still behaved like newlyweds. It always made Helen smile.

"Ben says that about all my pies."

"Well, I'm very happy to get these. I'll make a pie for

tonight's dessert." Helen automatically set the teakettle on the burner, dropping teabags in her best china pot.

"What time is your granddaughter getting here?"

Helen glanced at the kitchen clock. "Not for several hours. Around five."

Charlotte pulled out a chair and sat down, reaching into her voluminous bag for her knitting. Socks again. Charlotte was never without her knitting, and these days it was usually socks. Helen had recently made socks, too, but not ones you'd wear. She'd knit both Ruth and Paul Christmas stockings to hang by the fireplace. Because of the intricate pattern, it had taken her the better part of three months. She planned to give them their made-with-love Christmas stockings when they exchanged gifts that evening.

It wasn't long before the tea was ready and the two of them sat across the table from each other, a plate of the gingerbread cookies between them.

"I've met your granddaughter, haven't I?" Charlotte asked, picking up her teacup and frowning slightly.

"Yes, don't you recall? Ruth certainly remembers you."

"She does?"

"It was a few years ago. She was in quite a state when she came by to visit. She was absolutely beside herself because she wasn't sure what to do about Paul."

Charlotte looked confused.

"That was shortly after they met," Helen explained, surprised her friend had apparently forgotten the episode, since Charlotte had answered Ruth's knock at the door.

"They'd been corresponding for a while. Paul was in the marines. Well, he still is, but that's not the point."

Charlotte chose a cookie. "It's coming back to me now," she said. "They had a lovely romance, didn't they?"

"Oh, yes."

She took a bite. "Mmm. Delicious. Now, remind me again how they met."

Helen settled back in her chair and picked up her own cup of tea. This was such a wonderful story. Her own love story was part of it, too. All those years ago during the Second World War. There were fewer and fewer people who knew what that war had *really* been like.

For more than fifty years she'd refused to talk about that time, refused to even think about her adventures and ordeals. She'd lost so much—and yet, she'd gained, too. At the urging of the few friends she'd confided in, including Charlotte, she'd finally told Ruth what had happened. Ruth and her Paul. Afterward, her granddaughter had said that her experiences were more than family history; they were *history*.

"Helen," Charlotte murmured, shaking her out of her reverie. "You were going to tell me about Ruth and Paul."

"Oh, yes. The story of how they fell in love…" She settled back, listening to the comforting click of Charlotte's needles, and began.

One

Ruth Shelton hurried out of her classroom-management lecture at the University of Washington, where she was completing her master's of education degree. Clutching her books, she dashed across campus, in a rush to get home. By now the mail would have been delivered to her small rental house three blocks from the school.

"Ruth," Tina Dupont called, stopping her in midflight. "There's another antiwar rally this afternoon at—"

"Sorry, I've got to run," Ruth said, jogging past her friend and feeling more than a little guilty. Other students cleared a path for her; wherever she was headed must have seemed urgent—and it was, but only to her. Since Christmas, four months ago, she'd been corresponding with Sergeant Paul Gordon, USMC, who was stationed in Afghanistan. There'd been recent reports of fighting, and she hadn't received a letter or an email from Paul in three days. Three interminable days. Not since they'd initially begun their correspondence had there been such a lapse. Paul usually wrote every day and she did, too. They emailed as often as possible. Ruth had strong feelings about the war in Iraq, although her opinions didn't match those of her parents.

Earlier in the school year, Ruth had been part of a protest rally on campus. But no matter what her political views on the subject, she felt it was important to support American troops wherever they might be serving. In an effort to do that, Ruth had voluntarily mailed a Christmas card and letter to a nameless soldier.

Paul Gordon was the young man who'd received that Christmas card, and to Ruth's surprise he'd written her back and enclosed his photograph. Paul was from Seattle and he'd chosen her card because of the Seattle postmark. He'd asked her lots of questions—about her history, her family, her interests—and closed with a postscript that said he hoped to hear from her again.

When she first got his letter, Ruth had hesitated. She felt she'd done her duty, supported the armed services in a way she was comfortable doing. This man she'd never met was asking her to continue corresponding with him. She wasn't sure she wanted to become that involved. Feeling uncertain, she'd waited a few days before deciding.

During that time, Ruth had read and reread his letter and studied the head shot of the clean-cut handsome marine sergeant in dress uniform. His dark brown eyes had seemed to stare straight through her—and directly into her heart. After two days, she answered his letter with a short one of her own and added her email address at the bottom of the page. Ruth had a few concerns she wanted him to address before she could commit herself to beginning this correspondence. Being as straightforward and honest as possible, she explained her objections to the war in Iraq. She felt there was a more legitimate reason for troops to be in Afghanistan and wanted to know his stand. A few days later he emailed her. Paul didn't mince words. He told her he believed the United States had done the right thing in entering Iraq and gave his reasons. He left it up to her to decide if she wanted to continue their correspondence. Ruth emailed him back and once again listed her objections to the American presence in the Middle East. His response came a day later, suggesting they "agree to disagree." He ended the email with the same question he'd asked her earlier. Would she write him?

At first, Ruth wasn't going to. They were diametrically opposed in their political views. But in the end, even recognizing the conflict between their opinions, she did write. Their correspondence started slowly. She enjoyed his wry wit and his unflinching determination to make a difference in the world. His father had fought in Vietnam, he said, and in some ways the war in Afghanistan seemed similar—the hostile terrain, the unpredictability of the enemy, the difficult conditions. For her part, she mentioned that at twenty-five she'd returned to school to obtain her master's of education degree. Then, gradually, without being fully aware of how it had happened, Ruth found herself spending part of every day writing or emailing Paul. Despite the instant nature of email, and its convenience, they both enjoyed interspersing their online messages with more formal letters. There was something so…permanent about a real letter. As well, depending on his duty assignment, Paul didn't always have computer access.

After they'd been corresponding regularly for a couple of months, Paul asked for her picture. Eventually she'd mailed him her photograph, but only after she'd had her hair and makeup done at one of those "glamour" studios. Although she wasn't fashion-model beautiful, she considered herself fairly attractive and wanted to look her absolute best for Paul, although she didn't entirely understand why it mattered so much. For years, she'd been resigned to the fact that she wasn't much good at relationships. In high school she'd been shy, and while she was an undergraduate, she'd dated a little but tended to be reserved and studious. Her quiet manner didn't seem to appeal to the guys she met. It was only when she stepped in front of a classroom that she truly became herself. She loved teaching, every single aspect of it. In the process, Ruth lost her hesitation and her restraint, and to her astonishment discovered that this enthusiasm had begun to spill over into the rest of her life. Suddenly men started to notice her. She enjoyed the attention—who wouldn't?—and had dated more in the past few months than in the preceding four years.

For the picture, her short brown hair had been styled in loose curls. Her blue eyes were smiling and friendly, which was exactly the impression she hoped to convey. She was a little shocked by the importance of Paul's reaction—by her need that he find her attractive.

She waited impatiently for his response. A week later she received an email. Paul seemed to like what he saw in her photograph and soon they were writing and emailing back and forth at a feverish pace. A day without some form of communication from Paul felt empty now.

Ruth had never had a long-distance relationship before, and the growing intensity of her feelings for this man she'd never met took her by surprise. She wasn't a teenager with a schoolgirl crush. Ruth was a mature, responsible adult. Or at least she had been until she slipped a simple Christmas card into the mailbox—and got a reply from a handsome marine sergeant named Paul Gordon.

Ruth walked quickly to the rental house she shared with Lynn Blumenthal, then ran up the front steps to the porch. Lynn was eighteen and away from home and family for the first time. The arrangement suited both of them, and despite the disparity in their ages and interests, they'd gotten along fairly well. With her heart pounding hard, Ruth forced herself to draw in a deep breath as she started toward the mailbox.

The screen door flew open and Lynn came out. "What

are you doing home?" she asked, then shook her head. "Never mind, I already know. You're looking for a letter from soldier boy."

Ruth wasn't going to deny the obvious. "I haven't heard from him in three days."

Lynn rolled her eyes. "I don't understand you."

"I know." Ruth didn't want to get into another discussion with her roommate. Lynn had made her feelings about this relationship known from the outset, although as Ruth had gently tried to tell her, it was none of her business. That didn't prevent the younger woman from expressing her views. Lynn said that Ruth was only setting herself up for heartache. A part of Ruth actually agreed, but by the time she realized what was happening, she was emotionally involved with Paul.

"You hardly ever see Clay anymore," Lynn chastised, hands on her hips. "He called and asked about you the other night."

Ruth stared at the small black mailbox. "Clay and I are just friends."

"Not according to him."

It was true that they'd been seeing each other quite a bit following a Halloween party last October. Like her, Clay Matthews was obtaining his master's of education, and they seemed to have a lot in common. But her interest in him had started to wane even before she'd mailed that Christmas card to Paul. The problem was, Clay hadn't noticed.

"I'm sorry he's disappointed."

"Clay is decent and hardworking, and the way you've treated him the last few months is…is terrible." Lynn, who at five foot ten stood a good seven inches taller than Ruth, could be intimidating, especially with her mouth twisted in that grimace of disapproval.

Ruth had tried to let Clay down easily, but it hadn't worked. They'd gone to the library together last Thursday. Unfortunately, that had been a mistake. She'd known it almost right away when Clay pressured her to have coffee with him afterward. It would've been better just to end the relationship and forget about staying friends. He was younger, for one thing, and while that hadn't seemed important earlier, it did now. Perhaps it was wrong to compare him to Paul, but Ruth couldn't help it. Measured against Paul, Clay seemed immature, demanding and insecure.

"You said he phoned?" Frowning, she glanced at Lynn.

Lynn nodded. "He wants to know what's going on."

Oh, brother! Ruth couldn't have made it plainer had she handed him divorce papers. Unwilling to be cruel, she'd tried to bolster his ego by referring to all the positive aspects of his personality—but apparently, that had only led him to think the opposite of what she was trying to tell him. He'd refused to take her very obvious hints, and in her frustration, she'd bluntly announced that she wasn't interested in seeing him anymore. That seemed pretty explicit to her; how he could be confused about it left Ruth shaking her head.

The fact that he'd phoned and cried on her roommate's shoulder was a good example of what she found adolescent about his behavior. She was absolutely certain Paul would never do that. If he had a problem, he'd take it directly to the source.

"I think you're being foolish," Lynn said, and added, "Not that you asked my opinion."

"No, I didn't," Ruth reminded her, eyeing the mailbox again. There was an ornamental latticework design along the bottom, and looking through it, she could tell that the day's mail had been delivered. The envelope inside was white, and her spirits sank. There *had* to be something from Paul. If not a real letter, then an email.

"He wanted me to talk to you," Lynn was saying.

"Who did?" Ruth asked distractedly. She was dying to open the mailbox, but she wanted to do it in privacy.

"Clay," Lynn cried, sounding completely exasperated. "Who else are we talking about?"

Suddenly Ruth understood. She looked away from the mailbox and focused her attention on Lynn. "You're attracted to him, aren't you?"

Lynn gasped indignantly. "Don't be ridiculous."

"Sit down," Ruth said, gesturing toward the front steps where they'd often sat before. It was a lovely spring afternoon, the first week of April, and she needed to clear the air with her roommate before this got further out of hand.

"What?" Lynn said with a defensive edge. "You've got the wrong idea here. I was just trying to help a friend."

"Sit," Ruth ordered.

"I have class in twenty minutes and I—" Lynn paused, scowling at her watch.

"Sit down."

The eighteen-year-old capitulated with ill grace. "All right, but I know what you're going to say." She folded her arms and stared straight ahead.

"I'm fine with it," Ruth said softly. "Go out with him if you want. Like I said earlier, I'm not interested in Clay."

"You would be if it wasn't for soldier boy."

Ruth considered that and in all honesty felt she could say, "Not so."

"I don't understand you," Lynn lamented a second time. "You marched in the rally against the war in Iraq. Afghanistan isn't all that different, and now you're involved with Paul what's-his-face and it's like I don't even know you anymore."

"Paul doesn't have anything to do with this."

"Yes, he does," Lynn insisted.

"I'm not going to have this conversation with you. We agree on some points and disagree on others. That's fine. We live in a free society and we don't have to have the same opinion on these issues or anything else."

Lynn sighed and said nothing.

"I have the feeling none of this is really about Paul," Ruth said with deliberate patience. She hadn't known Lynn very long; they lived separate lives and so far they'd never had a problem. As roommates went, Ruth felt she was fortunate to have found someone as amicable as Lynn. She didn't want this difference of opinion about Clay—and Paul—to ruin that.

The other girl once again looked pointedly at her watch, as if to suggest Ruth say what she intended to say and be done with it.

"I don't want to see Clay," she said emphatically.

"You might have told him that."

"I tried."

Lynn glared at her. "You should've tried harder."

Ruth laughed, but not because she was amused. For whatever reason, Clay had set his sights on her and wasn't about to be dissuaded. Complicating matters, Lynn was obviously interested in him and feeling guilty and unsure of how to deal with her attraction.

"Listen," Ruth said. "I didn't mean to hurt Clay. He's a great guy and—"

"You shouldn't have lied to him."

Ruth raised her eyebrows. "When did I lie to him?"

"Last week you said you were going to visit your grand-mother in Cedar Cove and that was why you couldn't go out with him this weekend. I overheard you," she murmured.

Oh, that. "It was a white lie," Ruth confessed. She definitely planned to visit her grandmother, though. Helen Shelton lived across Puget Sound in a small community on the Kitsap Peninsula. Ruth had spent Thanksgiving with her grandmother and visited for a weekend before

Christmas and then again close to Valentine's Day. Her last visit had been early in March. She always enjoyed her time with Helen, but somehow the weeks had slipped away and here it was April already.

"A lie is a lie," Lynn said adamantly.

"Okay, you're right," Ruth agreed. "I should've been honest with Clay." Delaying had been a mistake, as she was now learning.

That seemed to satisfy her roommate, who started to get to her feet. Ruth placed her hand on Lynn's forearm, stopping her. "I want to know why you're so upset about this situation with Clay."

"I told you.... I just don't think this is how people should treat each other."

"I don't like the way Clay's put you in the middle. This is between him and me. He had no right to drag you into it."

"Yes, but—"

"You're defending him?"

Lynn shrugged. "I guess."

"Don't. Clay's a big boy. If he has something to say, then he can come to me all on his own. When and if he does, I'm going to tell him *again* that I'm no longer interested in dating him. I'm—"

"Stuck on some gun-wielding—"

A look from Ruth cut her off.

"Okay, whatever," Lynn muttered.

"What I want you to do is comfort him," Ruth said, patting Lynn's arm.

"I could, I suppose."

"Good," Ruth said, hoping to encourage her. "He might need someone to talk to, and since you're sensitive to his feelings, you'd be the perfect choice."

"You think so?"

Ruth nodded. Lynn stood up and went inside to get her books; she left with a cheerful goodbye as if they'd never had an argument. With her roommate gone, Ruth leaped off the step and across the porch to the mailbox. Lifting the top, she reached inside, holding her breath as she pulled out the electric bill in its white envelope, a sales flyer—and a hand-addressed air mail letter from Sergeant Paul Gordon.

Two

April 2

My Dear Ruth,

We've been out on a recon mission for the last four days and there wasn't any way I could let you know. They seemed like the longest four days of this tour, and not for the reasons you might think. Those days meant I couldn't write you or receive your letters. I've been in the marines for eight years now and I've never felt like this about mail before. Never felt this strongly about a woman I've yet to meet, either. Once we were back in camp, I sat down with your letters and read through each one. As I explained before, there are times we can't get online and this happened to be one of those times. I realize you've probably been wondering why I wasn't in touch. I hope you weren't too concerned. I would've written if I could.

I have good news. I'm coming home on leave....

Ruth read Paul's letter twice. Yes, he'd definitely said he was headed home, to Seattle, for two weeks before flying to Camp Pendleton in California for additional training. He hoped to spend most of his leave with her. His one request was that Ruth make as much time for him as her studies would allow and, if possible, keep her weekends free.

If Ruth thought her heart had been beating hard a few minutes earlier, it didn't compare to the way it pounded now. She could barely breathe. Never had she looked forward to meeting anyone more.

Sitting on the edge of her bed, Ruth picked up the small framed photograph she kept on her nightstand. Paul's image was the first thing she saw when she woke and the last before she turned off her light. In four months, he'd become an important part of her life. Now, with his return to Seattle, their feelings for each other would stand the real test. Writing letters and email messages was very different from carrying on a face-to-face conversation....

At the end of his letter, Paul suggested they meet at 6:00 p.m. on Saturday, April 16, at Ivar's restaurant on the Seattle waterfront. She didn't care what else was on her schedule; any conflicting arrangement would immediately be canceled.

Rather than begin her homework, Ruth sat down and wrote Paul back, her fingers flying over the computer keys as she composed her response. Yes, she would see him there. Nothing could keep her away. While she was nervous at the prospect of meeting Paul, she was excited, too.

Her letter was coming out of the printer when the phone rang. Absently Ruth grabbed the receiver, holding it against her shoulder as she opened the desk drawer and searched for an envelope.

"Hello?"

"Ruth, it's your grandmother."

"Grandma," Ruth said, genuinely pleased to hear from Helen. "I've been meaning to call you and I haven't. I'm sorry."

Her grandmother chuckled. "I didn't call to make you feel guilty. I'm inviting you to lunch."

"When?"

"In a couple of weeks—on Sunday the seventeenth if that works for you. I figured I'd give you plenty of time to fit me into your schedule. I thought we'd sit out on the patio, weather permitting, and enjoy the view of the cove."

Her grandmother's duplex was on a hill overlooking the water with the lighthouse in the distance. Her grandparents had lived in Cedar Cove for as long as Ruth could remember, and Helen had stayed there after her husband's death. Because Ruth had been born and raised in Oregon, she'd visited the small Washington town often through the years. "I've wanted to get over to see you."

"I know, I know, but unless we both plan ahead, it won't happen. In no time you'll have your master's degree and then you'll move on and we'll both regret the missed opportunities. I don't want that."

"I don't, either." Her Grandma Shelton was Ruth's favorite relative. She was highly educated, which wasn't particularly common for a woman her age, and spoke French and German fluently. She'd worked as a translator from the 1950s through the '80s, specializing in French novels, which she translated into English. Her father hadn't said much about his mother's life prior to her marriage, and one of the reasons Ruth had chosen to attend the University of Washington was so she could get to know her grandmother better.

"I can put you down for lunch, then?"

"Yes, that would be lovely." Her gaze fell on Paul's letter and Ruth realized that the date her grandmother had suggested was the first weekend Paul would be in town. He'd specifically asked her to keep as much of that two-week period free as she could. She wanted to spend time with him and yet she couldn't refuse her grandmother. "Grandma, I'm looking at my calendar and—"

"Is there a conflict?"

"Not…exactly. I've sort of got a date," she said, assuming she and Paul would be seeing each other. It would be ideal if he could join her. "It isn't anything official, so I—"

"Then you do have another commitment."

"No…" This was getting complicated. "Well, not exactly," she said again.

"I wasn't aware that you were dating anyone special. Who is he?"

The question hung there for a moment before Ruth answered. "His name is Paul Gordon and we aren't really dating." She would've continued, except that her grandmother broke in.

"Your parents didn't say anything about this." The words were spoken as if there must be something untoward about Paul that Ruth didn't want to divulge.

"No, Mom and Dad wouldn't," Ruth said, not adding that she hadn't actually mentioned Paul to her parents. She'd decided it wasn't necessary to enlighten them about this correspondence yet. Explaining her feelings about Paul to her family would be difficult when everyone knew her political views. More importantly, she wasn't sure how she felt about him and wouldn't be until they'd met.

So far, they were only pen pals, but this was the man she dreamed about every night, the man who dominated her thoughts each and every day.

"Grandma, I haven't said anything to Mom and Dad because I haven't officially met Paul yet."

"Is this…" Her grandmother hesitated. "Is this one of those…those *internet* relationships?" She spit out the word as though meeting a man via the internet was either illegal or unseemly—most likely both.

"No, Grandma, it's nothing like that."

"Then why don't your parents know about him?"

"Well, because…because he's a soldier in Afghanistan." There—it was out.

Her announcement was greeted by silence. "There's something wrong with that?" she eventually asked.

"No…"

"You say it like you're ashamed."

"I'm *not* ashamed," Ruth insisted. "I like Paul a great deal and I'm proud of his service to our country." She downplayed her political beliefs as she expanded on her feelings. "I enjoy his letters and like him more than I probably should, but I don't like the fact that he's a soldier."

"You sound confused."

Ruth sighed. That was certainly an accurate description of how she felt.

"So this Paul will be in Seattle on leave?"

"Yes. For two weeks."

"He's coming here to meet you?"

"His family also lives in the area."

"Invite him along for lunch," her grandmother said. "I want to meet him, too."

"You do?" Ruth's enthusiasm swelled. "That's great. I thought of it, but I wasn't sure how you'd feel about having him join us."

"I meant what I said. I want to meet him."

"We've only been writing for a few months. I don't know him well, and…" She let the rest fade.

"It'll be fine, Ruth," her grandmother assured her. Helen

always seemed to understand what Ruth was feeling. She'd found ways to encourage the special bond between them.

"Grandpa was a soldier when you first met him, wasn't he?" Ruth remembered her father telling her this years ago, although he'd also said his mother didn't like to talk about those years. Ruth assumed that was because of Grandpa Sam's bad memories of the war, the awful things he'd seen and experienced in Europe. She knew her grandparents had met during the Second World War, fallen in love and married soon afterward. Ruth's father had been born in the baby boom years that followed, and her uncle Jake had arrived two years later. Ruth was Helen's only granddaughter, but she had three grandsons.

"Oh, yes." She sighed wistfully. "My Sam was so handsome, especially in his uniform." Her voice softened perceptibly.

"How long did you know him before you were married?"

Her grandmother laughed. "Less than a year. In wartime everything's very intense. People married quickly because you never knew if you'd still be alive tomorrow. It was as if those of us who were young had to cram as much life into as short a time as possible."

"The war was terrible, wasn't it?"

Helen sighed before whispering, "All war is terrible."

"I agree," Ruth said promptly.

"So you and this soldier you've never met are discussing marriage?" her grandmother asked after a moment.

"No!" Ruth nearly choked getting out her denial. "Paul

and me? No, of course not. I promise you the subject has never even come up." They hadn't written about kissing or touching or exchanged the conventional romantic endearments. That didn't mean she hadn't *dreamed* about what it would be like to be held by Paul Gordon. To kiss him and be caressed by him. She'd let her imagination roam free....

"So you say," her grandmother said with amusement in her voice. "By all means, bring your friend. I'll look forward to meeting him."

That was no doubt true, Ruth thought, but no one looked forward to meeting Paul Gordon more than she did.

Three

"How do I look?" Ruth asked her roommate. She hated to sound so insecure, but this was perhaps the most important meeting of her life and Ruth was determined to make a perfect impression.

"Fabulous," Lynn said, her face hidden behind the latest issue of *People* magazine.

"I might believe you if you actually looked at me." Ruth held on to her patience with limited success. The relationship with her roommate had gone steadily downhill since the confrontation on the porch steps two weeks earlier. Apparently Clay wasn't interested in dating Lynn. What Ruth did know was that Clay hadn't contacted either of them since, and her roommate had been increasingly cold and standoffish. Ruth had tried to talk to her but that hadn't done any good. She suspected that Lynn *wanted* to be upset, so Ruth had decided to go about her own business and ignore her roommate's disgruntled mood. This might not be the best strategy, but it was the only way she could deal with Lynn's attitude.

Her roommate heaved a sigh; apparently lifting her head a couple of inches required immense effort. Her eyes were devoid of emotion as she gave Ruth a token appraisal. "You look all right, I guess."

These days, that was high praise coming from Lynn. Ruth had spent an hour doing her hair, with the help of a curling iron and two brushes. And now it was raining like crazy. This wasn't the drizzle traditionally associated with the Pacific Northwest, either. This was *rain*. Real rain. Which spelled disaster for her hair, since her umbrella wouldn't afford much protection.

If her hair had taken a long time, choosing what to wear had demanded equal consideration. She had a pretty teal-and-white summer dress from last year that made her eyes look soft and dreamy, but the rain had altered *that* plan. Now she was wearing black pants and a white cashmere sweater with a beige overcoat.

"You're meeting at Ivar's, right?"

"Right." Ruth didn't remember telling her roommate. They were barely on speaking terms.

"Too bad."

"Too bad what?"

Lynn sighed once more and set aside the magazine. "If you must know, soldier boy phoned and said you should meet him outside the restaurant." She grinned nastily. "And in case you haven't noticed, it's pouring out."

"I'm supposed to meet him outside?"

"That's what he said."

Ruth made an effort not to snap at her. "You didn't think to mention this before?"

Lynn shrugged. "It slipped my mind."

Ruth just bet it did. Rather than start an argument, she collected her raincoat, umbrella and purse. Surely she would receive a heavenly reward for controlling her temper. Lynn would love an argument but Ruth wasn't going to give her one; she wasn't going to play childish games with her roommate. The difference in their ages had never seemed more pronounced than it had in the past two weeks.

Because of the rain, Ruth couldn't find convenient street parking and was forced to pay an outrageous amount at a lot near the restaurant. She rushed toward Ivar's, making sure she arrived in plenty of time. Lynn's sour disposition might have upset Ruth if not for the fact that she was finally going to meet the soldier who'd come to mean so much to her.

Focusing on her hair, dress and makeup meant she'd paid almost no attention to something that was far more important—what she'd actually say when she saw Paul for the first time. Ideas skittered through her mind as she crossed the street.

Ruth hoped to sound witty, articulate and well informed. She so badly wanted to impress Paul and was afraid she'd stumble over her words or find herself speechless. Her other fear was that she'd take one look at him and burst into tears. It could happen; she felt very emotional about meeting this man she'd known only through letters and emails.

Thankfully, by the time she reached Ivar's, the rain had slowed to a drizzle. But it was still wet out and miserably gray. Her curls, which had been perfectly styled, had turned into tight wads of frizz in the humid air. She was sure she resembled a cartoon character more than the fashion model she'd strived for earlier that afternoon.

After the longest ten-minute wait of her life, Ruth checked her watch and saw that it was now one minute past six. Paul was late. She pulled her cell phone from her bag; unfortunately Paul didn't answer *his* cell, so she punched out her home number. Perhaps he'd been delayed in traffic and had called the house, hoping to connect with her.

No answer. Either Lynn had left or purposely chosen not to pick up the receiver. Great, just great.

To her dismay, as she went to toss her cell phone back inside her purse, she realized the battery was low. Why hadn't she charged it? Oh, no, that would've been *much* too smart.

All at once Ruth figured it out. Paul wasn't late at all. Somehow she'd missed him, which wouldn't be that difficult with all the tourist traffic on the waterfront. Even in the rain, people milled around the area as if they were on the sunny beaches of Hawaii. Someone needed to explain to these tourists that the water dripping down from the sky was cold rain. Just because they'd dressed for sunshine didn't mean the weather would cooperate.

Despite her umbrella, her hair now hung in tight ringlets all around her head. Either of two things had happened, she speculated. Perhaps her appearance was so drastically changed from the glamour photo she'd sent him that Paul hadn't recognized her and assumed she'd stood him up. The other possibility was even less appealing. Paul had gotten a glimpse of her and decided to escape without saying a word.

For a moment Ruth felt like crying. Rather than waste the last of her cell phone battery phoning her roommate again, she stepped inside the restaurant to see if Paul had left a message for her.

She opened the door and lowered her umbrella. As she did, she saw a tall, lean and very handsome Paul Gordon get up from a chair in the restaurant foyer.

"Ruth?"

"Paul?" Without a thought, she dropped the umbrella and moved directly into his embrace.

Then they were in each other's arms, hugging fiercely.

When it became obvious that everyone in the crowded foyer was staring at them, Paul finally released her.

"I was outside—didn't you tell Lynn that's where we were meeting?"

"No." He brushed the wet curls from her forehead and smiled down at her. "I said inside because I heard on the weather forecast that it was going to rain. And—" he rolled his eyes "—I forgot my cell phone. I'm not used to carry-ing one around."

"Of *course* you said inside." Ruth wanted to kick her-self for being so dense. She should've guessed what Lynn was up to; instead, she'd fallen right into her roommate's petty hands. "I'm so sorry to keep you waiting."

A number of people were still watching them but Ruth didn't care. She couldn't stop looking at Paul. He seemed unable to break eye contact with her, too.

The hostess came forward. "Since your party's arrived," she said with a smile, "I can seat you now."

"Yes, please." Paul helped Ruth off with her coat and set the umbrella beside several others so it could dry. Then, as if they'd known and loved each other all their lives, he reached for her hand and linked her fingers with his as they walked through the restaurant.

The hostess seated them by the window, which over-looked the dark, murky waters of Puget Sound. Rain ran in rivulets down the tempered glass, but as far as Ruth was concerned it could have been the brightest, sunniest day in Seattle's history.

Paul continued to hold her hand on top of the table.

"I was worried about what I'd say once we met," she said. "Then when we did, I just felt so glad, the words didn't seem important."

"I'd almost convinced myself you'd stood me up." He yawned, covering his mouth with the other hand, and she realized he was probably functioning on next to no sleep.

"Stood you up? I would've found a way to get here no matter what." She let the truth of that show in her eyes. She had the strongest feeling of *certainty,* and an involuntary sense that he was everything she'd dreamed.

He briefly looked away. "I would've found a way to get to you, too." His fingers tightened around hers.

"When did you last sleep?" she asked.

His mouth curved upward in a half smile. "I forget. A long time ago. Maybe I should've suggested we meet tomorrow instead, but I didn't want to wait a minute longer than I had to."

"Me, neither," she confessed.

He smiled again, that wonderful, intoxicating smile.

"When did you land?" she asked, because if she didn't stop staring at him she was going to embarrass herself.

"Late this morning," he told her. "My family—well, you know what families are like. Mom's been cooking for days and there was a big family get-together this afternoon. I wanted to invite you but—"

"No, I understand. You couldn't because—well, how could you?" That didn't come out right, but Paul seemed to know what she was trying to say.

"You're exactly like I pictured you," he said, leaning forward to touch her cheek.

"You imagined me drenched?"

He chuckled. "I imagined you beautiful, and you are."

His words made her blush. "I'm having a hard time believing you're actually here," she said.

"I am, too."

The waitress came for their drink order. Ruth hadn't even looked at her menu or thought about what she'd like to drink. Because she was wet and chilled, she ordered hot tea and Paul asked for a bottle of champagne.

"We have reason to celebrate," he announced. Then, as if it had suddenly occurred to him, he said, "You do drink alcohol, don't you?"

She nodded quickly. "Normally I would've asked for wine, but I wanted the tea so I could warm up. I haven't decided what to order yet." She picked up the menu and scanned the entrées.

The waitress brought the champagne and standing ice bucket to the table. "Is there something special you're celebrating?" she asked in a friendly voice.

Paul nodded and his eyes met Ruth's. "We're celebrating the fact that we found each other," he said.

"Excellent." She removed the foil top and wire around the cork and opened the bottle with a slight popping sound. After filling the two champagne flutes, she left.

Ruth took her glass. "Once again, I'm so sorry about what happened. Let me pay for the champagne, please. You wouldn't have had a problem finding me if I'd—"

"I wasn't talking about this evening," he broke in. "I was talking about your Christmas card."

"Oh."

Paul raised his glass; she raised hers, too, and they

clicked the rims gently together. "Do you believe in fate?" he asked.

Ruth smiled. "I didn't, but I've had a change of heart since Christmas."

His smile widened. "Me, too."

Dinner was marvelous. Ruth didn't remember what she'd ordered or anything else about the actual meal. For all she knew, she could've been dining on raw seaweed. It hardly mattered.

They talked and talked, and she felt as if she'd known Paul her entire life. He asked detailed questions about her family, her studies, her plans after graduation, and seemed genuinely interested in everything she said. He talked about the marines and Afghanistan with a sense of pride at the positive differences he'd seen in the country. After dinner and dessert, they lingered over coffee and at nine-thirty Paul paid the tab and suggested they walk along the waterfront. She eagerly agreed. Her umbrella was now merely an encumbrance because the rain had stopped, so they brought it back to her car before they set off.

The clouds had drifted away and the moon was glowing, its light splashing against the pier as they strolled hand in hand. Although she knew Paul had to be exhausted from his long flight and the family gathering, she couldn't deny herself these last few minutes.

"You asked me to keep the weekends free," Ruth murmured, resting her head against his shoulder.

"Did you?"

She sighed. "Not tomorrow."

"Do you have a date with some other guy?"

She leaned back in order to study his face, trying to discern whether he was serious. "You're joking, right?" she said hesitantly.

He shrugged. "Yes and no. You have no obligation to me and vice versa."

"Are *you* seeing someone else?"

"No." His response was immediate.

"I'm not, either," she told him. She wanted to ask how he could even *think* that she would be. "I promised my grandmother I'd visit tomorrow."

"Your grandmother?" he repeated.

"She invited you, too."

He arched his brows.

"In fact, she insisted I bring you."

"So you've mentioned me to your family."

She'd told him in her letters that she hadn't. "Just her. We've become really close. I'm sure you'll enjoy meeting her."

"I'm sure I will, too."

"You'll come, won't you?"

Paul turned Ruth into his arms and gazed down at her. "I don't think I could stay away."

And then he kissed her. Ruth had fantasized about this moment for months. She'd wondered what it would be like when Paul kissed her, but nothing she'd conjured up equaled this reality. Never in all her twenty-five years had she experienced anything like the sensation she felt when Paul's mouth descended on hers. Stars fell from the sky. She saw it happen even with her eyes tightly closed. She heard triumphant music nearby; it seemed to surround her. But once she opened her eyes, all the stars seemed to be exactly where they'd been before. And the music came from somebody's car radio.

Paul wore a stunned look.

"That was…very nice," Ruth managed.

Paul nodded in agreement, then cleared his throat. "Very."

"Should I admit I was afraid of what would happen when we met?" she asked.

"Afraid why? Of what?"

"I didn't know what to expect."

"I didn't either." He slid his hand down her spine and moved a step away. "I'd built this up in my mind."

"I did, too," she whispered.

"I was so afraid you could never live up to my image of you," Paul told her. "I figured we'd meet and I'd get you out of my system. I'd buy you dinner, thank you for your letters and emails—and that would be the end of it. No woman could possibly be everything I'd envisioned you to be. But you are, Ruth, you are."

Although the wind was chilly, his words were enough to warm her from head to foot.

"I didn't think you could be what I'd imagined, either, and I was right," Ruth said.

"You were?" He seemed crestfallen.

She nodded. "Paul, you're even more wonderful than I'd realized." At his relieved expression, she said, "I underestimated how strong my feelings for you are. Look at me, I'm shaking." She held out her hand as evidence of how badly she was trembling after his kiss.

He shook his head. "I feel the same way—nervous and jittery inside."

"That's lack of sleep."

"No," he said, and took her by the shoulders. "That's what your kiss did to me." His eyes glittered as he stared down at her.

"What should we do?" she asked uncertainly.

"You're the one with reservations about falling for a guy in the service."

Her early letters had often referred to her feelings about exactly that. Ruth lowered her gaze. "The fundamental problem hasn't changed," she said. "But you'll eventually get out, won't you?"

He hesitated, and his dark eyes—which had been so warm seconds before—seemed to be closing her out. "Eventually I'll leave the marines, but you should know it won't be anytime in the near future. I'm in for the long haul, and if you want to continue this relationship, the sooner you accept that, the better."

Ruth didn't want their evening to end on a negative note. When she'd answered his letter that first time, she'd known he was a military man and it hadn't stopped her.

She'd gone into this with her eyes wide open. "I don't have to decide right away, do I?"

"No," he admitted. "But—"

"Good," she said, cutting him off. She couldn't allow their differences to come between them so quickly. She sensed that Paul, too, wanted to push all that aside. When she slipped her arms around his waist and hugged him, he hugged her back. "You're exhausted. Let's meet in the morning. I'll take you over to visit my grandmother and we can talk some more then."

Ruth rested her head against his shoulder again and Paul kissed her hair. "You're making this difficult," he said.

"I know. I'm sorry."

"Me, too," he whispered.

Ruth knew they'd need to confront the issue soon. She could also see that settling it wasn't going to be as easy as she'd hoped.

Four

Paul met Ruth at the Seattle terminal at ten the next morning and they walked up the ramp to board the Bremerton ferry. The hard rain of the night before had yielded to glorious sunshine.

Unlike the previous evening, when Paul and Ruth had talked nonstop through a three-hour dinner, it seemed that now they had little to say. The one big obstacle in their relationship hung between them. They sat side by side on the wooden bench and sipped hot coffee as the ferry eased away from the Seattle dock.

"You're still thinking about last night, aren't you?" Ruth said, carefully broaching the subject after a lengthy silence. "About you being in the military, I mean, and my objections to the war in Iraq?"

He nodded. "Yeah, there's the political aspect and also

the fact that you don't seem comfortable with the concept of military life," he said.

"I'm not, really, but we'll work it out," she told him, and reached for his free hand, entwining their fingers. "We'll find a way."

Paul didn't look as if he believed her. But after a couple of minutes, he seemed to come to some sort of decision. He brought her hand to his lips. "Let's enjoy the time we have today, all right?"

Ruth smiled in agreement.

"Tell me about your grandmother."

Ruth was more than willing to change the subject. "This is my paternal grandmother, and she's lived in Cedar Cove for the past thirty years. She and my grandfather moved there from Seattle after he retired because they wanted a slower pace of life. I barely remember my grandfather Sam. He died when I was two, before I had any real memories of him."

"He died young," Paul commented sympathetically.

"Yes… My grandmother's been alone for a long time."

"She probably has good friends in a town like Cedar Cove."

"Yes," Ruth said. "And she's still got friends she's had since the war. It's something I admire about my grandmother," she continued. "She's my inspiration, and not only because she speaks three languages fluently and is one of the most intelligent women I know. Ever since I can remember, she's been helping others. Although she's in her eighties, Grandma's involved with all kinds of charities and social groups. When I enrolled at the University of Washington, I intended for the two of us to get together often, but I swear her schedule's even busier than mine."

Paul grinned at her. "I know what you mean. It's the same in my family."

By the time they stepped off the Bremerton ferry and took the foot ferry across to Cedar Cove, it was after eleven. They stopped at a deli, where Paul bought a loaf of fresh bread and a bottle of Washington State gewürztraminer to take with them. At quarter to twelve, they trudged up the hill toward her grandmother's duplex on Poppy Lane.

When they arrived, Helen greeted them at the front door and ushered Paul and Ruth into the house. Ruth hugged her grandmother, whose white hair was cut stylishly short. Helen was thinner than the last time Ruth had visited and seemed more fragile somehow. Her grandmother paused to give Paul an embarrassingly frank look. Ruth felt her face heat as Helen spoke.

"So, you're the young man who's captured my granddaughter's heart."

"Grandma, this is Paul Gordon," Ruth said hurriedly, gesturing toward Paul.

"This is the soldier you've been writing to, who's fighting in Afghanistan?"

"I am." Paul's response sounded a bit defensive, Ruth thought. He obviously preferred not to discuss it.

In an effort to ward off any misunderstanding, Ruth added, "My grandfather was a soldier when Grandma met him."

Helen nodded, and a faraway look stole over her. It took her a moment to refocus. "Come, both of you," she said, stepping between them. She tucked her arm around Ruth's waist. "I set the table outside. It's such a beautiful afternoon, I thought we'd eat on the patio."

"We brought some bread and a bottle of wine," Ruth said. "Paul got them."

"Lovely. Thank you, Paul."

While Ruth sliced the fresh-baked bread, he opened the wine, then helped her grandmother carry the salad plates outside. An apple pie cooled on the kitchen counter and the scent of cinnamon permeated the sunlit kitchen.

They chatted throughout the meal; the conversation was light and friendly as they lingered over their wine. Every now and then Ruth caught her grandmother staring at Paul with the strangest expression on her face. Ruth didn't know what to make of this. It almost seemed as if her grandmother was trying to place him, to recall where she'd seen him before.

Helen had apparently read Ruth's mind. "Am I embarrassing your beau, sweetheart?" she asked with a half smile.

Ruth resisted informing her grandmother that Paul wasn't her anything, especially not her beau. They'd had one lovely dinner together, but now their political differences seemed to have overtaken them.

"I apologize, Paul." Helen briefly touched his hand, which rested on the table. "When I first saw you—" She stopped abruptly. "You resemble someone I knew many years ago."

"Where, Grandma?" Ruth asked.

"In France, during the war."

"You were in France during World War II?" Ruth couldn't quite hide her shock.

Helen turned to her. "I haven't spoken much about those days, but now, toward the end of my life, I think about them more and more." She pushed back her chair and stood.

Ruth stood, too, thinking her grandmother was about to carry in their empty plates and serve the pie.

Helen motioned her to sit. "Stay here. There's something I want you to see. I think perhaps it's time."

When her grandmother had left them, Ruth looked at Paul and shrugged. "I have no idea what's going on."

Paul had been wonderful with her grandmother, thoughtful and attentive. He'd asked a number of questions during the meal—about Cedar Cove, about her life with Sam—and listened intently when she responded. Ruth knew his interest was genuine. Together they cleared the table and returned the dishes to the kitchen, then waited for Helen at the patio table.

It was at least five minutes before she came back. She held a rolled-up paper that appeared to be some kind of poster, old enough to have yellowed with age. Carefully she opened it and laid it flat on the cleared table. Ruth saw that the writing was French. In the center of the poster, which measured about eighteen inches by twenty-four, was a pencil sketch of two faces: a man and a woman, whose names she didn't recognize. Jean and Marie Brulotte.

"Who's that?" Ruth asked, pointing to the female.

Her grandmother smiled calmly. "I am that woman."

Ruth frowned. Helen had obviously used a false name, and although she'd seen photographs of her grandmother as a young woman, this sketch barely resembled the woman she knew. The man in the drawing, however, seemed familiar. Gazing at the sketch for a minute, she realized the face was vaguely like Paul's. Not so much in any similarity of features as in a quality of…character, she supposed.

"And the man?"

"That was Jean-Claude," Helen whispered, her voice full of pain.

Paul turned to Ruth, but she was at a complete loss and didn't know what to tell him. Her grandfather's name was Sam and she'd never heard of this Jean or Jean-Claude. Certainly her father had never mentioned another man in his mother's life.

"This is a wanted poster," Paul remarked. "I speak some French—studied it in school."

"Yes. The Germans offered a reward of one million francs to anyone who turned us in."

"You were in France during the war and you were

wanted?" This was more than Ruth could assimilate. She sat back down; so did her grandmother. Paul remained standing for a moment longer as he studied the poster.

"But…it said Marie. Marie Brulotte."

"I went by my middle name in those days. Marie. You may not be aware that it was part of my name because I haven't used it since."

"But…"

"You and Jean-Claude were part of the French Resistance?" Paul asked. It was more statement than question.

"We were." Her grandmother seemed to have difficulty speaking. "Jean-Claude was my husband. We married during the war, and I took his name with pride. He was my everything, strong and handsome and brave. His laughter filled a room. Sometimes, still, I think I can hear him." Her eyes grew teary and she dabbed at them with her linen handkerchief. "That was many years ago now and, as I said, I think perhaps it's time I spoke of it."

Ruth was grateful. She couldn't let her grandmother leave the story untold. She suspected her father hadn't heard any of this, and she wanted to learn whatever she could about this unknown episode in their family history before it was forever lost.

"What were you doing in France?" Ruth asked. She couldn't comprehend that the woman she'd always known as a warm and loving grandmother, who baked cookies and knit socks for Christmas, had been a freedom fighter in a foreign country.

"I was attending the Sorbonne when the Germans invaded. You may recall that my mother was born in France, but her own parents were long dead. I was studying French literature. My parents were frantic for me to book my passage home, but like so many others in France, I didn't believe the country would fall. I assured my mother I'd leave when I felt it was no longer safe. Being young and foolish, I thought she was overreacting. Besides, I was in love. Jean-Claude had asked me to marry him, and what woman in love wishes to leave her lover over rumors of war?" She laughed lightly, shaking her head. "France seemed invincible. We were convinced the Germans wouldn't invade, convinced they'd suffer a humiliating defeat if they tried."

"So when it happened you were trapped," Paul said.

Her grandmother drew in a deep breath. "There was the Blitzkrieg.... People were demoralized and defeated when France surrendered after only a few days of fighting. We were aghast that such a thing could happen. Jean-Claude and a few of his friends decided to resist the occupation. I decided I would, too, so we were married right away. My parents knew nothing of this."

"How did you join the Resistance?" Paul asked as Ruth looked at her grandmother with fresh eyes.

"Join," she repeated scornfully. "There was no place to *join,* no place to sign up and be handed a weapon and an instruction manual. A group of us students, naive and foolish, offered resistance to the German occupation. Later we learned there were other groups, eventually united under the leadership of General de Gaulle. We soon found one another. Jean-Claude and I—we were young and too stupid to understand the price we'd pay, but by then we'd already lost some of our dearest friends. Jean-Claude and I refused to let them die in vain."

"What did you do?" Ruth breathed. She leaned closer to her grandmother.

"Whatever we could, which in the beginning was pitifully little. The Germans suffered more casualties in traffic accidents. At first our resistance was mostly symbolic." A slow smile spread across her weathered face. "But we learned, oh yes, we learned."

Ruth was still having difficulty taking it all in. She pressed her hand to her forehead. She found it hard enough to believe that the sketch of the female in this worn poster was her own grandmother. Then to discover that the fragile, petite woman at her side had been part of the French Resistance...

"Does my dad know any of this?" Ruth asked.

Helen sighed heavily. "I'm not sure, but I doubt it. Sam might have mentioned it to him. I've only told a few of my friends. No one else." She shook her head. "I didn't feel I could talk to my sons about it. There was too much that's disturbing. Too many painful memories."

"Did you...did you ever have to kill anyone?" Ruth had trouble even getting the question out.

"Many times," Helen answered bluntly. "Does that surprise you?"

It shocked Ruth to the point that she couldn't ask anything else.

"The first time was the hardest," her grandmother said. "I was held by a French policeman." She added something derogatory in French, and although Ruth couldn't understand the language, some things didn't need translation. "Under Vichy, some of the police worked hard to prove to the Germans what good little boys they were," she muttered, this time in English. "I'd been stopped and questioned, detained by this pig of a man. He said he was taking me to the police station. I had a small gun with me that I'd hidden, a seven millimeter."

Ruth's heart raced as she listened to Helen recount this adventure.

"The pig didn't drive me to the police station. Instead he headed for open country and I knew that once he was outside town and away from the eyes of any witnesses, he would rape and murder me."

Ruth pressed her hand to her mouth, holding back a gasp of horror.

"You'd trained in self-defense?" Paul asked.

Her grandmother laughed. "No. How could we? There was no time for such lessons. But I realized that I didn't need technique. What I needed was nerve. This beast of a man pulled his gun on me but I was quicker. I shot him in the head." She paused at the memory of that terrifying moment. "I buried him myself in a field and, as far as I know, he was never found." She wore a small satisfied look. "His mistake," she murmured, "was that he tightened his jaw when he reached for his gun—and I saw. I'd been watching him closely. He was thinking of what might happen, of what could go wrong. He was a professional, and I was only nineteen, and yet I knew that if I didn't act then, it would've been too late."

"Didn't *you* worry about what could happen?" Ruth asked, unable to grasp how her grandmother could ever shoot another human being.

"No," Helen answered flatly. "I *knew* what would happen. We all did. We didn't have a chance of surviving, none of us. My parents would never have discovered my fate—I would simply have disappeared. They didn't even know I'd married Jean-Claude or changed my name." She stared out at the water. "I don't understand why I lived. It makes no sense that God would spare me when all my friends, all those I loved, were killed."

"Jean-Claude, too?"

Her eyes filled and she slowly nodded.

"Where was he when you were taken by the policeman?" Paul asked.

Her grandmother's mouth trembled. "By then, Jean-Claude had been captured."

"The French police?"

"No," she said in the thinnest of whispers. "Jean-Claude was being held by the Gestapo. That was the first time they got him—but not the last."

Ruth had heard about the notorious German soldiers and their cruelty.

Helen straightened, and her back went rigid. "I could only imagine how those monsters were torturing my husband." Contempt hardened her voice.

"What did you do?" Ruth glanced at Paul, whose gaze remained riveted on her grandmother.

At first Helen didn't answer. "What else could I do? I had to rescue him."

"You?" Paul asked this with the same shock Ruth felt.

"Yes, me and…" Helen's smile was fleeting. "I was very clever about it, too." The sadness returned with such intensity that it brought tears to Ruth's eyes.

"They eventually killed him, didn't they?" she asked, hardly able to listen to her grandmother's response.

"No," Helen said as she turned to face Ruth. "I did."

Five

"You killed Jean-Claude?" Ruth repeated incredulously.

Tears rolling down her cheeks, Helen nodded. "God forgive me, but I had no choice. I couldn't allow him to be tortured any longer. He begged me to do it, begged me to end his suffering. That was the second time he was captured, and they were more determined than ever to break him. He knew far too much."

"You'd better start at the beginning. You went into Gestapo headquarters?" Paul moved closer as if he didn't want to risk missing even one word. "Was that the first time or the second?"

"Both. The first time, in April 1943, I rescued him. I pretended I was pregnant and brought a priest to the house the Gestapo had taken over. I insisted with great bravado that they force Jean-Claude to marry me and give my baby a name. I didn't care if they killed him, I said, but before he died I wanted him to give my baby his name." She paused. "I was very convincing."

"So you weren't really pregnant?" Ruth asked.

"No, of course not," her grandmother replied. "It was a ploy to get into the house."

"Was the priest a real priest?"

"Yes. He didn't know I was using him, but I had no alternative. I was desperate to get Jean-Claude out alive."

"The priest knew nothing," Ruth said, meeting Paul's eyes, astounded by her grandmother's nerve and cunning.

"The Father knew nothing," the older woman concurred, smiling grimly. "But I needed him, so I used him. Thankfully the Gestapo believed me, and because they wanted to keep relations with the Church as smooth as possible, they brought Jean-Claude into the room."

Ruth could picture the scene, but she didn't know if she'd ever possess that kind of bravery.

"Jean-Claude was in terrible pain, but he nearly laughed out loud when the priest asked him if he was the father of my child. Fortunately he didn't have to answer because our friends had arranged a distraction outside the house. A firebomb was tossed into a parked vehicle, which exploded. All but two Gestapo left the room. I shot them both right in front of the priest, and then Jean-Claude and I escaped through a back window."

"Where did you find the courage?" Ruth asked breathlessly.

"Courage?" her grandmother echoed. "That wasn't courage. That was fear. I would do anything to save my husband's life—and I did. Then, only a few weeks later, I was the one who killed him. What took courage was finding the will to live after Jean-Claude died. *That* was courage, and I would never have managed if it hadn't been for the American soldier who saved my life. If it hadn't been for Sam."

"He was my grandfather," Ruth explained to Paul.

"I want to know more about Jean-Claude," Paul said, placing his arm around Ruth's shoulders. It felt good to be held by him and she leaned into his strength, his solid warmth.

Her grandmother's eyes grew weary and she shook her head. "Perhaps another day. I'm tired now, too tired to speak anymore."

"We should go," Paul whispered.

"I'll do the dishes," Ruth insisted.

"Nonsense. You should leave now," Helen said. "You have better things to do than talk to an old lady."

"But we *want* to talk to you," Ruth told her.

"You will." Helen looked even more drawn. "Soon, but not right now."

"You'll finish the story?"

"Yes," the old woman said hoarsely. "I promise I'll tell you everything."

While her grandmother went to her room to rest, Ruth and Paul cleaned up the kitchen. At first they worked in silence, as if they weren't quite sure what to say to each other. Ruth put the food away while Paul rinsed the dishes and set them inside the dishwasher.

"You didn't know any of this before today?" he asked, propping himself against the counter.

"Not a single detail."

"Your father never mentioned it?"

"Never." Ruth wondered again how much her father actually knew about his mother's wartime adventures. "I'm sure you were the one who prompted her."

"Me?" Paul asked. "How?"

"More than anything, I think you reminded her of Jean-Claude." Ruth tilted her head to one side. "It's as if this woman I've known all my life has suddenly become a stranger." Ruth finished wiping down the counters. She knew they'd need to leave soon if they were going to catch the ferry.

"Maybe you'd better check on her before we go," Paul said.

She agreed and hurried out of the kitchen. Her grandmother's eyes opened briefly when Ruth entered the cool, silent room. Reaching for an afghan at the foot of the bed, Ruth covered her with it and kissed the papery skin of her cheek. She'd always loved Helen, but she had an entirely new respect for her now.

"I'll be back soon," Ruth promised.

"Bring your young man."

"I will."

Helen's response was low, and at first Ruth didn't understand her and strained to hear. Gradually her voice drifted off. Ruth waited until Helen was asleep before she slipped out of the room.

"She's sleeping?" Paul asked, setting aside the magazine he was reading when Ruth returned to the kitchen.

Ruth nodded. "She started talking to me in French. I so badly wish I knew what she said."

They left a few minutes later. Absorbed in her own thoughts, Ruth walked down the hill beside Paul, neither of them speaking as they approached the foot ferry that would take them from Cedar Cove to Bremerton.

Once they were aboard, Paul went to get them coffee from the concession stand. While he was gone, Ruth decided she had to find out how much her family knew about her grandmother's war exploits. She opened her purse and rummaged for her cell phone.

Paul brought the coffee and set her plastic cup on the table.

Ruth glanced up long enough to thank him with a smile. "I'm calling my parents."

Paul nodded, tentatively sipping hot coffee. Then, in an obvious effort to give her some privacy, he moved to stand by the rail, gazing out at the water.

Her father answered on the third ring. "Dad, it's Ruth," she said in a rush.

"Ruthie! It's nice to hear from you."

Her father had never enjoyed telephone conversations and generally handed the phone off to Ruth's mother.

"Wait—I need to talk to you," Ruth said.

"What's up?"

That was her dad, too. He didn't like chitchat and wanted to get to the point as quickly as possible.

"I went over to see Grandma this afternoon."

"How is she? We've been meaning to get up there and see her *and* you. I don't know where the time goes. Thanksgiving was our last visit."

How is she? Ruth wasn't sure what to say. Her grandmother seemed fragile and old, and Ruth had never thought of her as either. "I don't know, Dad. She's the same, except—well, except she might have lost a few pounds." Ruth looked over at Paul and bit her lip. "I...brought a friend along with me."

"Your roommate? What's her name again?"

"Lynn Blumenthal. No, this is a male friend."

That caught her father's attention. "Someone from school?"

"No, we met sort of...by accident. His name is Paul Gordon and he's a sergeant in the marines. We've been corresponding for the past four months. But Paul isn't the reason I'm phoning."

"All right, then. What is?"

Ruth dragged in a deep breath. "Like I said before, I was visiting Grandma."

"With this marine you're seeing," he reiterated.

"Yes." Ruth didn't dare look at Paul a second time. Nervously, she tucked a strand of hair behind her ear and leaned forward, lowering her voice. "Grandma was in France during World War II. Did you know that?"

Her father paused. "Yes, I did."

"Were you aware that she was a member of the French Resistance?"

Again he paused. "My father said something shortly before he died, but I never got any more information."

"Didn't you ask your mother?"

"I tried, but she refused to talk about it. She said some things were better left buried and deflected all my questions. Do you mean to say she told you about this?"

"Yes, and, Dad, the stories were incredible! Did you know Grandma was married before she met Grandpa Sam?"

"What?"

"Her husband's name was Jean-Claude."

"A Frenchman?"

"Yes." She tried to recall his surname from the poster. "Jean-Claude...Brulotte. That's it. He was part of the movement, too, and Grandma, your *mother,* went into a Gestapo headquarters and managed to get him out."

"My mother?" The question was loud enough for Paul to hear from several feet away, because his eyebrows shot up as their eyes met.

"Yes, Dad, *your* mother. I was desperate to learn more, but she got tired all of a sudden, and neither Paul nor I wanted to overtax her. She's taking a nap now, and Paul and I are on the ferry back to Seattle."

Ruth heard her father take a long, ragged breath.

"All these years and she's never said a word to me. My dad did, as I told you, but he didn't give me any details, and I never believed Mom's involvement amounted to much—more along the lines of moral support, I always figured. My dad was over there and we knew that's where he met Mom."

"Did they ever go back to France?" Ruth asked.

"No. They did some traveling, but mostly in North America—Florida, Mexico, Quebec…"

"I guess she really was keeping the past buried," Ruth said.

"She must realize she's getting near the end of her life," her father went on, apparently thinking out loud. "And she wants us to know. I'm grateful she was willing to share this with you. Still, it's pretty hard to take in. My mother…part of the French Resistance. She told me she was in school over there."

"She was." Ruth didn't want her father to think Helen had lied to him.

"Then how in heaven's name did she get involved in that?"

"It's a long story."

"What made her start talking about it now?" her father asked.

"I think it's because she knows she's getting old, as you suggested," Ruth said. "And because of Paul."

"Ah, yes, this young man you're with."

"Yeah."

Her father hesitated. "I know you can't discuss this with Paul there, so give us a call later, will you? Your mother's going to want to hear about this young man."

"Yes, Daddy," she said, thinking with some amusement that she sounded like an obedient child.

"I'll call Mom this evening," her father said. "We need to set up a visit ourselves, possibly for the Memorial Day weekend."

After a quick farewell, she clicked off the phone and put it back in her purse.

Paul, still sipping his coffee, approached her again. She picked up her own cup as he sat down beside her.

"I haven't enjoyed an afternoon more in years," Paul said. "Not in years," he added emphatically.

Ruth grinned, then drank some of her cooling coffee. "I'd like to believe it was my company that was so engaging, but I know you're enthralled with my grandmother."

"And her granddaughter," Paul murmured, but he said it as if he felt wary of the fact that he found her appealing.

Ruth took his hand. "We haven't settled anything," he reminded her, tightening his hold on her fingers.

"Do we have to right this minute?"

He didn't answer.

"I want to see you again," she told him, moving closer.

"That's the problem. I want to see you again, too."

"I'm glad." Ruth didn't hide her relief.

Paul's responding smile was brief. "Fine. We'll do this your way—one day at a time. But remember, I only have two weeks' leave."

She could sense already that these would be the shortest two weeks of her life.

"By the time I ship out, we should know how we feel. Agreed?"

"Agreed."

He nodded solemnly. "Do you own a pair of in-line skates?" he asked unexpectedly.

"Sure, but I don't have them in Seattle. I can easily rent a pair, though."

"Want to go skating?"

"When?"

"Now?"

Ruth laughed. "I'd love to, with one stipulation."

"What's that?"

Ruth hated to admit how clumsy she was on skates. "If I fall down, promise you'll help me up."

"I can do that."

"If I get hurt…"

"If you get hurt," Paul said, "I promise to kiss you and make it better."

Ruth had the distinct feeling that she wasn't going to mind falling, not one little bit.

Six

Helen Shelton
5-B Poppy Lane
Cedar Cove, Washington
April 23

Dearest Charlotte,
Forgive me for writing rather than calling. It must
seem odd, since we're neighbors as well as friends.
It's just that sometimes writing things out makes it
easier to think them through....
I have some news, by the way. You haven't met my
granddaughter, Ruth, but you've heard me speak of
her. Well, she was over last week with a soldier she's
been writing to, who's on leave from Afghanistan.
He's a delightful young man and it was easy to see

that her feelings for him are quite intense. His name is Paul Gordon. When Ruth first introduced us, I'm afraid I embarrassed us both by staring at him. Paul could've been Jean-Claude's grandson, the resemblance is that striking.

For the past few weeks, I've been remembering and dreaming about my war experiences. You've encouraged me for years to write them down. I've tried, but couldn't make myself do it. However… I don't know if this was wise but I told Ruth and her young man some of what happened to me in France. I know I shocked them both.

My son phoned later the same day, and John was quite upset with me, especially since I'd told Ruth and not him. I tried to explain that these were memories I've spent most of my life trying to forget. I do hope he understands. But Pandora's box is open now, and my family wants to learn everything they can. I've agreed to allow Ruth to tape our conversations, which satisfies everyone. I'm afraid you're right, my dear friend—I should've told my children long ago.

Do take care of yourself and Ben. I hope to see you soon.

Bless you, dear Charlotte,

Your friend always,

Helen

"I want you to meet my family," Paul said a little more than a week after their first date. They'd spent every available moment together; they'd been to the Seattle Center and the Space Needle, rowing on Lake Washington, out to dinner and had seen a couple of movies. Sitting on the campus lawn, he'd been waiting for Ruth after her last class of the day. He stood when she reached him, and Ruth saw that he wasn't smiling as he issued the invitation.

"When?"

"Mom and Dad are at the house."

"You mean you want me to meet them *now?*" Ruth asked as they strolled across the lush green grass toward the visitors' parking lot. If she'd known she was meeting Paul's parents she would've been better prepared. She would've done something about her hair and worn a different outfit and…

"Yeah," Paul muttered.

Ruth stopped and he walked forward two or three steps before he noticed. Frowning, he glanced back.

"What's going on here?" she asked, clutching her books to her chest.

Paul looked everywhere but at her. "My parents feel they should meet you, since I'm spending most of my time in your company. The way they figure it, you must be someone important in my life."

Ruth's heart did a happy little jig. "Am I?" she asked flirtatiously.

A rigid expression came over him, betraying none of his feelings. "I don't know the answer to that yet."

"Really?" she teased.

"Listen, Ruth, I'm not handing you my heart so you can break it. You don't want to be involved with a soldier. Well, I'm a soldier, and either you accept that or at the end of these two weeks, it's over."

He sounded so...so military. As if he thought a relationship could be that simple, that straightforward. Life didn't divide evenly into black and white. There were plenty of gray areas, too. All right, so Paul had a point. In the back of her mind, Ruth hoped that, given time, Paul would decide to get out of the war business. She wasn't the kind of woman who'd be content to sit at home while the man she loved was off in some faraway country risking his life. Experiencing dreadful things. Suffering. Maybe dying.

"You'd rather I didn't meet your family?" she asked.

"Right."

That hurt. "I see."

Some of her pain must have been evident in her voice, because Paul came toward her and tucked his finger beneath her chin. Their eyes met for the longest moment. "If my family meets you, they'll know how much I care about you," he said quietly.

Ruth managed to smile. "I'm glad you care, because I care about you, too," she admitted. "A *lot*."

"That doesn't solve anything."

"No, it doesn't," she said, leaning forward so their lips could meet. She half expected Paul to pull away, but he didn't.

Instead, he groaned and forcefully brought his mouth

to hers. Their kiss was passionate, deep—honest. She felt the sharp edges of her textbooks digging painfully into her breasts, and still Ruth melted in his arms.

"You're making things impossible," he mumbled when he lifted his head from hers.

"I've been known to do that."

Paul reached for her hand and led her into the parking lot. "I mentioned your grandmother to my parents," he said casually as he unlocked the car doors.

"Ah," Ruth said, slipping into the passenger seat. "That explains it."

"Explains what?"

"Why your family wants to meet me. I've brought you to *my* family. They feel cheated."

Paul shook his head solemnly. "I really don't think that's it. But…speaking of your grandmother, when can we see her again?"

"Tomorrow afternoon, if you like. I talked to her this morning before my classes and she asked when we could make a return visit."

"You're curious about what happened, aren't you?" Paul asked as he inserted the key into the ignition.

"Very much," Ruth said. Since their visit to Cedar Cove, she'd thought about her grandmother's adventures again and again. She'd done some research, too, using the internet and a number of library books on the war. In fact, Ruth was so fascinated by the history of the Resistance movement, she'd found it difficult to concentrate on the psychology essay she was trying to write.

She'd had several days to become accustomed to the idea of Helen's exploits during the Second World War. And yet she still had trouble imagining the woman she knew as a fighter for the French Resistance.

"She loved Jean-Claude," Paul commented.

Ruth nodded. Her grandmother had loved her husband enough to kill him—a shocking reality that would not have made sense at any other time in Helen's life. And then, at some point after that, Helen had met her Sam. How? Ruth wondered. Helen said he'd rescued her, but what were the circumstances? When did they fall in love? Family history told her that Sam Shelton had fought in the European campaign during the Second World War. He'd been in France toward the end of the war, she recalled. How much had he known about Helen's past?

Ruth could only hope her grandmother would provide some answers tomorrow.

The meeting with Paul's family was going well. Ruth was charmed by his parents, who immediately welcomed her. Barbara, his mother, had an easy laugh and a big heart. She brought Ruth into the kitchen and settled her on a stool at the counter while she fussed with the dinner salad.

Paul and his father, Greg, were on the patio, firing up the grill and chatting. Every now and then, Ruth caught Paul stealing a glance in her direction.

"I want to help," Ruth told his mother.

"Nonsense," Barbara Gordon said as she tore lettuce leaves into a large wooden bowl. "I'm just so pleased to finally meet you. It was as if Paul had some secret he was keeping from us."

Ruth smiled and sipped her glass of iced tea.

"My father was career military—in the marines," Barbara said, chopping tomatoes for the salad. "I don't know if that was what induced Paul to join the military or not, but I suspect it had an influence."

"How do you feel about him being stationed so far from home?" Ruth asked, curious to hear his mother's perspective. She couldn't imagine any mother wanting to see her son or daughter at that kind of risk.

Barbara sighed. "I don't like it, if that's what you're asking. Every sane person hates war. My father didn't want to fight in World War II, and I cried my eyes out the day Greg left for Vietnam. Now here's my oldest son in Afghanistan."

"It seems most generations are called upon to serve their country, doesn't it?" Ruth said.

Barbara agreed with a short nod. "Freedom isn't free—for us or for the countries we support. Granted, in hindsight some of the conflicts we've been involved in seem misguided, but unfortunately war appears to be part of the human condition."

"Why?" Ruth asked, although she didn't really expect a response.

"I think every generation has asked that same question," Barbara said thoughtfully, putting the salad aside. She began to prepare a dressing, pouring olive oil and balsamic vinegar into a small bowl. "Paul told me you have a problem with his unwillingness to leave the marines at the end of his commitment. Is that right?"

A little embarrassed by the question, Ruth nodded. "I do."

"The truth is, as his mother, I want Paul out of the marines, too, but that isn't a decision you or I can make for him. My son has always been his own person. That's how his father and I raised him."

Ruth's gaze followed Paul as he stood with his father by the barbecue. He looked up and saw her, frowning as if he knew exactly what she and his mother were talking about. Ruth gave him a reassuring wave.

"You're in love with him, aren't you?" his mother asked, watching her closely.

The question took Ruth by surprise. "I'm afraid I am." Ruth didn't *want* to be—something she hadn't acknowledged openly until this moment. He'd described his reluctance to hand her his heart to break. She felt the same way and feared he'd end up breaking hers.

There seemed to be a tacit agreement not to broach these difficult subjects during dinner.

The four of them sat on the patio around a big table, shaded by a large umbrella. His mother had made corn bread as well as the salad, and the steaks were grilled to perfection. After dinner, Ruth helped with the cleanup and then Paul made their excuses.

"We're going to a movie?" she whispered on their way out the door, figuring he'd used that as a convenient pretext for leaving.

"I had to get you out of there before my mother started showing you my baby pictures."

"I'll bet you were a real cutie."

"You should see my brother and sister, especially the nude photos."

Ruth giggled.

Instead of the theater, they headed for Lake Washington and walked through the park, licking ice-cream cones, talking and laughing. Ruth couldn't remember laughing with anyone as much as she did with Paul.

He dropped her off after ten, walked her up to the front porch and kissed her good-night.

"I'll pick you up at noon," he said. "After your morning class."

"Noon," she repeated, her arms linked around his neck. That seemed too long. Despite her fears, despite the looming doubts, she *was* in love with him.

"You're sure your grandmother's up to having company so soon?" he asked.

"Yes." Ruth pressed her forehead against his shoulder. "I think the real question's whether we're ready for the next installment. I don't know if I can bear to hear exactly what happened to Jean-Claude."

"Perhaps not, but she needs to tell us."

"Yes," Ruth said. "She couldn't talk about it before."

"I know." Paul kissed her again.

Ruth felt at peace in his arms. Only when she stopped to think about the future, *their* future, did she become uncertain and confused.

Seven

Ruth and Paul sat with Helen at the kitchen table in her Cedar Cove house as rain dripped rhythmically against the windowpane. The day was overcast and dreary, as it frequently was during spring in the Pacific Northwest.

Helen reached for the teapot in the middle of the table and filled each of their cups, then offered them freshly baked peanut-butter cookies arranged on a small dessert plate. Ruth recognized the plate from her childhood. She and her grandmother had often had tea together when she was a youngster. Her visits to Cedar Cove were special; her grandmother had listened while Ruth chattered endlessly, sharing girlish confidences. It was during those private little tea parties that they'd bonded, grandmother and granddaughter.

Today the slow ritual of pouring tea and passing around

cookies demanded patience. Ruth badly wanted to throw questions at Helen, but she could see that her grandmother would resume her story only when she was ready. Helen seemed to be bracing herself for this next installment.

"I've been thinking about the things I mentioned on your last visit," Helen finally said, sipping her tea. Steam rose from the delicate bone-china cup. "It was a lot for you to absorb at one time."

"I didn't know *anything* about your adventures, Grandma." And they truly were adventures, of a kind few people experienced these days. *Real* adventures, with real and usually involuntary risks.

Helen grimaced. "My children didn't, either. But as I said before, it's time." Helen set the fragile cup back in its saucer. "Your father phoned and asked me about all of this." She paused, a look of distress on her face. "I hope he'll forgive me for keeping it from him all these years."

"I'm sure he will," Ruth told her.

Helen obviously wanted to believe that. "He asked me to tell him more, but I couldn't," she said sadly.

"I'm sure Dad understood."

"I couldn't relive those memories again so soon."

Ruth laid a comforting hand on her grandmother's arm. This information of Helen's was an important part of her family history. Today, with Helen's agreement, she'd come prepared with a small tape recorder. Now nothing would be lost.

"Jean-Claude had a wonderful gift," her grandmother

said, breaking into the story without preamble. "He was a big man who made friends easily—a natural leader. Our small group trusted him with our lives."

Paul smiled encouragingly.

"Within a few minutes of meeting someone, he could figure out if he should trust that person," Helen continued. "More and more people wanted to join us. We started with a few students like ourselves, who were determined to resist the Nazis. Soon, others found us and we connected with groups across France. We all worked together as we lit fires of hope."

"Tell me about the wanted poster with your picture and Jean-Claude's," Ruth said.

Her grandmother smiled ruefully, as if that small piece of notoriety embarrassed her. "I'm afraid Jean-Claude and I acquired a somewhat exaggerated reputation. Soon almost everything that happened in Paris as part of the Resistance movement was attributed to us, whether we were involved or not."

"Such as?"

"There was a fire in a supply depot. Jean-Claude and I wished we'd been responsible, but we weren't. Yet that was what prompted the Germans to post our pictures." A smile brightened her eyes. "It was a rather unflattering sketch of Jean-Claude, he told me, although I disagreed."

"Can you tell me some of the anti-Nazi activities you were able to undertake?" Ruth asked, knowing her father would want to hear as much of this as his mother could recall.

Helen considered the question. "Perhaps the most daring adventure was one of Jean-Claude's. There was an SS officer, a horrible man, a pig." This word was spit out, as if even the memory of him disgusted her. "Jean-Claude discovered that this officer had obtained information through torturing a fellow Resistance member, information that put us all at risk. Jean-Claude decided the man had to die and that he would be the one to do it."

Paul glanced at Ruth, and he seemed to tell her that killing an SS officer would be no easy task.

Helen sipped her tea once more. "I feared for Jean-Claude."

"Is this when he…died?" Ruth asked.

"No." For emphasis, her grandmother shook her head. "That came later."

"Go on," Paul urged.

"One night Jean-Claude left me and another woman in a garden in the suburbs, at the home of a sympathetic schoolteacher who'd made contact with our group. He and his wife went out for the evening. Jean-Claude instructed us to dig a grave and fill it with quicklime. We were to wait there for his return. He left with two other men and I was convinced I'd never see him again."

"But you did," Ruth said.

The old woman nodded. "According to Jean-Claude, it

was either kill the SS officer or he would take us all down. He simply knew too much."

"What did Jean-Claude do?"

"That is a story unto itself." Helen sat even straighter in her chair. "This happened close to the final time he was captured. He knew, I believe, that he would die soon, and it made him fearless. He took more and more risks. And he valued his own life less and less." Her eyes shone with tears as she gazed out the rain-blurred window, lost in a world long since past.

"The SS officer had taken a room in a luxury hotel on the outskirts of Paris," Helen went on a minute later. "He was in the habit of sipping a cognac before retiring for the evening. When he called for his drink, it was Jean-Claude who brought it to him wearing a waiter's jacket. I don't know how he killed the SS man, but he did it without alerting anyone. He made sure there was no blood. The problem was getting the body out of the hotel without anyone seeing."

"Why? Couldn't he just leave it there?"

"Why?" Helen repeated, shaking her head. "If the man's body had been discovered, the entire staff would have been tortured as punishment. Eventually someone would have broken. In any event, Jean-Claude smuggled the body out."

"How did he do it?"

"Jean-Claude was clever. His friends hauled him and the body of the SS officer up the chimney. First the dead man and then the live one. That was necessary, you see, because there was a guard at the end of the hallway."

"But once they got to the rooftop, how did he manage?"

"It was an effort," Helen said. "Jean-Claude told me they tossed the body from that rooftop to the roof of another building and then another—an office building. They lowered him down in the elevator. When the men arrived with the body, we all worked together and buried him quickly."

"The SS officer's disappearance must have caused trouble for the Resistance," Paul said.

Helen nodded ardently. "Oh, yes."

"When was Jean-Claude captured the second time?" Ruth asked. She was intensely curious and yet she dreaded hearing about the death of this brave man her grandmother had loved.

Helen's eyes glistened and she lifted her teacup with an unsteady hand. "It isn't what you think," she prefaced, and the cup made a slight clinking sound as it rattled against the saucer. Helen placed both hands in her lap and took a moment to compose herself. "We were headed for the Metro—the subway. By then I'd bleached my hair and we'd both changed our appearances as much as possible. I don't think my own mother would have recognized me. Jean-Claude's, either," she added softly, her voice a mere whisper.

Paul reached for Ruth's hand, as if sensing that she needed his support.

When her grandmother began to speak again, it was

in French. She switched languages naturally, apparently without realizing she'd done so. All at once, she covered her face and broke into sobs.

Although Ruth hadn't understood a word, she started crying, too, and gently wrapped her arms around her grandmother's thin shoulders. Hugging her was the only thing she could do to ease this remembered pain.

"It's all right, it's all right," Ruth cooed over and over. "You don't need to tell us any more."

Paul agreed. "This is too hard on her—and you," he said.

They stayed for another hour, but it was clear that reliving the past had exhausted her grandmother. She seemed so frail now, even more than during the previous visit.

While her grandmother rested in her room, Ruth cleared the table. As she took care of the few dishes, her eyes brimmed with tears again. It was agonizing to think about the horrors her grandmother had endured.

"When she was speaking French, she must've been reliving the day Jean-Claude died," Ruth said, turning so her back was pressed against the kitchen counter.

Paul nodded. "She was," he answered somberly.

Ruth studied him as she returned to the kitchen table, where he sat. "You said you speak French. Could you understand what she was saying?"

He nodded again. "At the Metro that day, Jean-Claude was picked up in a routine identity check by the French police. Through pure luck, Helen was able to get on the train without being stopped. She had to stand helplessly inside the subway car and watch as the police hauled him to Gestapo headquarters." Paul paused long enough to give her an odd smile. "The next part was a tirade against the police, whom she hated. Remember last week when she explained that some of the French police were trying to prove their worth to the Germans? Well, apparently Jean-Claude was one of their most wanted criminals."

"They tortured him, didn't they?" she asked, although she already knew the answer.

"Yes." Paul met her eyes. "Unmercifully."

Ruth swallowed hard.

"Helen tried to save him. Disregarding her own safety, she went in after him, only this time she went alone. No sympathetic priest." Paul's face hardened. "They dragged her into the basement, where Jean-Claude was being tortured. They had him strung up by his arms. He was bloody and his face was unrecognizable."

"No!" Ruth hid her eyes with both hands.

"They taunted him. Said they had his accomplice and now he would see her die."

Ruth could barely talk. "They...were going to...kill Helen—in front of Jean-Claude?"

"From what she said, it wouldn't have been an easy death. The point was for Jean-Claude to watch her suffer— to watch her die a slow, agonizing death."

"Dear God in heaven."

"She didn't actually say it," Paul continued. "She didn't have to spell it out, but Jean-Claude obviously hadn't been broken. Seeing her suffer would have done it, though, and your grandmother knew that. She also knew that if he talked, it would mean the torture and death of others in the Resistance." Paul looked away for a moment. "Apparently he and his friends had helped a number of British pilots escape German detection. At risk was the entire underground effort. Jean-Claude knew more than anyone suspected."

"Helen couldn't let that happen," Ruth said.

"No, and Jean-Claude understood that, too."

"Remember when she said she was the one who killed him? She didn't mean that literally, did she?"

"She did."

This was beginning not to make sense. "But...how?"

Paul braced his elbows on the table. "Her voice started to break at that point and I didn't catch everything. She talked about a cyanide tablet. I'm not sure how she got hold of it. But I know she kissed him.... A final kiss goodbye. By this stage she was too emotional to understand clearly."

The pieces started to fall together for Ruth. "She gave him the pill—you mean instead of taking it herself?"

"That's what it sounded like to me," he said hoarsely.

"Was this when he asked her to kill him? And then she kissed him and transferred the pill?"

"I think so." Paul cleared his throat, but his voice was still rough. "She said Jean-Claude had begged her to kill him. He spoke to her in English, which the Germans couldn't understand."

Ruth pictured the terrible scene. Helen and Jean-Claude

arguing. If Helen swallowed the pill, she'd be dead and the Gestapo would lose their bargaining chip. Even knowing that, Jean-Claude couldn't bear to see his wife die. It truly would have broken him.

"Speaking in another language added enough confusion that she had the opportunity to do what he asked," Ruth speculated.

"Last time she told us about being driven by fear instead of courage," Paul reminded her. "I'm sure she didn't stop to think about what she was doing—she couldn't. Nor could she refuse Jean-Claude."

Ruth wanted to bury her face in her hands and weep.

"Jean-Claude thanked her," Paul said.

"She would have refused." Ruth could see it all in her mind, the argument between them.

"I'm convinced she did refuse at first. She loved Jean-Claude—he was her husband."

Ruth couldn't imagine a worse scenario.

Paul's voice dropped slightly. "She said Jean-Claude had never begged for mercy, never pleaded for anything, but he told her he couldn't bear any more pain. Above all, he couldn't bear it if they killed her. He begged her to let him die."

"He loved her that much," Ruth said in a hushed whisper.

"And she loved him that much, enough to spare him any more torture, even at the risk of her own death."

"They didn't kill her, though," Ruth said, stating the obvious. "Even though they must have figured out that she was responsible for his death?"

Paul's eyes widened as if he couldn't explain that any more than she could. "She didn't say what happened next."

Ruth stood, anxious now to see her grandmother before they left. "I'm going to check on her."

Ruth went to her grandmother's room to find her resting fitfully. Helen's eyes fluttered open when Ruth stepped quietly past the threshold.

"Have I shocked you?" Helen asked, holding out her hand to Ruth.

"No," Ruth told her grandmother, who had to be the bravest woman she'd ever know. She sat on the edge of the bed and whispered, "Thank you, Grandma—for everything you did. And for doing Paul and me the honor of sharing it with us."

Helen smiled and touched her cheek. "You've been crying."

Taking her grandmother's hand between her own, she kissed the old woman's knuckles. A lump filled her throat and she couldn't find the words to express her love.

"When did you meet Grandpa?" she finally asked.

Helen smiled again and her eyes drifted shut. "Two years later. He was one of the American soldiers who came with Patton's army to free us from the concentration camp."

This was a completely different aspect of the story.

"When it was learned that I was an American citizen, I

was immediately questioned and when my citizenship was verified, I was put on a ship and sent home."

"Two years," Ruth said in a choked voice. "You were in a camp for *two years?*" Just when she thought there was nothing more to horrify her, Helen revealed something else.

"Buchenwald... I don't want to talk about it," Helen muttered.

No wonder her grandmother had never spoken of those years. The memories were far worse than the worst Ruth had been able to imagine.

Her grandmother brushed the hair from Ruth's forehead. "I want you to know I like your young man."

"He reminded you of Jean-Claude, didn't he?"

Her smile was weak, which told Ruth how drained this afternoon's conversation had left Helen. "Not at first, but then he smiled and I saw Jean-Claude in Paul's eyes." She swallowed a couple of times and added, "I wanted to die after Jean-Claude did. I would've done anything if only the Germans had put me out of my living hell. They knew that and decided it was better to let me live and remember, each and every day, that I'd killed my own husband." A tear slid down her face. "I can't speak of it anymore."

Ruth understood. "I'll leave you to rest. Try to sleep."

Her grandmother's answering sigh told Ruth how badly she needed that just then.

"Come back and see me soon," she called as Ruth stood.

"I will, I promise." She bent down to kiss the soft cheek.

Paul was waiting for her in the living room, flipping

through the *Cedar Cove Chronicle,* but he got up when she returned. "Is she all right?"

Ruth shrugged. "She's tired." Her eyes were watering again, despite her best efforts not to cry. She couldn't stop thinking about the pain her grandmother had endured and kept hidden all these years.

Paul held open his arms and she walked into his embrace as naturally as she slipped on a favorite coat. Once there, she began to cry—harsh, broken sobs she thought would never end.

Eight

As before, Ruth and Paul spoke little on the ferry ride back to Seattle.

Ruth's entire perspective on her grandmother had changed. Until now, she'd always viewed the petite, gentle woman as...well, her grandmother. All of a sudden Ruth was forced to realize that Helen had been young once, and deeply involved in events that had changed or destroyed many lives. She'd been an ordinary young woman from a fairly privileged background. She'd been a student, fallen in love, enjoyed a carefree existence. Then this ordinary young woman had been caught up in extraordinary circumstances—and risen to their demands.

Ruth was curious about the connection between her grandmother's life during the war and her life afterward.

Clearly the link was her grandfather, whom she'd never had a chance to know.

Paul stood with Ruth at the railing as the ferry glided through the relatively smooth waters of Puget Sound. The rain had stopped, and although the sky remained cloudy and gray, the air was fresh with only the slightest hint of brine.

"Every story I hear leaves me amazed that this incredible woman is my grandmother," Ruth said fervently, grateful that Paul was beside her.

"I know. I'm overwhelmed, and I just met her."

They exchanged tentative smiles, and then they both sighed—in appreciation, Ruth thought, of everything Helen Shelton had been and done.

"I wish I'd known my grandfather," she said. "He seems to have been the one who gave my grandmother a reason to live. He loved her and she loved him." Ruth knew that from every word her grandmother and her dad had said about Sam Shelton.

"How old were you when he died?" Paul asked.

"Two or so." She turned so she could look directly at Paul. "When I saw my grandmother in her bedroom, she said he was with a group of soldiers who freed the prisoners in the concentration camp."

"She was in a concentration camp?"

Ruth nodded. "She was there at least a couple of years."

Paul frowned, obviously upset.

"I can't *bear* to think what her life was like in one of those obscene places," Ruth said.

"It would've been grim. You're right—they were obscene. Places of death."

Ruth didn't welcome the reminder. "I'm so glad you've been with me on these visits," she told him. Paul's presence helped her assimilate the details her grandmother had shared. He'd given her a feeling of comfort and companionship as they'd listened to these painful wartime experiences. Ruth believed there was something about Paul that had led Helen to divulge her secrets.

After the ferry docked, they walked along the Seattle waterfront, where they ate clam chowder, followed by fish and chips, for dinner. Their mood was somber, and yet, strangely, Ruth felt a sense of peace.

The next day, after her classes, she hurried back to her rental house and ran into Lynn. As much as possible, Ruth had avoided her roommate. Her relationship with Lynn had been awkward ever since the argument over Clay. Lynn's lie, which she'd told in an effort to keep Ruth from meeting Paul, hadn't helped.

Lynn was coming out just as Ruth leaped up the porch steps. Her roommate hesitated.

Ruth did, too. She'd never said anything to Lynn about her intentional mix-up that first night she was meeting Paul. Her classes would be over in June, and she was more than ready to move out.

"Hi," Lynn offered uncertainly.

Ruth's pace slowed as she waited, half expecting Lynn to make some derogatory remark about Paul. Because Ruth had been with him so often lately, she'd had very little contact with her roommate.

"Are you seeing Paul again?" The question lacked the scornful tone she'd used when referring to him previously. She seemed more prompted by curiosity than anything else.

"We're meeting some friends of his later. Why?" Ruth couldn't help being suspicious. If he'd phoned with a change of plan, she needed to know about it. She knew from experience that Lynn couldn't be trusted to relay the message.

Lynn shrugged. "No reason."

"Is there something you aren't telling me?" Ruth's voice was calm.

Her roommate had the grace to blush. "He didn't call, if that's what you're asking."

"Like I could believe you."

"You can—okay, maybe what I did that night was stupid."

"Maybe?" Ruth echoed.

"All right, it was. I was upset because of Clay." She didn't meet Ruth's eyes. "I thought Clay was really hot and you dumped him for soldier boy, and I thought that was just wrong."

"I don't need you to decide who I'm allowed to date." Ruth couldn't keep the anger out of her voice. What Lynn had tried to do still rankled. If her cell phone battery hadn't been low, she and Paul might have missed each other completely. That sent chills down her spine.

Lynn released a long sigh. "I'll admit it—you were right about Clay."

"How so?"

"He's…he's stuck on himself."

Ruth suspected that meant he wasn't interested in Lynn.

"I…I like Paul," her roommate confessed.

Ruth wasn't even aware that Lynn had met him and said so.

"He stopped by one afternoon when he thought you were back from class, only you weren't, and I was here. We talked for a bit. Then he left to look for you at the library."

Funny that neither had mentioned the incident earlier. "I had the impression you were dead set against him."

"Not him," Lynn said. "I'm against the war in Iraq.… I thought you were, too."

"I don't like war of any kind. This war or any war, including Afghanistan. Still, the United States is involved in the Middle East, and no matter what, it's our young men and women who are fighting there. Politics aside, I want to support our troops."

"I know." Lynn suddenly seemed to find something absolutely mesmerizing about her shoes.

Ruth moved past her on the porch. "I'd better go in and change."

"Ruth," Lynn said sharply. Ruth turned to face her. "I'm

sorry about the other night. That really was an awful thing to do. I was upset and I took it out on you."

Ruth had pretty much figured that out on her own. "Paul and I connected, so no harm done."

"I know, and I'm glad you did because I think Paul is great. I know he's a soldier and all, but he's a nice guy. I only met him once, but I could see he's ten times the man Clay will ever be. He's the kind of guy I hope to meet."

Paul had obviously impressed her during their brief exchange. She wondered what they'd talked about.

"All's well that ends well," Ruth said.

"Shakespeare, right?" Lynn asked. "In other words, all is forgiven?"

Ruth laughed and nodded, then started into the house.

Paul picked her up at five-thirty and they drove to a Mexican restaurant in downtown Kent. Paul had arranged for her to meet his best friend.

Brian Hart and his wife, Carley, were high school sweethearts and Brian had known Paul for most of his life.

"We go way back," Brian said when they were introduced. He slid out of the booth and they exchanged handshakes, with Paul standing just behind Ruth, his hand on her shoulder.

"I'm pleased to meet you both." They were a handsome couple. Carley was a delicate blonde with soulful blue eyes, and her husband was tall and muscular, as if he routinely worked out.

"We're pleased to meet you, too," Carley said when Ruth slipped into the booth across from her.

Paul got in beside Ruth.

"I insisted Paul introduce us," Carley said as she reached for a chip and dipped it in the salsa. "Every time we tried to get together during his leave, he already had plans with you."

Ruth hadn't thought of it that way, but realized she'd monopolized his time. "I guess I should apologize for that."

"We only have the two weeks," Paul explained.

"You'll be back in Seattle after the training, won't you?" Brian asked.

"Maybe, but…" Paul hesitated and glanced at Ruth.

"We only just met and…" Ruth let the rest fade. He would be back and they'd see each other again, but only if she could accept his career in the military.

This fourteen-day period was a testing time for them both, and at the end they had a decision to make.

"I'm giving Ruth two weeks to fall head over heels in love with me." Paul said it as if it were a joke.

"If she doesn't, there's definitely something wrong with her," Carley joked back.

Ruth smiled, but she felt her heart sinking. She hadn't made her decision yet; the truth was, she'd been putting it off until the last possible minute.

Time was dwindling and soon, in a matter of days, Paul would be leaving. She wasn't ready—wasn't ready to decide and wasn't ready for him to go.

Brian and Carley had to be home before eight because of their babysitter, so they left the restaurant first.

Ruth had enjoyed the spicy enchiladas, the margarita and especially the teasing between Paul and Brian. Carley had told story after story of the two boys and their high school exploits, and they'd all laughed and joked together.

Paul and Ruth lingered in the booth over cups of dark coffee, gazing into each other's eyes. He'd switched places so he could sit across from her. If she'd met him under any other circumstance, there'd be no question about her feelings. None! It was so easy to fall in love with this man. In fact, it was already too late; even Paul's mother had seen that. Ruth *knew* him. After all the letters and emails, all the conversations, she felt as if he'd become part of her life.

"I know what you're thinking," Paul said unexpectedly.

"What am I thinking?" she asked with amusement.

"You're wondering why I find life in the military so attractive."

She shrugged. "Close."

"Do you want to know my answer?"

Ruth was aware of his reasons, but wanted to hear him out, anyway. "Sure, go ahead."

"I like the structure, the discipline, the knowledge that I'm doing something positive to bring about freedom and democracy in the world."

This was where it got troubling for Ruth.

Before she could state her own feelings, Paul stopped

her. "I know you don't agree with me, and I accept that, but I am who I am."

"I didn't challenge that—I wouldn't."

He stiffened, then reached for his coffee and held it at arm's length, cupping his hands around the mug. "True enough, but the minute I started talking, you looked like you wanted to challenge my answer."

She hadn't known her feelings were that transparent.

"I guess now is as good a time as any to ask where I stand with you."

"What do you mean?" An uneasy feeling began to creep up her spine. They had only a couple of days before he was scheduled to leave, and she was going to need every minute of that time to concentrate on this relationship.

"You know what I'm asking, Ruth."

She did. She met his eyes. "I'm in love with you, Paul."

"I'm in love with you, too." He stretched his hand across the table and intertwined their fingers.

Her heart nearly sprang out of her chest with happiness and yet tears filled her eyes.

To her astonishment, Paul laughed. "This is supposed to be a happy moment," he told her.

"I *am* happy, but I'm afraid, too."

"Of what?"

"Of you leaving again. Of your involvement in the military. Of you fighting in a war, any war."

"It's what I do."

"I know." Still, she had difficulty reconciling her emotions and beliefs with the way Paul chose to make his living.

"But you don't like it," he said, his voice hard.

"No."

He sighed harshly. "Then tell me where we go from here."

Ruth wished she knew. "I can't answer that."

His eyes pleaded with her. "I can't answer it for you, Ruth. You're going to have to make up your mind about us."

She'd known it would come down to this. "I'm not sure I can. Not yet."

He considered her words. "When do you think you'll be able to decide?"

"Let's wait until you've finished your training and we see each other again.... We'll both have a better idea then, don't you think?"

"No. I might not be coming back to Seattle. I have to know soon. Now. Tonight." He paused. "I realize I sound unfair and pushy, and I apologize."

"Apologize for what?" she asked. Her hand tightened around his fingers. She could feel him pulling away from her, if not physically, then emotionally.

"I've been trained to be decisive. Putting things off only leads to confusion. We've been writing for months."

"Yes, I know, but—"

"We've spent every possible minute of my leave together."

"Yes..."

"I love you, Ruth, but I won't lie to you. I'm not leaving the marines. I've chosen the military as my career and that means I could be involved in conflicts all over the world. I have to know if you can accept that."

"I..."

"If you can't, we need to walk away from each other right now. I don't want to drag this out. You decide."

Ruth didn't want a part-time husband. "I want a man who'll be a husband to me and a father to my children. A man of peace, not war." She didn't mean to sound so adamant.

Paul didn't respond for a long moment. "I think we have our answer." He slid out of the booth and waited for her. They'd paid earlier, so there was nothing to do but go out to the parking lot.

Ruth wasn't finished with the conversation, even if Paul was. "I need time," she told him.

"The decision's made."

"You're pressuring me," she protested. "I've still got two days, remember?"

"It doesn't work that way," he said.

"But this isn't fair!"

"I already admitted it wasn't." He opened the passenger door, and a moment later, he joined her in the car. "I wish now I'd waited and we still had those two days," he said bleakly. "But we don't."

He started the car and Ruth noticed that his fingers had tensed on the steering wheel.

Ruth bit her lip. "Sure we do. Let's just pretend we didn't have this conversation and enjoy the time we have left. You can do that, can't you?" Her voice took on a pleading quality.

"I wish I could, but…I can't." He inhaled deeply. "The decision is made," he said again.

They didn't have much to say during the rest of the ride to the university district. When Paul pulled up in front of the rental house, Ruth noticed the lights were on, which meant Lynn was home.

They sat side by side in the car without speaking until Paul roused himself to open his door. He walked around to escort her from the passenger side, then accompanied her to the porch.

Ruth half expected him to kiss her. He didn't.

"Will I see you again?" she asked as he began to leave.

He turned back and stood there, stiff and formal. "Probably not."

"You mean this is it? This is goodbye…as if I meant nothing…as if we were strangers?" She felt outraged that he could abandon her like this, without a word. It was unkind and unfair…and life wasn't that simple.

"Is there anything left to say?" he asked.

"Of course there is," she cried. She didn't know what, but surely there was *something*. Hurting and angry, Ruth gestured wildly with her arms. "You can't be serious! Are you really going to walk away? Just like that?"

"Yes." The word was devoid of emotion.

"You aren't going to write me again?"

"No."

This was unbelievable.

"Call me?"

"No."

She glared at him. "In other words, you're going to act as if you'd never even met me, as if I'd never mailed that Christmas card."

A hint of a smile flickered over his tightly controlled features. "I'm certainly going to give it my best shot."

"Fine, then," she muttered. If he thought so little of her, then he could do as he wished. She didn't want to be with a man who didn't care about her feelings, just his own.

Nine

True to his word, Paul didn't get in touch with her after their Tuesday-night dinner. The first day, her anger carried her. Then she convinced herself that he'd contact her before he left for Camp Pendleton. Not so. Paul Gordon—correction, *Sergeant* Paul Gordon, USMC—was out of her life and that was perfectly fine with her. Only it wasn't.

A week later, as she sat in her "Theories of Learning" class, taking notes, her determination faltered. She wanted to push all thoughts of Paul out of her mind forever; instead, he was constantly there.

What upset her most was the cold-blooded way he'd dismissed her from his life. It seemed so easy for him, so... simple. She was gone for him, as if she meant nothing. That hurt, and it didn't stop hurting.

Ruth blinked, forcing herself to listen to the lecture. If she flunked this course, Paul Gordon would be to blame.

After class she walked across campus, her steps slow and deliberate. She felt no urge to hurry. But when her cell phone rang, she nearly dropped her purse in her eagerness. Could it be Paul? Had he changed his mind? Had he found it impossible to forget her, the same way she couldn't forget him? A dozen more questions flew through her mind before she managed to answer.

"Hello?" She sounded excited and breathless at the same time.

"Ruth." The familiar voice of a longtime friend, Tina Dupont, greeted her. They talked for a few minutes, and arranged to meet at the library at the end of the week. Four minutes after she'd answered her cell, it was back in her purse.

She was too restless to sit at home and study, which was how she'd spent every night since her last date with Paul, so she decided to go out. That was what she needed, she told herself with forced enthusiasm. Find people, friends, a party. Something to do, somewhere to be.

Although it was midafternoon, she took the bus down to the waterfront, where she'd met Paul the first night. That wasn't a smart idea. She wasn't up to dealing with memories. Before she could talk herself out of it, Ruth hopped on the Bremerton ferry. A visit with her grandmother would lift her spirits in a way nothing else could. Besides, if Helen felt strong enough, she wanted to hear the rest of the story, especially the role her grandfather had played.

As she stepped off the foot ferry from Bremerton to Cedar Cove, it occurred to Ruth that she should've phoned first. But it was unlikely her grandmother would be out. And if she was, Ruth figured she could wander around Cedar Cove for a while. That would help fill the void threatening to swallow her whole.

The trudge up the hill to her grandmother's house seemed twice as steep and three times as long. Funny, when she'd been with Paul, the climb hadn't even winded her. That was because she'd been laughing and joking with him, she remembered—and wished she hadn't. Alone, hands shoved in her pockets, she felt drained of energy.

Reaching 5-B Poppy Lane, she saw that the front door to her grandmother's duplex stood open, although the old-fashioned wooden screen was shut. The last remaining tulips bloomed in primary colors as vivid as the rainbow. Walking up the steps, Ruth rang the doorbell. "Grandma! Are you home?"

No one answered. "Grandma?"

Alarm jolted through her. Had something happened to her grandmother? She pounded on the door and was even more alarmed when a white-haired woman close to her grandmother's age came toward her.

"Hello," the older lady said pleasantly. "Can I help you?"

"I'm looking for my grandmother."

The woman unlatched the screen door and swung it

open. "You must be Ruth. I don't think Helen was expecting you. I'm Charlotte Rhodes."

"Charlotte," Ruth repeated. "Helen's spoken of you so often. It's wonderful to meet you."

"You, too," Charlotte said, taking Ruth's hand. "I'm happy to make your acquaintance."

Ruth nodded, but she couldn't stop herself from blurting out, "Is anything wrong with my grandmother?"

"Oh, no, not at all. We're sitting on the patio, talking and knitting. Helen's counting stitches and asked me to get the door. She assumed it was a salesman and my job was to get rid of him...or her." Charlotte laughed. "Not that *I'm* much good at that. Just the other day, a Girl Scout came to my door selling cookies. When I bought four boxes, she announced that every kid comes to my house first, because I'll buy anything. Especially for charity."

Ruth grinned. "I think my grandmother must be like that, too."

"Why do you suppose she sent *me* to the door?" Charlotte joked. "Your grandmother's knitting a Fair Isle sweater. It's her first one and she asked me over to get her started."

"Perhaps I should come back at a more convenient time?" Ruth didn't want to interrupt the two women.

"Nonsense! She'd never forgive me if you left. Besides, I was just gathering my things to head on home. My husband will be wondering what's kept me so long." Charlotte led the way through the house.

As soon as Ruth stepped onto the brick patio, her grandmother's eyes lit up with pleasure. "Ruth! What a welcome surprise."

Ruth bent forward and kissed Helen's cheek.

Charlotte Rhodes collected her knitting, saying she'd talk to Helen at the Senior Center on Monday, and left.

"Sit down, sit down," Helen urged, motioning at the chair next to her. "Help yourself to iced tea if you'd like." Strands of yarn were wrapped around both index fingers as she held the needles. One was red, the other white. "You can find a glass, can't you?"

"Yes, of course, but I'm fine," Ruth assured her, enjoying the sunshine and the sights and sounds of Cedar Cove. The earth in her grandmother's garden smelled warm and clean—the way it only smelled in spring. Inhaling deeply, Ruth sat down, staring at the cove with its sparkling blue water.

"Where's Paul?" her grandmother asked, as if noticing for the first time that he wasn't with her.

Ruth's serenity was instantly destroyed and she struggled to disguise her misery. "He went to the marines' camp in California."

"Oh." Her grandmother seemed disappointed. "I imagine you miss him."

Ruth decided to let the comment slide.

"I liked him a great deal," her grandmother said, rubbing salt into Ruth's already wounded heart. Helen's focus was on her knitting, but when Ruth didn't immediately respond, she looked up.

Ruth met her eyes and exhaled forcefully. "Would you mind if we didn't discuss Paul?"

Her request was met with a puzzled glance. "Why?"

Ruth decided she might as well tell her. "We won't be seeing each other again."

"Really?" Her grandmother's expression was downcast. "I thought highly of that young man. Any particular reason?"

"Actually," Ruth said, "there are several. He's in the military, which you already know."

Her grandmother carefully set her knitting aside and reached for her glass of iced tea, giving Ruth her full attention. "You knew that when you first met, I believe."

"Yes, I did, but I assumed that in time he'd be released from his commitment and return to civilian life. He told me that won't be the case, that the military's his career." *In for the long haul,* as he'd put it. Granted, she'd known about his dedication to the marines from the beginning, but he'd known about her feelings, too. Did her preferences matter less than his?

"I see." Her grandmother studied her.

Ruth wondered if she truly did. "What really upsets me is the heartless way he left. I told him I wasn't sure I could live with the fact that he'd chosen the military." The memory angered her, and she raised her voice. "Then Paul had the audacity to say I wouldn't be hearing from him again and he...he just walked away." Ruth hadn't planned to spill out the whole story minutes after she arrived, but she couldn't hold it inside a second longer.

Her grandmother's response shocked her into silence. Helen *smiled*.

"Forgive me," her grandmother said gently, leaning forward to give Ruth's hand a small squeeze. "Sam did something similar, you see."

The irritation died instantly. "I wanted to ask you about my grandfather."

A peaceful look came over Helen. "He was a wonderful man. And he saved me."

"From the Germans, you mean?"

Helen shook her head. "Technically, it was General Patton and the Third Army who saved us. Patton knew what Buchenwald was. He knew that a three-hour wait meant twenty-thousand lives because the Germans had been given orders to kill all prisoners before surrendering. Against every rule of caution, Patton mounted an attack, cutting off the SS troops from the camp. Because of his decisive move, the Germans were forced to flee or surrender. By that time, the German soldiers knew they were defeated. They threw down their guns and surrendered. Sam was with Patton on the march, so, yes, he contributed to my rescue and that of countless others. But when I say your grandfather saved me, I mean he saved me from myself."

"I want to hear about him, if you're willing to tell me." Ruth straightened, perching on the edge of her seat.

Her grandmother closed her eyes. "I cannot speak about the years in Buchenwald, not even to you."

Ruth reached for Helen's hand, stroking the soft skin over the gnarled and prominent knuckles. "That's fine, Grandma."

"I wanted to die, wished it with all my heart. Without Jean-Claude, it was harder to live than to die. Living was the cruelest form of punishment." Tears pooled in her eyes and she blinked them away.

"When the Americans came," Helen continued, "the gates were opened and we were free. It was a delicious feeling—freedom always is—but one never appreciates it until it's taken away. The soldiers spoke English, and I went to them and explained that I was an American. I had no identification or anything to prove my claim, so I kept repeating the address where my parents lived in New York. I was desperate to get word to them that I was alive. They hadn't heard from me in almost five years.

"One of the soldiers brought me to their headquarters. I was completely emaciated, and I'm sure my stench was enough to nauseate anyone standing within twenty feet. The young man then took me to his lieutenant, whose name was Sam Shelton. From that moment forward, Sam took care of me. He saw that I had food and water, clothes and access to showers and anything else I needed."

Ruth shuddered at the thought of her grandmother's physical and mental condition following her release.

Her grandmother paused to take a deep breath, and when

she spoke again, it was in another language, what Ruth assumed was German. Pressing her hand on Helen's, she stopped her. "Grandma, English, please."

Her grandmother frowned. "Sorry."

"Was that German?"

She shrugged, eyes wild and confused. "I don't know."

After all those years inside a German camp, it made sense that she'd revert to the language. In her mind she'd gone back to that time, was reliving each incident.

"Go on. Please," Ruth urged.

Helen sighed. "I don't remember much about those first days of freedom."

Ruth could easily understand that.

"Still, every memory I have is of the lieutenant at my side, watching over me. I was hospitalized, and I think I slept almost around the clock for three days straight, waking only long enough to eat and drink. Yet every time I opened my eyes, Sam was there. I'm sure that's not possible, but that's how I remember it."

She picked up her tea with a trembling hand and sipped the cool liquid. "After a week—maybe more, I don't know, time meant nothing to me—I was transported out of Germany and placed on a ship going to America. Sam wrote out his name and home address in Washington State and gave it to me. I didn't know why he'd do that."

"Did you keep it?" Ruth asked.

"I did," Helen confessed, "although I didn't think I'd ever need it. By the time I got back to New York, I was still skin and bones. My own parents didn't even recognize me. My mother looked at me and burst into tears. I was twenty-four years old, and I felt sixty."

Ruth was in her twenties and couldn't imagine living through any of what her grandmother had described.

"Five months after I got home, Sam Shelton knocked on the door of my parents' brownstone. I'd gained weight and my hair had grown back, and when I saw him I barely remembered who he was. He visited for two days and we talked. He'd come to see how I was adjusting to life in America."

Ruth had wondered about that, too. It couldn't have been easy.

"I hadn't done very well. My parents owned a small bakery and I worked at the counter, but I had no life in me, no joy. Now that I was free, I felt I had nothing to live for. My husband was dead, and I was the one who'd killed him. I told this American soldier, whom I hardly knew, all of this. I told him I preferred to die. I told him everything—not one thing did I hold back. He listened and didn't interrupt me with questions, and when I was finished he took my hand and kissed it." The tears came again, spilling down her cheeks. "He said I was the bravest woman he'd ever known."

"I think you are, too," Ruth said, her voice shaky.

"Sam told me he was part of D-day," Helen said. "His company was one of the first to land on Omaha Beach. He spoke of the fighting there and the bravery of his men. He'd seen death the same way I had. Later, in the midst of the fighting, he'd stumbled across the body of his own brother. He had no time to mourn him. He didn't understand why God had seen fit to spare him and not his brother.

"This lieutenant asked the very questions I'd been asking myself. I didn't know why I should live when I'd rather have died with Jean-Claude—or instead of him." She paused again, as if to regain her composure.

"After that, Sam said he'd needed to do a lot of thinking, and praying, and it came to him that his brother, his men, had sacrificed their lives so that others could live in freedom. God had spared him, and me, too, and it wasn't up to either of us to question why. As for Jean-Claude and Tim, Sam's brother, they had died in this terrible but necessary *war*. For either of us to throw away our lives now would be to dishonor them—my husband and Sam's brother."

"He was right, you know."

Her grandmother nodded. "Sam left after that one visit. He wished me well and said he hoped I'd keep in touch. I waited a week before I wrote the first letter. Sam hadn't given me many details of his war experiences, but deep down I knew they'd been as horrific as my own. In that, we had a bond."

"So you and Grandpa Sam wrote letters to each other."

Helen nodded again. "For six months we wrote, and every day I found more questions for him to answer. His letters were messages of encouragement and hope for us both. Oh, Ruth, how I wish you'd had the opportunity to know your grandfather. He was wise and kind and loving. He gave me a reason to live, a reason to go on. He taught me I could love again—and then he asked me to marry him." Helen drew in a deep breath. "Sam wrote and asked me to be his wife, and I said no."

"You refused?" Ruth asked, incredulous.

"I couldn't leave my parents a second time.… Oh, I had a dozen excuses, all of them valid."

"How did he convince you?"

Her smile was back. "He didn't. In those days, one didn't hop on a plane or even use the phone unless it was a dire emergency. For two weeks he was silent. No letters and no contact. Nothing. When I didn't hear from him, I knew I never would again."

This was the reason her grandmother had smiled when Ruth told her she hadn't heard from Paul.

"I couldn't stand it," Helen admitted. "This soldier had become vitally important to me. For the first time since Jean-Claude died, I could *feel*. I could laugh and cry. I knew Sam was the one who'd taken this heavy burden of pain from my shoulders. Not only that, he loved me. Loved me," she repeated, "and I'd turned him down when he asked me to share his life."

"What did you do next?"

Helen smiled at the memory. "I sent a telegram that said three words. *Yes. Yes. Yes.* Then I boarded a train and five days later, I arrived in Washington State. When I stepped off the platform, my suitcase in hand, Sam was there with his entire family. We were married two weeks later. I knew no one, so he introduced me to his best friends and the women they loved. Those four became my dearest friends. They were the people who helped me adjust to normal life. They helped me find my new identity." She shook her head slowly. "Not once in all the years your grandfather and I were together did I have a single regret."

Ruth's eyes were teary. "That's a beautiful love story."

"Now you're living one of your own."

Ruth didn't see it like that. "I don't want to be a military wife," she said. "I can't do it."

"You love Paul."

Ruth noted that her grandmother hadn't made it a question. Helen knew that Ruth's heart was linked with Paul's. He was an honorable man, and he loved her. They didn't need to have the same political beliefs as long as they respected each other's views.

"Yes, Grandma, I love him."

"And you miss him the same way I missed Sam."

"I do." It was freeing to Ruth to admit it. The depression that had hung over her for the past week lifted.

All at once Ruth knew exactly what she was going to do. Her decision was made.

Ten

Barbara Gordon answered the doorbell, and the moment she saw Ruth, her eyes lit with delight. "Ruth, I'm so glad to see you!"

Ruth was instantly ushered into the house. She hadn't been sure what kind of reception she'd get. After all, she'd disappointed and possibly hurt the Gordons' son.

"I was so hoping you'd stop by," Barbara continued as she led her into the kitchen.

Obediently Ruth followed. "I came because I don't have a current address for Paul."

"You plan on writing him?" Barbara seemed about to leap up and down and clap her hands.

"Actually, no."

The happiness drained from the other woman's eyes.

"I know it's a bit old-fashioned, but I thought I'd send him a telegram."

The delight was back in place. "Greg," she shouted over her shoulder. "Ruth is here."

Almost immediately Paul's father joined them in the kitchen. His grin was as wide as his wife's had been. "Good to see you, good to see you," he said expansively.

"What did I tell you?" Barbara insisted.

The two of them stood there staring at her.

"About Paul's address?" Ruth prodded.

"Oh, yes." As if she'd woken from a trance, Barbara Gordon hurried into the other room, leaving Ruth alone with Paul's father.

It was awkward at first, and Ruth felt the least she could do was explain the reason for her visit. "I miss Paul so much," she told him. "I need his address."

Greg Gordon nodded. "He's missing you, too. Big-time."

Ruth's heart filled with hope. "He said that?"

"Not in those exact words," Greg stated matter-of-factly. "But rest assured, my son is pretty miserable."

"That's *wonderful*." Now it was Ruth who wanted to leap up and down and clap her hands.

"My son is miserable and you're happy?" Greg asked, but a teasing light glinted in his eyes.

"Yes...no... Yes," she quickly amended. "I just hope he's been as miserable as I have."

Greg's smile faded. "No question there."

The phone rang once; Barbara must have answered

it right away. Within a few minutes she returned to the kitchen, carrying a portable phone. "It's for you."

Greg started toward her.

"Not you, honey," she said, gesturing at Ruth. "The call is for Ruth."

"Me?" She was startled. No one knew she'd come here. Anyone wanting to reach her would automatically call her cell. Her frown disappeared as she realized who it must be.

"Is it Paul?" she asked, her voice low and hopeful.

"It is. He thinks Greg's about to get on the line." She clasped her husband's elbow. "Come on, honey, let's give Ruth and Paul some privacy." She was halfway out of the room when she turned back, caught Ruth's eye and winked.

That was just the encouragement Ruth needed. Still, she felt decidedly nervous as she picked up the phone resting on the kitchen counter. After the way they'd parted, she didn't know what to expect or how to react.

"Hello, Paul," she said, hoping to sound calm and confident, neither of which she was.

Her greeting was followed by a slight hesitation. "Ruth?"

"Yes, it's me." Her voice was downright cheerful—and more than a little forced.

"What are you doing at my parents' place?" he asked gruffly.

"Visiting."

Again he paused, as if he wasn't sure what to make of this. "I'd like to speak to my father."

"I'm sorry, he and your mother left the room so you and I could talk."

"About what?" He hadn't warmed to her yet.

"Your calling ruins everything," she told him. "I was going to send you a telegram. My grandmother sent one to my grandfather sixty years ago."

"A telegram?"

"I know it's outdated. It's also rather romantic, I thought."

"What did you intend to say in this telegram?"

"I hadn't decided. My first idea was to say the same thing Helen said to my grandfather. It was a short message—just three little words."

"I love you?" He was warming up now.

"No."

"No?" He seemed skeptical. "What else could it be? Helen loved him, didn't she?"

"Oh, yes, but that was understood. Oh, Paul, I heard the rest of the story and it's so beautiful, so compelling, you'll see why she loved him as much as she did. Sam helped her look to the future and step out of the past."

"You're avoiding the question," he said.

That confused her for a moment. "What's the question?"

"Do you love me enough to accept me as a marine?"

"I wasn't sending *that* answer by way of Western Union." The answer that was going to change her life....

"You can tell me now," he said casually.

"Before I do, you have to promise, on your word of

honor as a United States marine, that you'll never walk away from me like that again."

"You think it was easy?" he demanded.

"I don't care if it was easy or not, you can't ever do it again." His abandonment had hurt too much.

"All right," he muttered. "I promise I'll never walk away from you again."

"Word of honor?"

"Word of honor."

He'd earned it now. "I'm crazy about you, Paul Gordon. *Crazy.* Crazy in love with you. If having the marines as your career means that much to you, then I'll adjust. I'll find a way to make it work. But you need to compromise, too, when it comes to my career. I can't just leave a teaching job in order to follow you somewhere."

The last thing Ruth expected after her admission was a long stretch of silence.

Then, "Are you serious? You'll accept my being in the military?"

"Yes. Do you think I'd do this otherwise?"

"No," he told her. "But what you don't know is that I've been thinking about giving up the marines."

"Because of me?"

"Yes."

"You were?" Never once had it occurred to Ruth that he'd consider such a thing.

"My dad and I have had a couple of long talks about it," he went on to say.

"Tell me more."

"You already know this part—I'm crazy about you, too. I wasn't convinced I could find a way to live the rest of my life without you. One option I've looked into is training. I've talked to my commander about it, and he thinks it's a good possibility. I'd be able to stay in the marines, but I'd be stationed in one place for a while."

Ruth slumped onto a kitchen stool, feeling deliciously weak, too weak to stay upright. "Oh, Paul, that's wonderful!"

"I felt like a fool," he said. "I made my big stand, and I honestly felt I was right, but I didn't have to force you to decide that very minute. My pride wouldn't allow me to back off, though."

"Pride carried me the first week," she said. "Then I went to see my grandmother, and she told me how she met my grandfather at the end of the war. Their romance was as much of an adventure as everything else she told us."

"She's a very special woman," Paul said. "Just like her granddaughter."

"I'll tell you everything later."

"I can't wait to hear it. I'm just wondering if history might repeat itself."

"How?"

"I'm wondering if you'll be my wife."

"That's the perfect question," Ruth said, and it *was* perfect for what she had in mind.

She closed her eyes and sighed deeply. "I do believe I'll send you that telegram after all."

Yes. Yes. Yes.

Epilogue

Paul reached for Ruth's hand beneath the dining-room table. Ruth smiled and gave his hand a squeeze.

"Dinner was fabulous, Grandma," Ruth said. She'd never expected her grandmother to go to all this effort. "I wish you hadn't worked so hard, though. Paul and I would've taken you out to eat."

"Nonsense. It's Christmas Eve. Besides, I rarely get the opportunity to cook for anyone these days. I enjoyed it. And it's such a treat to have the two of you all to myself."

"Thank you so much for everything—especially the stockings. You know we'll treasure them."

"And thank *you,* my darling, for the beautiful memoir you've created."

Ruth had made a new version of Helen's story, including a number of photographs she'd found through her research. She'd scanned the poster declaring Helen and her first husband, Jean-Claude, criminals. She'd also inserted some details Helen had remembered more recently. Finally, she'd had it professionally bound and it was, even if she said so herself, a beautiful piece of work. The memoir was for her grandmother, true, but it was also for everyone in the Shelton family, now and in the future.

Ruth stood and carried the empty dinner plates to the sink. "Paul and I will do the dishes."

"No need."

"We insist," Paul said.

"I don't want to waste a minute of our time together with dishes," Helen told him. "I hardly ever see you as it is."

"Well, that should be changing soon," Ruth said with a smile.

"I've requested Seattle as my next duty station," Paul explained. "My parents are here, too, and we both love the Pacific Northwest."

"California is fine, but this is where we want to make our home," Ruth added.

"Let me get coffee—and the pie," Helen said, walking into the kitchen behind them.

"You mean, there's pie, as well as those yummy cookies?" Paul's eyes lit up.

"Green tomato mincemeat. The tomatoes are from Charlotte Rhodes's garden. It's the best you'll ever taste."

"I love mincemeat," Ruth said, resisting the urge to poke her husband, who was making a face.

Helen smiled. "Give it a try and if you don't like it, I also have fruitcake."

"I believe I'll pass on both."

Ruth's grandmother ignored his comment and quietly dished up three small slices of pie with vanilla ice cream. Ruth helped her bring the plates into the dining room. Paul followed, carrying two cups and saucers, steaming with freshly brewed coffee. Ruth had declined, saying the pie was enough for her.

"One taste," she said, waving her fork at him.

Paul grinned. "I doubt anyone could refuse you, Ruth. Especially me."

"You keep thinking that, okay?"

Ruth watched as her husband sliced off a sliver of the pie. She laughed when she saw his expression change.

"Hey, this is *good*."

Helen looked equally pleased. "I'll tell Charlotte she made a convert out of you." She paused to sip her coffee. "What are your plans for Christmas Day?"

Paul reached for Ruth's hand once more. "First, we're making you breakfast tomorrow morning. It's the least we can do." Helen had invited them to stay the night, and they'd accepted. "Then we're driving to Seattle to spend the day with my parents."

"And we're going to visit Mom and Dad for New Year's," Ruth said.

"Our Christmas vacation worked out perfectly, since I was able to get a week's leave at the same time Ruth finished teaching for the semester."

"There's nothing like being with family over the holidays." Helen nodded.

"I couldn't agree more." Ruth turned to her husband, who sent her a smile. "Besides, we have news to share... the kind of news we wanted to tell you in person."

Helen stared at them expectantly.

"We're going to make you a great-grandma," Ruth announced, and awaited her grandmother's reaction. To her surprise, Helen said nothing.

"Grandma Shelton, did you hear?" Paul prodded.

Helen's face broke into a huge smile. "Congratulations. When are you due?"

"Not until June."

"June? What a perfect month for a birthday."

"Oh, Grandma, you'd say that about any month."

"Probably," Helen agreed. "I apologize for not responding right away. I was trying to calculate if I had enough time to knit you a special baby blanket and an extra Christmas stocking before then. I suspect I do."

"Oh, Grandma," Ruth said, struggling not to laugh.

"This is a blessed Christmas," Helen said simply, happiness radiating from her face. "There was a time I didn't believe I'd ever know joy again and yet I feel it every single day."

"Merry Christmas, Grandma."

"Merry Christmas to both of you. No—" she raised her coffee cup in a toast "—to all *three* of you."

* * * * *

*Can a single moment change
your entire life?*

International lawyer Sophie Bellamy has dedicated
her life to helping people in war-torn countries.
But when she survives a hostage situation, she
remembers what matters most—the children she
loves back home. Haunted by regrets, she returns
to the idyllic Catskills village of Avalon on the
shores of Willow Lake, determined to repair
the bonds with her family.

www.mirabooks.co.uk